Praise for
Nancy Culpepper

"[Bobbie Ann Mason] returns to her greatest strength, the short story. . . . She is able to capture in subtle detail . . . fault lines as they appear in her characters' lives."   —Louisville *Courier-Journal*

"A book of short stories by a masterful author really is the perfect summer read. . . . If you're from the South or wish you were, go get Mason's *Nancy Culpepper* and soak in the heat with her. . . . Mason's stories are like settling down under the AC and a fan with a cool glass of lemonade and Grandma's quilt draped over your legs—everything's familiar and comfortable, but you keep remembering Grandma, and it hurts sometimes that she's gone. . . . [Mason] knows Dixie."
—Fort Worth *Star-Telegram*

"Poignant . . . [Mason] is a nimble storyteller, with a knack for dialogue. She also has an instinctual ability to capture the ambience of home."   —Minneapolis *Star Tribune*

"Mason writes with quiet authority about that most unfashionable of American subjects, class differences. . . . [A] quiet, gently moving collection."   —*Kirkus Reviews*

"Authentic and fresh . . . Bobbie Ann Mason's great talent is that she is a Southern writer without contrivance. . . . Her characters talk the way Southerners talk, when their roots are deep in the country and they are perhaps somewhere else. . . . The characters and their conversations ring true. . . . Mason uses her heroine the way a songwriter uses his bridge. . . . In a Bobbie Ann Mason book, then, maybe it's not just how the characters talk that makes them so bona fide Southern. It's also what they know."   —*The Atlanta Journal-Constitution*

"Illuminating . . . honors our ideas of home, and the efforts we make to keep it safe, to remake it and to find it again."   —*Chicago Tribune*

Also by Bobbie Ann Mason

Nancy Culpepper

Nancy Culpepper

Stories

BOBBIE ANN MASON

RANDOM HOUSE TRADE PAPERBACKS
NEW YORK

2007 Random House Trade Paperback Edition

Copyright © 2006 by Bobbie Ann Mason
Reading group guide copyright © 2007 by Random House, Inc.

Published in the United States by Random House Trade Paperbacks, an imprint of The Random House Publishing Group, a division of Random House, Inc., New York.

RANDOM HOUSE TRADE PAPERBACKS and colophon are trademarks of Random House, Inc.

READER'S CIRCLE and colophon are trademarks of Random House, Inc. Originally published in hardcover in the United States by Random House, an imprint of The Random House Publishing Group, a division of Random House, Inc., in 2006.

"Nancy Culpepper" was first published in *The New Yorker* in 1980. "Blue Country" was published and syndicated by Fiction Network. Copyright © 1985 by Bobbie Ann Mason. "Proper Gypsies" was first published in *The Southern Review* in 1995.

"Lying Doggo" was published in *Shiloh and Other Stories* by Bobbie Ann Mason, published by Harper & Row. Copyright © 1982 by Bobbie Ann Mason. *Spence + Lila* by Bobbie Ann Mason was published by Harper & Row in 1988; Ecco Press edition 1998. Copyright © 1988 by Bobbie Ann Mason.

ISBN 978-0-8129-7667-0

LIBRARY OF CONGRESS CATALOGING-IN-PUBLICATION DATA
Mason, Bobbie Ann.
Nancy Culpepper: stories / Bobbie Ann Mason.
p. cm.
Contents: Nancy Culpepper—Blue country—Lying doggo—Spence + Lila—Proper Gypsies—The heirs—The prelude.
ISBN 978-0-8129-7667-0
1. Kentucky—Social life and customs—Fiction. 2. Women—Kentucky—Fiction. 3. Domestic fiction, American. I. Title.
PS3563.A7877N36 2006
813'.54—dc22 2005541241

www.thereaderscircle.com

Book design by Dana Leigh Blanchette

147028622

*Dedicated
to the
memory
of my
parents*

CONTENTS

1980—1982

Nancy Culpepper

When Nancy received her parents' letter saying they were moving her grandmother to a nursing home, she said to her husband, "I really should go help them out. And I've got to save Granny's photographs. They might get lost." Jack did not try to discourage her, and she left for Kentucky soon after the letter came.

Nancy has been vaguely wanting to move to Kentucky, and she has persuaded Jack to think about relocating his photography business. They live in the country, near a small town an hour's drive from Philadelphia. Their son, Robert, who is eight, has fits when they talk about moving. He does not want to leave his room or his playmates. Once, he asked, "What about our chickens?"

"They have chickens in Kentucky," Nancy explained. "Don't worry. We're not going yet."

Later he asked, "But what about the fish in the pond?"

"I don't know," said Nancy. "I guess we'll have to rent a U-Haul."

When Nancy arrives at her parents' farm in western Kentucky, her mother says, "Your daddy and me's both got inner ear and nerves. And we couldn't lift Granny, or anything, if we had to all of a sudden."

"The flu settled in my ears," Daddy says, cocking his head at an angle.

"Mine's still popping," says Mom.

In a few days they plan to move Granny, and they will return to their own house, which they have been renting out. For nine years, they have lived next door, in Granny's house, in order to care for her. There Mom has had to cook on an ancient gas range, with her mother-in-law hovering over her, supervising. Granny used only lye soap on dishes, and it was five years before Nancy's mother defied her and bought some Joy. By then, Granny was confined to her bed, crippled with arthritis. Now she is ninety-three.

"You didn't have to come back," Daddy says to Nancy at the dinner table. "We could manage."

"I want to help you move," Nancy says. "And I want to make sure Granny's pictures don't get lost. Nobody cares about them but me, and I'm afraid somebody will throw them away."

Nancy wants to find out if Granny has a picture of a great-great-aunt named Nancy Culpepper. No one in the family seems to know anything about her, but Nancy is excited by the thought of an ancestor with the same name as hers. Since she found out about her, Nancy has been going by her maiden name, but she has given up trying to explain this to her mother, who persists in addressing letters to "Mr. and Mrs. Jack Cleveland."

"There's some pictures hid behind Granny's closet wall," Daddy tells Nancy. "When we hooked up the coal-oil stove through the fireplace a few years ago, they got walled in."

"That's ridiculous! Why would you do that?"

"They were in the way." He stands up and puts on his cap, preparing to go out to feed his calves.

"Will Granny care if I tear the wall down?" Nancy asks, joking.

Daddy laughs, acting as though he understood, but Nancy knows he is pretending. He seems tired, and his billed cap looks absurdly small perched on his head.

When Nancy and Jack were married, years ago, in Massachusetts, Nancy did not want her parents to come to the wedding. She urged them not to make the long trip. "It's no big deal," she told them on the telephone. "It'll last ten minutes. We're not even going on a honeymoon right away, because we both have exams Monday."

Nancy was in graduate school, and Jack was finishing his B.A. For almost a year they had been renting a large old house on a lake. The house had a field-rock fireplace with a heart-shaped stone centered above the mantel. Jack, who was studying design, thought the heart was tasteless, and he covered it with a Peter Max poster.

At the ceremony, Jack's dog, Grover, was present, and instead of organ music, a stereo played *Sgt. Pepper's Lonely Hearts Club Band*. It was 1967. Nancy was astonished by the minister's white robe and his beard and by the fact that he chain-smoked. The preachers she remembered from childhood would have called him a heathen, she thought. Most of the wedding pictures, taken by a friend of Jack's, turned out to be trick photography—blurred faces and double exposures.

The party afterwards lasted all night. Jack blew up two hundred balloons and kept the fire going. They drank too much wine–and–7-Up punch. Guests went in and out, popping balloons with cigarettes, taking walks by the lake. Everyone was looking for the northern lights, which were supposed to be visible that evening. Holding on to Jack, Nancy searched the murky sky, feeling that the two of them were lone travelers on the edge of some outer-space adventure. At the same time, she kept thinking of her parents at home, probably watching *Gunsmoke*.

"I saw them once," Jack said. "They were fantastic."

"What was it like?"

"Shower curtains."

"Really? That's amazing."

"Luminescent shower curtains."

"I'm shivering," Nancy said. The sky was blank.

"Let's go in. It's too cloudy anyway. Someday we'll see them. I promise."

Someone had taken down the poster above the fireplace and put up the picture of Sgt. Pepper—the cutout that came with the album. Sgt. Pepper overlooked the room like a stern father.

"What's the matter?" a man asked Nancy. He was Dr. Doyle, her American History 1861–1865 professor. "This is your wedding. Loosen up." He burst a balloon and Nancy jumped.

When someone offered her a joint, she refused, then wondered why. The house was filled with strangers, and the Beatles album played over and over. Jack and Nancy danced, hugging each other in a slow two-step that was all wrong for the music. They drifted past the wedding presents, lined up on a table Jack had fashioned from a door—hand-dipped candles, a silver roach clip, *Joy of Cooking*, signed pottery in nonfunctional shapes. Nancy wondered what her parents had eaten for supper. Possibly fried steak, two kinds of peas, biscuits, blackberry pie. The music shifted and the songs merged together; Jack and Nancy kept dancing.

"There aren't any stopping places," Nancy said. She was crying. "Songs used to have stopping places in between."

"Let's just keep on dancing," Jack said.

Nancy was thinking of the blackberry bushes at the farm in Kentucky, which spread so wildly they had to be burned down every few years. They grew on the banks of the creek, which in summer shrank to still, small occasional pools. After a while Nancy realized that Jack was talking to her. He was explaining how he could predict exactly when the last, dying chord on the album was about to end.

"Listen," he said. "*There.* Right there."

Nancy's parents had met Jack a few months before the wedding, during spring break, when Jack and Nancy stopped in Kentucky on their way to Denver to see an old friend of Jack's. The visit involved some elaborate lies about their sleeping arrangements on the trip.

At the supper table, Mom and Daddy passed bowls of food self-consciously. The table was set with some napkins left over from Christmas. The vegetables were soaked in bacon grease, and Jack took small helpings. Nancy sat rigidly, watching every movement, like a cat stationed near a bird feeder. Mom had gathered poke, because it was spring, and she said to Jack, "I bet you don't eat poke salet up there."

"It's weeds," said Nancy.

"I've never heard of it," Jack said. He hesitated, then took a small serving.

"It's poison if it gets too big," Daddy said. He turned to Nancy's mother. "I think you picked this too big. You're going to poison us all."

"He's teasing," Nancy said.

"The berries is what's poison," said Mom, laughing. "Wouldn't that be something? They'll say up there I tried to poison your boyfriend the minute I met him!"

Everyone laughed. Jack's face was red. He was wearing an embroidered shirt. Nancy watched him trim the fat from his ham as precisely as if he were using an X-Acto knife on mat board.

"How's Granny?" asked Nancy. Her grandmother was then living alone in her own house.

"Tolerable well," said Daddy.

"We'll go see her," Jack said. "Nancy told me all about her."

"She cooks her egg in her oats to keep from washing a extry dish," Mom said.

Nancy played with her food. She was looking at the pink dining room wall and the plastic flowers in the window. On the afternoon Jack and Nancy first met, he took her to a junk shop, where he bought a stained-glass window for his bathroom. Nancy would never have thought of going to a junk shop. It would not have occurred to her to put a stained-glass window in a bathroom.

"What do you aim to be when you graduate?" Daddy asked Jack abruptly, staring at him. Jack's hair looked oddly like an Irish setter's ears, Nancy thought suddenly.

"Won't you have to go in the Army?" Mom asked.

"I'll apply for an assistantship if my grades are good enough," Jack said. "Anything to avoid the draft."

Nancy's father was leaning into his plate, as though he were concentrating deeply on each bite.

"He makes good grades," Nancy said.

"Nancy always made all A's," Daddy said to Jack.

"We gave her a dollar for ever' one," said Mom. "She kept us broke."

"In graduate school they don't give A's," said Nancy. "They just give S's and U's."

Jack wadded up his napkin. Then Mom served fried pies with white sauce. "Nancy always loved these better than anything," she said.

After supper, Nancy showed Jack the farm. As they walked through the fields, Nancy felt that he was seeing peaceful land-scapes—arrangements of picturesque cows, an old red barn. She had never thought of the place this way before; it reminded her of prints in a dime store.

While her mother washes the dishes, Nancy takes Granny's dinner to her, and sits in a rocking chair while Granny eats in bed. The food is on an old TV-dinner tray. The compartments hold chicken and dress-ing, mashed potatoes, field peas, green beans, and vinegar slaw. The servings are tiny—six green beans, a spoonful of peas.

Granny's teeth no longer fit, and she has to bite sideways, like a cat. She wears the lower teeth only during meals, but she will not get new ones. She says it would be wasteful to be buried with a new three-hundred-dollar set of teeth. In between bites, Granny guzzles iced tea from a Kentucky Lakes mug. "That slaw don't have enough sugar in it," she says. "It makes my mouth draw up." She smacks her lips.

Nancy says, "I've heard the food is really good at the Orchard Acres Rest Home."

Granny does not reply for a moment. She is working on a chicken gristle, which causes her teeth to clatter. Then she says, "I ain't going nowhere."

"Mom and Daddy are moving back into their house. You don't want to stay here by yourself, do you?" Nancy's voice sounds hollow to her.

"I'll be all right. I can do for myself."

When Granny swallows, it sounds like water spilling from a bucket into a cistern. After Nancy's parents moved in, they covered Granny's old cistern, but Nancy still remembers drawing the bucket up from below. The chains made a sound like crying.

Granny pushes her food with a piece of bread, cleaning her tray. "I can do a little cooking," she says. "I can sweep."

"Try this boiled custard, Granny. I made it just for you. Just the way you used to make it."

"It ain't yaller enough," says Granny, tasting the custard. "Store-bought eggs."

When she finishes, she removes her lower teeth and sloshes them in a plastic tumbler on the bedside table. Nancy looks away. On the wall are Nancy's high school graduation photograph and a picture of Jesus. Nancy looks sassy; her graduation hat resembles a tilted lid. Jesus has a halo, set at about the same angle.

Now Nancy ventures a question about the pictures hidden behind the closet wall. At first Granny is puzzled. Then she seems to remember.

"They're behind the stovepipe," she says. Grimacing with pain, she stretches her legs out slowly, and then, holding her head, she sinks back into her pillows and draws the quilt over her shoulders. "I'll look for them one of these days—when I'm able."

Jack photographs weeds, twigs, pond reflections, silhouettes of Robert against the sun with his arms flung out like a scarecrow's. Sometimes he works in the evenings in his studio at home, drinking tequila sunrises and composing bizarre still lifes with lightbulbs, wine bottles, Tinkertoys, Lucite cubes. He makes arrangements of gourds look like breasts.

On the day Nancy tried to explain to Jack about her need to save Granny's pictures, a hailstorm interrupted her. It was the only hailstorm she had ever seen in the North, and she had forgotten all about them. Granny always said a hailstorm meant that God was cleaning out his icebox. Nancy stood against a white Masonite wall mounted with a new series of photographs and looked out the window at tulips being smashed. The ice pellets littered the ground like shattered glass. Then, as suddenly as it had arrived, the hailstorm was over.

"Pictures didn't used to be so common," Nancy said. Jack's trash can was stuffed with rejected prints, and Robert's face was crumpled on top. "I want to keep Granny's pictures as reminders."

"If you think that will solve anything," said Jack, squinting at a negative he was holding against the light.

"I want to see if she has one of Nancy Culpepper."

"That's *you.*"

"There was another one. She was a great-great-aunt or something, on my daddy's side. She had the same name as mine."

"There's another one of you?" Jack said with mock disbelief.

"I'm a reincarnation," she said, playing along.

"There's nobody else like you. You're one of a kind."

Nancy turned away and stared deliberately at Jack's pictures, which were held up by clear-headed pushpins, like translucent eyes dotting the wall. She examined them one by one, moving methodically down the row—stumps, puffballs, tree roots, close-ups of cat feet.

Nancy first learned about her ancestor on a summer Sunday a few years before, when she took her grandmother to visit the Culpepper graveyard, beside an oak grove off the Paducah highway. The old oaks had spread their limbs until they shaded the entire cemetery, and the tombstones poked through weeds like freak mushrooms. Nancy wandered among the graves, while Granny stayed beside her husband's gravestone. It had her own name on it too, with a blank space for the date.

Nancy told Jack afterwards that when she saw the stone marked "NANCY CULPEPPER, 1833–1905," she did a double take. "It was like time-lapse photography," she said. "I mean, I was standing there looking into the past and the future at the same time. It was weird."

"She wasn't kin to me, but she lived down the road," Granny explained to Nancy. "She was your granddaddy's aunt."

"Did she look like me?" Nancy asked.

"I don't know. She was real old." Granny touched the stone, puzzled. "I can't figure why she wasn't buried with her husband's people," she said.

On Saturday, Nancy helps her parents move some of their furniture to the house next door. It is only a short walk, but when the truck is loaded they all ride in it, Nancy sitting between her parents. The truck's muffler sounds like thunder, and they drive without speaking. Daddy backs up to the porch.

The paint on the house is peeling, and the latch of the storm door is broken. Daddy pulls at the door impatiently, saying, "I sure wish I could burn down these old houses and retire to Arizona." For as long as Nancy can remember, her father has been sending away for literature on Arizona.

Her mother says, "We'll never go anywhere. We've got our dress tail on a bedpost."

"What does that mean?" asks Nancy, in surprise.

"Use to, if a storm was coming, people would put a bedpost on a child's dress tail, to keep him from blowing away. In other words, we're tied down."

"That's funny. I never heard of that."

"I guess you think we're just ignorant," Mom says. "The way we talk."

"No, I don't."

Daddy props the door open, and Nancy helps him ease a mattress over the threshold. Mom apologizes for not being able to lift anything.

"I'm in your way," she says, stepping off the porch into a dead canna bed.

Nancy stacks boxes in her old room. It seems smaller than she remembered, and the tenants have scarred the woodwork. Mentally, she refurnishes the room—the bed by the window, the desk opposite. The first time Jack came to Kentucky he slept here, while Nancy slept on the couch in the living room. Now Nancy recalls the next day, as they headed west, with Jack accusing her of being dishonest, foolishly trying to protect her parents. "You let them think you're such a goody-goody, the ideal daughter," he said. "I bet you wouldn't tell them if you made less than an A."

Nancy's father comes in and runs his hand across the ceiling, gathering up strings of dust. Tugging at a loose piece of door facing, he says to Nancy, "Never trust renters. They won't take care of a place."

"What will you do with Granny's house?"

"Nothing. Not as long as she's living."

"Will you rent it out then?"

"No. I won't go through that again." He removes his cap and smooths his hair, then puts the cap back on. Leaning against the wall, he talks about the high cost of the nursing home. "I never thought it would come to this," he says. "I wouldn't do it if there was any other way."

"You don't have any choice," says Nancy.

"The government will pay you to break up your family," he says. "If I get like your granny, I want you to just take me out in the woods and shoot me."

"She told me she wasn't going," Nancy says.

"They've got a big recreation room for the ones that can get around," Daddy says. "They've even got disco dancing."

When Daddy laughs, his voice catches, and he has to clear his throat. Nancy laughs with him. "I can just see Granny disco dancing. Are you sure you want me to shoot you? That place sounds like fun."

They go outside, where Nancy's mother is cleaning out a patch of weed-choked perennials. "I planted these iris the year we moved," she says.

"They're pretty," says Nancy. "I haven't seen that color up North."

Mom stands up and shakes her foot awake. "I sure hope y'all can move down here," she says. "It's a shame you have to be so far away. Robert grows so fast I don't know him."

"We might someday. I don't know if we can."

"Looks like Jack could make good money if he set up a studio in town. Nowadays people want fancy pictures."

"Even the school pictures cost a fortune," Daddy says.

"Jack wants to free-lance for publications," says Nancy. "And there aren't any here. There's not even a camera shop within fifty miles."

"But people want pictures," Mom says. "They've gone back to decorating living rooms with family pictures. In antique frames."

Daddy smokes a cigarette on the porch, while Nancy circles the house. A beetle has infested the oak trees, causing clusters of leaves to turn brown. Nancy stands on the concrete lid of an old cistern and watches crows fly across a cornfield. In the distance a series of towers slings power lines across a flat sea of soybeans. Her mother is talking about Granny. Nancy thinks of Granny on the telephone, the day of her wedding, innocently asking, "What are you going to cook for your wedding breakfast?" Later, seized with laughter, Nancy told Jack what Granny had said.

"I almost said to her, 'We usually don't eat breakfast, we sleep so late!' "

Jack was busy blowing up balloons. When he didn't laugh, Nancy said, "Isn't that hilarious? She's really out of the nineteenth century."

"You don't have to make me breakfast," said Jack.

"In her time, it meant something really big," Nancy said helplessly. "Don't you see?"

Now Nancy's mother is saying, "The way she has to have that milk of magnesia every night, when I know good and well she don't need it. She thinks she can't live without it."

"What's wrong with her?" asks Nancy.

"She thinks she's got a knot in her bowels. But ain't nothing wrong with her but that head-swimming and arthritis." Mom jerks a long morning glory vine out of the marigolds. "Hardening of the arteries is what makes her head swim," she says.

"We better get back and see about her," Daddy says, but he does not get up immediately. The crows are racing above the power lines.

Later, Nancy spreads a Texaco map of the United States out on Granny's quilt. "I want to show you where I live," she says. "Philadelphia's nearly a thousand miles from here."

"Reach me my specs," says Granny, as she struggles to sit up. "How did you get here?"

"Flew. Daddy picked me up at the airport in Paducah."

"Did you come by the bypass or through town?"

"The bypass," says Nancy. Nancy shows her where Pennsylvania is on the map. "I flew from Philadelphia to Louisville to Paducah. There's California. That's where Robert was born."

"I haven't seen a geography since I was twenty years old," Granny says. She studies the map, running her fingers over it as though she were caressing fine material. "Law, I didn't know *where* Floridy was. It's way down there."

"I've been to Florida," Nancy says.

Granny lies back, holding her head as if it were a delicate china bowl. In a moment she says, "Tell your mama to thaw me up some of them strawberries I picked."

"When were you out picking strawberries, Granny?"

"They're in the freezer of my refrigerator. Back in the back. In a little milk carton." Granny removes her glasses and waves them in the air.

"Larry was going to come and play with me, but he couldn't come," Robert says to Nancy on the telephone that evening. "He had a stomachache."

"That's too bad. What did you do today?"

"We went to the Taco Bell and then we went to the woods so Daddy could take pictures of Indian pipes."

"What are those?"

"I don't know. Daddy knows."

"We didn't find any," Jack says on the extension. "I think it's the wrong time of year. How's Kentucky?"

Nancy tells Jack about helping her parents move. "My bed is gone, so tonight I'll have to sleep on a couch in the hallway," she says. "It's really dreary here in this old house. Everything looks so bare."

"How's your grandmother?"

"The same. She's dead set against that rest home, but what can they do?"

"Do you still want to move down there?" Jack asks.

"I don't know."

"I know how we could take the chickens to Kentucky," says Robert in an excited burst.

"How?"

"We could give them sleeping pills and then put them in the trunk so they'd be quiet."

"That sounds gruesome," Jack says.

Nancy tells Robert not to think about moving. There is static on the line. Nancy has trouble hearing Jack. "We're your family too," he is saying.

"I didn't mean to abandon you," she says.

"Have you seen the pictures yet?"

"No. I'm working up to that."

"Nancy Culpepper, the original?"

"You bet," says Nancy, a little too quickly. She hears Robert hang up. "Is Robert O.K.?" she asks through the static.

"Oh, sure."

"He doesn't think I moved without him?"

"He'll be all right."

"He didn't tell me goodbye."

"Don't worry," says Jack.

"She's been after me about those strawberries till I could wring her neck," says Mom as she and Nancy are getting ready for bed. "She's talking about some strawberries she put up in nineteen seventy-*one*. I've told her and told her that she eat them strawberries back then, but won't nothing do but for her to have them strawberries."

"Give her some others," Nancy says.

"She'd know the difference. She don't miss a thing when it comes to what's *hers*. But sometimes she's just as liable to forget her name."

Mom is trembling, and then she is crying. Nancy pats her mother's hair, which is gray and wiry and sticks out in sprigs. Wiping her eyes, Mom says, "All the kinfolks will talk. 'Look what they done to her, poor helpless thing.' It'll probably kill her, to move her to that place."

"When you move back home you can get all your antiques out of the barn," Nancy says. "You'll be in your own house again. Won't that be nice?"

Mom does not answer. She takes some sheets and quilts from a closet and hands them to Nancy. "That couch lays good," she says.

When Nancy wakes up, the covers are on the floor, and for a moment she does not remember where she is. Her digital watch says 2:43. Then it tells the date. In the darkness she has no sense of distance, and it seems to her that the lighted numerals could be the size of a billboard, only seen from far away.

Jack has told her that this kind of insomnia is a sign of depression, while the other kind—inability to fall asleep at bedtime—is a sign of anxiety. Nancy always thought he had it backwards, but now she thinks he may be right. A flicker of distant sheet lightning exposes the bleak walls with the suddenness of a flashbulb. The angles of the hall seem unfamiliar, and the narrow couch makes Nancy feel small and alone. When Jack and Robert come to Kentucky with her, they all sleep in the living room, and in the early morning Nancy's parents pass through to get to the bathroom. "We're just one big happy family," Daddy announces, to disguise his embarrassment when he awakens them. Now, for some reason, Nancy recalls Jack's strange still lifes, and she thinks of the black irises and the polished skulls of cattle suspended in the skies of O'Keeffe paintings. The irises are like thunderheads. The night they were married, Nancy and Jack collapsed into bed, falling asleep immediately, their heads swirling. The party was still going on, and friends from New York were staying over. Nancy woke up the next day saying her new name, and feeling that once again, in another way, she had betrayed her parents. "The one time they really thought they knew what I was doing, they didn't at all," she told Jack, who was barely awake. The visitors had gone out for the Sunday newspapers, and they brought back doughnuts. They had doughnuts and wine for breakfast. Someone made coffee later.

In the morning, a slow rain blackens the fallen oak branches in the yard. In Granny's room the curtains are gray with shadows. Nancy places an old photograph album in Granny's lap. Silently, Granny turns pages of blank-faced babies in long white dresses like wedding gowns. Nancy's father is a boy in a sailor suit. Men and women in pictures the color of café au lait stand around picnic tables. The immense trees in these settings are shaggy and dark. Granny cannot find Nancy Culpepper in the album. Quickly, she flips past a picture of her husband. Then she almost giggles as she points to a girl. "That's me."

"I wouldn't have recognized you, Granny."

"Why, it looks just *like* me." Granny strokes the picture, as though she were trying to feel the dress. "That was my favorite dress," she says. "It was brown poplin, with grosgrain ribbon and self-covered buttons. Thirty-two of them. And all those tucks. It took me three weeks to work up that dress."

Nancy points to the pictures one by one, asking Granny to identify them. Granny does not notice Nancy writing the names in a notebook. Aunt Sass, Uncle Joe, Dove and Pear Culpepper, Hortense Culpepper.

"Hort Culpepper went to Texas," says Granny. "She had TB."

"Tell me about that," Nancy urges her.

"There wasn't anything to tell. She got homesick for her mammy's cooking." Granny closes the album and falls back against her pillows, saying, "All those people are gone."

While Granny sleeps, Nancy gets a flashlight and opens the closet. The inside is crammed with the accumulation of decades—yellowed newspapers, boxes of greeting cards, bags of string, and worn-out stockings. Granny's best dress, a blue bonded knit she has hardly worn, is in plastic wrapping. Nancy pushes the clothing aside and examines the wall. To her right, a metal pipe runs vertically through the closet. Backing up against the dresses, Nancy shines the light on the corner and discovers a large framed picture wedged behind the pipe. By tugging at the frame, she is able to work it gradually through the narrow space between the wall and the pipe. In the picture a man and woman, whose features are sharp and clear, are sitting expectantly on a brocaded love seat. Nancy imagines that this is a wedding portrait.

In the living room, a TV evangelist is urging viewers to call him, toll-free. Mom turns the TV off when Nancy appears with the picture, and Daddy stands up and helps her hold it near a window.

"I think that's Uncle John!" he says excitedly. "He was my favorite uncle."

"They're none of my people," says Mom, studying the picture through her bifocals.

"He died when I was little, but I think that's him," says Daddy. "Him and Aunt Lucy Culpepper."

"Who was she?" Nancy asks.

"Uncle John's wife."

"I figured that," says Nancy impatiently. "But who *was* she?"

"I don't know." He is still looking at the picture, running his fingers over the man's face.

Back in Granny's room, Nancy pulls the string that turns on the ceiling light, so that Granny can examine the picture. Granny shakes her head slowly. "I never saw them folks before in all my life."

Mom comes in with a dish of strawberries.

"Did I pick these?" Granny asks.

"No. You eat yours about ten years ago," Mom says.

Granny puts in her teeth and eats the strawberries in slurps, missing her mouth twice. "Let me see them people again," she says, waving her spoon. Her teeth make the sound of a baby rattle.

"Nancy Hollins," says Granny. "She was a Culpepper."

"That's Nancy Culpepper?" cries Nancy.

"*That*'s not Nancy Culpepper," Mom says. "That woman's got a rat in her hair. They wasn't in style back when Nancy Culpepper was alive."

Granny's face is flushed and she is breathing heavily. "She was a real little-bitty old thing," she says in a high, squeaky voice. "She never would talk. Everybody thought she was curious. Plumb curious."

"Are you sure it's her?" Nancy says.

"If I'm not mistaken."

"She don't remember," Mom says to Nancy. "Her mind gets confused."

Granny removes her teeth and lies back, her bones grinding. Her chest heaves with exhaustion. Nancy sits down in the rocking chair, and as she rocks back and forth she searches the photograph, exploring the features of the young woman, who is wearing an embroidered white dress, and the young man, in a curly beard that starts below his chin, framing his face like a ruffle. The woman looks frightened—of the camera perhaps—but nevertheless her deep-set eyes sparkle like shards of glass. This young woman would be glad to dance to "Lucy in the Sky with Diamonds" on her wedding day, Nancy thinks. The man seems bewildered, as if he did not know what to expect, marrying a woman who has her eyes fixed on something so far away.

Blue Country

"The Blue Lantern Inn—that's a name straight out of a Nancy Drew book," said Nancy.

"Is Nancy Drew your namesake?" teased Jack.

Nancy laughed. "Nancy Drew always stopped at some quaint wayside inn for tea, and there would be a mystery to solve. The inns were just like this. I feel I've been here before."

Nancy and Jack were at the Blue Lantern Inn on the coast above Boston. They had come for the weekend to attend the wedding of a friend from graduate school who was finally getting married to the man she had lived with for five years. Nancy and Jack had driven for six hours from Pennsylvania. On the way Jack had said, "Why couldn't the wedding be two weeks from now, when the autumn leaves are just right?" They used to live in New England, and Jack was crazy about the fall foliage. He was always critical of autumn in Pennsylvania. He would complain about the brown-and-gold splendor on the mountain ridge near their home. Not a single flaming red sugar maple on the whole mountain, he would point out, like someone judging a parade.

That evening, in a seafood house on a wharf, Jack and Nancy ripped apart bright lobsters and laughed. They drank a bottle of rosé—

to match the lobster, Jack said. But the colors didn't match at all. Jack acted silly, calling her "Toots," the way he did to tease her when they were first married. Nancy called him "Mr. Toots" in return and giggled. Jack had been teasing her all day. Going to a wedding made them happy. Water leaked from the boiled lobster into Nancy's lap. Jack splintered a claw and a tender orange hand slithered out.

Afterwards, they walked in the dark on the beach in front of the Blue Lantern Inn. The tide had gone so far out they had to hike to meet it. The sand was wet and marshy in places, and it was too dark to see the water. Some birds skittered by quietly.

"I had forgotten how much I love the ocean," Jack said. "I can't wait till Sunday."

"I'm not sure I want to go out there in a little boat to watch whales," Nancy said. "The idea is terrifying."

"It won't be terrifying in the daytime," Jack said. "Whales are friendly."

"But they're so big."

"They're like horses. Horses are very careful not to step on cats and chickens."

"Tell that to Ahab," said Nancy, squeezing his hand.

In the inn during the night, she heard the sea whispering, and toward morning she heard a gurgling sound—rain falling from the drain spouts. Suddenly, there was a sharp tapping on the door and an urgent voice: "Phone call. Phone call." Nancy was in her jeans and sweat shirt and downstairs in the lobby before she could realize what she had heard. She was afraid something had happened to their child, Robert, who was staying with friends at home.

It was Nancy's mother, in Kentucky. "Nancy? Did I get you up? Granny passed away last night, about eleven o'clock."

Nancy had expected this phone call for years. But now she was stunned and her mother sounded bewildered. Nancy's grandmother was ninety-four and had been arthritic and senile for several years. During the past summer her health had deteriorated, and for many months Nancy had not traveled without notifying her parents where to reach her.

Nancy's mother said, "She had mass-matter on the brain."

"What in the world is mass-matter on the brain?" Nancy cried. A tall man in a blue blazer turned his head in her direction.

Mom said, "Sometimes the blood vessels running to your brain mat together in a pocket? They call it mass-matter."

"You mean she had a stroke."

"She was acting wild on us all day," Mom went on. "Hollering and carrying on. Trying to walk for the first time in a year. I went in about ten-thirty to give her a pill and I thought she was dead. But she wasn't completely dead yet."

While her mother described the funeral plans, Nancy looked out the front window and saw that the ocean was still far away. The tide had come in and gone out again. She should leave for Kentucky immediately, for the funeral was the next day.

"I don't know how soon I can get there," she said. "I'll have to check with the airlines." She suddenly looked down, wondering if she had remembered to dress. Guests were entering the dining room for breakfast.

She spoke with her father, who sounded weary and distant.

"Can't you wait till Monday?" Nancy asked him.

"Nobody would come on Monday. They'd have to work."

"I'll try to get there," she said. "I just woke up. I'm looking out at the sea. It's beautiful. We're at this nice inn—"

"I know how much you always cared for Granny, and you had always planned to come back for her funeral," said Daddy.

"Yes," Nancy said.

Jack was still sleeping. Telephone calls never alarmed him. Nancy instinctively feared bad news from the telephone. She was fourteen, on the farm in Kentucky, when the family first got a telephone, the same year they got television. Jack came from a different world—private school, summer camps. How did we ever get together? Nancy thought wildly, as she woke him up and told him the news.

"Granny had some kind of fit," she said. "It sounded unreal." She remembered the way her grandmother lay curled up, barely able to turn, for so long. Nancy's father had once said, "Old people get that way, drawed up like a baby in the womb." They had attempted once to take her to a nursing home, but she had refused to go.

Jack sat up on his elbows, looking disappointed. Jack, a photographer, had planned to make a wedding album for Laurie and Ed as a present.

"Do you want me to fly down with you?" he asked.

"No. It's not necessary." Jack was always uncomfortable in the South. The first time he went with her, in the late sixties, a truck driver had threatened to beat him up. It was Jack's hair. Nancy said now, "You don't have to go. I don't want you to miss the wedding, and you were counting on seeing whales tomorrow."

"You may not even be able to get there because of the airline strike," Jack said, getting out of bed and parting the curtains. "Oh, it's raining," he said. "I was going to run."

"Well, if I can't get there, then I can't get there," said Nancy.

"How would they feel if you didn't go?"

"I don't know." She pulled her sweat shirt over her head. Her face was still in her sweat shirt when Jack drew her to him and held her, waiting for her to cry.

"Would you call the airlines for me while I take a shower?" Nancy asked. "This hasn't registered yet. Look at me. I'm not even crying."

In the shower, Nancy realized that everything in the Blue Lantern Inn was blue. The wallpaper was blue. The rugs were blue. In the lobby downstairs, seashells on blue tiles were mounted on the wall. The inn seemed to be the ideal place she had aspired toward since her childhood, when she read about the pleasant, cozy tearooms in the storybooks. She tried to picture her grandmother's face—the gentle woman she loved—but all she could see was a silhouette of an old woman hunched over her dishpan set on the gas stove to heat. In the stove, in a compartment next to the oven, would be food from dinner saved for supper. Miraculously, no one in the family had ever had food poisoning. Nancy pushed open the clouded-glass window in the shower and saw the ocean beating, gray in the rain. She dreaded the thought of flying in the rain.

"The only plane that will get you to Louisville with decent connections leaves Boston in two hours," Jack told Nancy when she came out of the shower. "And you'll have to fly standby. There's one from New York at six, but we'd have to drive to New York, and there's nothing out of Louisville until noon tomorrow. I don't think that one would get you home in time for the funeral. Anyway, all the flights are booked solid, and you'd have to take a chance on getting a seat."

"Let's eat and think about this," said Nancy. She had hoped for an evening flight so she would not have to miss the wedding. It occurred to her that Jack would have to drive back to Pennsylvania alone.

"What are you feeling?" he asked.

"I don't know." She spread cold lotion on her legs. "I feel inconvenienced," she said. "I mean, it doesn't seem personal. She was so old."

Jack said, "I hope you're relieved, Nancy. She's been a terrible strain on your parents."

"I know it," Nancy said, pulling on corduroy slacks. "She's driven my mother crazy. If I cry, it will be for my mom."

"Maybe you should wait and go down in a week or two and spend some time with your parents. They might need you more then."

"That might be better—and I have that important meeting at work on Tuesday." Nancy began to relax. Jack was always so clear-headed. She put on an Icelandic wool sweater she had bought in Scotland once when she and Jack went looking for the Loch Ness monster. Jack called the sweater her "sheep."

"Why *don't* you go down later?" he said, looking happier. He did a few deep knee bends.

Nancy gazed at snapshots of previous guests on a bulletin board in the dining room. On a paper plate thumbtacked next to the tide tables, someone had scrawled, YES, THE MOONIES ARE HERE. A smiling gray-haired man in a striped sweater said to Jack, "We come here every year. We were here all week and the weather was *glorious* until today."

"There's an artists' colony here as good as on the Cape," a short woman, his wife, said, beaming.

Nancy took orange juice, coffee, and a blueberry muffin from a sideboard and sat at the corner of the long table, facing the ocean. Jack sat down and handed her a napkin and silverware. "You forgot these," he said gently. He chatted with the cheerful couple while Nancy ate and gazed out the window at the vacant sky and water. Her appetite surprised her. The muffins were homemade, according to the other guests.

Jack brought Nancy another muffin. "Are you O.K.?" he asked.

"I think so."

"Do you know what you want to do?"

"I don't want to travel in the rain." She spread butter on the muffin and watched it crumble. She said, "When my parents were young, they wanted to build a house of their own half a mile down the road. They wanted to buy a piece of land and build. Instead, they built that house next door, on Granddaddy's land. Mom remembers how Granny fretted at the idea of Daddy moving half a mile away. She said, 'Well, what if he was to get sick? Who would take care of him?' She didn't want her precious son out of her sight and didn't trust my mother to look out for him. Mom bore that insult to this day. And she ended up taking care of Granny all those years."

"Think of how free your parents are going to be now," Jack said.

Nancy ate a bite of muffin. "I know I should go," she said slowly. "But it seems to me that if you have a choice between a wedding and a funeral, you should go to the wedding."

"It's up to you."

"I know you want to take pictures, and we drove so far."

More guests were entering the dining room, talking about the weather.

Nancy said to Jack, "Later I'll double-check and see if there's some way I could get there late tonight or tomorrow morning. And I'll call home later today. They'll be at the funeral home all afternoon anyway."

Suddenly, a small blond dog rushed into the dining room, followed by the woman who ran the guesthouse. She cried, "Tuffie—get back here! You know you're not supposed to be in Blue Country!"

The gray-haired man said to her, "It's too bad you have to live in the back of the house, without this beautiful view."

"Oh, in the winter we always move into Blue Country," she said, smiling and scooping up the dog from the blue rug. She tugged the dog's ribboned topknot. "Bad boy, Tuffie."

"That dog doesn't look half as guilty as I do," Nancy said to Jack.

The wedding had been planned for the beach, but because of the rain it was moved to a summer camp nearby. The redwood cottages, with elaborately carved cornices and red-painted trim, resembled a Russian peasant village. "Everything in New England is quaint," said Nancy as Jack's umbrella exploded into shape. They could hear the ocean roaring beyond a low, tree-lined hill. The clouds were rushing by, like something chased, so near they looked transparent as smoke.

The art studio, where the crowd was gathering, was unfinished inside, and spider plants dangled from two-by-fours braced together overhead. Some stretched canvases faced the wall, and the floor was paint-splotched. Nancy sat in a folding chair and scanned the crowd for familiar faces while Jack began photographing Laurie and Ed, who were already there. Nancy had not seen Laurie in four years, and they had met Ed only once, at a restaurant in Philadelphia when he was attending a computer conference. Someone was adjusting the flowers in Laurie's hair. Nancy did not remember ever seeing Laurie in a dress. Laurie kept hitching up her waistband. Ed, in a dark tuxedo with red, embroidered lapels, was greeting friends and smiling broadly. Nancy remembered that at the restaurant in Philadelphia he had ordered baby octopus and that it had arrived intact, on a bed of pasta. Jack, who found Ed somewhat pretentious, had thought it was vulgar to order such a thing, but Nancy thought it had been adventurous.

When the musicians—two guitarists and a violinist—began playing, Nancy recognized Gypsy music in the wail of the violin. She recalled a Nancy Drew mystery involving Gypsies. She used to read those books on Granny's front porch. She sat on the porch swing, swinging as high as she could go and wishing hard that she could go someplace Nancy Drew went, and she begged Granny to run away with her, but Granny warned her against Gypsies and did not have a high opinion of unknown places. The violin was mournful at first, then sweet, then ecstatic, before shivering and retreating into a low moan.

Jack sat down beside Nancy. "I think I got some good shots," he said. "Doesn't Laurie look incredible?"

Two tall men walked with Laurie and Ed to the front of the room.

One of the men took a white gown from his briefcase and fluffed it up. He threw it up in the air like pizza dough and caught it, then pulled it over his head. The other man, a rabbi, draped an embroidered vestment around his shoulders. Laurie tugged at her skirt.

"The minister must be a friend of theirs," said the woman sitting next to Nancy.

The rabbi spoke in Hebrew and offered Laurie and Ed a glass of wine. Suddenly, in the front row, a man stood up and began talking to Laurie. She turned to listen. Then he faced the audience and said apologetically, "I couldn't give Laurie away, because I don't own her. But I ran across some things last week that I wanted to share on this occasion." He thumbed through the papers in his hand, explaining that they were report cards and drawings he had saved from Laurie's childhood. "I have this Valentine here," he said. "It's signed, 'Love, Laurie.' " He cried, and Laurie, looking embarrassed, embraced him. When he sat down, a woman next to him stood up, her back to the audience, and read a poem titled "The Outermost Limits." Nancy saw the rain splatter the stained glass, and somewhere a baby cried. The rabbi raised a glass of wine and sang. Laurie and Ed took turns reading parts of their marriage contract. Laurie had a theatrical voice; she was an actress and had once had a part in a soap opera.

She read, "We join together in the bond of marriage, but we do so in protest against the established institution of marriage, an institution that enslaves women by making them property, thus denying them economic equality. We also protest against laws that prevent homosexual couples from marrying. Yet we join together, formally, in this bond, as an affirmation of the love that individual human beings can feel for one another."

Suddenly, Laurie and Ed were stomping on wine glasses wrapped in cloth napkins, and then with a cry of relief that the glasses broke successfully, they virtually leaped into each other's arms. The Gypsy music began. Nancy was crying, at last.

At the reception in the cafeteria, she found a price tag dangling on a nylon thread inside the cuff of her silk blouse. Jack bit it off, discreetly, and she pulled out the end of the thread.

"Minnie Pearl," he teased. Nancy smiled nervously. Umbrellas drifted past the windows. The stained glass over the doorway was an abstract design—broken lines like shattered glass.

During the day, while Jack took more pictures, and the people milled around her, Nancy forgot for indeterminate stretches of time the news from home. When it occurred to her, rushing forward in a little replay of the conversation with her mother, she still felt awkward, almost puzzled. The rain was pounding harder outside, and the hum of voices blended with it. Everyone seemed happy. Two older women were thrilled to learn that Nancy lived in Pennsylvania. One of them cried, "Oh, we go to Pennsylvania! Once a year we go down to New Hope, and sometimes at midnight our friends take us across the state line to play Midnight Beano."

"It's lots of fun!" said her companion, who had red lipstick smeared around her lips.

"And then after that they take us shopping at a discount store there." The woman grasped Nancy's arm and said, "It was such a lovely ceremony, especially when Laurie's father made that little speech."

"That was touching," said the other woman. "I clean for Laurie. Ed has allergics and can't stand a speck of dust."

"That poem was odd, though. Wasn't it odd?"

"Ed is very sensitive."

Nancy found Jack changing a lens. "The lighting's wrong," he said. "I need my bright lights. Look at all the shadows."

"It's appropriate, though, for the weather today," said Nancy, seeing the shadows, the jewel-light of the stained glass. The people, dressed for the autumn beach in wool and corduroy, looked like faded autumn leaves. She said, "I just talked to some women who go to New Jersey to play Midnight Beano after they go discount shopping! Can you imagine! They were delightful."

"You seem to be enjoying yourself," Jack said.

"Should I?"

"Sure. It's a wedding."

"It's a wonderful wedding."

Nancy and Jack were laughing the way they had the previous day.

They ate at a table with Karen Bordon, an acquaintance from graduate school. Nancy barely remembered her, but Karen said Nancy had once given her a ride to Pittsfield. Karen operated a camera for a Boston television station. She called herself a camera person. The man she was with, Malcolm, worked in color processing, and Jack and Malcolm and Karen talked in technicalities about film while Nancy concentrated on the food, which had been catered by a Beacon Hill restaurant Nancy and Jack used to go to. There was food at funerals too, Nancy thought. The neighbors would bring hams and pies and cakes.

Later, Nancy telephoned the airlines, rechecking the schedule. There were still no seats available, and now flights were being canceled because of the weather.

Nancy sat with the telephone in front of a window. She saw Jack out on the beach with his camera, aiming at the foggy scene. She imagined gray, empty space in the pictures.

On the telephone, Nancy's father didn't protest when Nancy explained the difficulty of the travel schedule. She promised to come down later to help them get adjusted and to help her mother clean out Granny's room.

Nancy repeated to her mother, "The airline schedules are erratic because of the strike. I wish you'd put it off till Monday."

"We'll get a better crowd on Sunday. We'll just have a handful anyway. Everybody her age has died off. All the pallbearers on her list are dead, or else they're down in their back. Remember that list she used to keep under her pillow? Oh, I wish you could see her! She's beautiful, the way they've got her fixed up. She told your daddy she didn't want an open casket—she didn't want people to see her looking so pitiful. But she'd be proud if she could see herself. Those big flower sprays you put on top of the casket have gone up, so we couldn't afford a big one. They cost about a hundred dollars, so we got the small one for fifty. If we'd had a closed casket with just that little spray on it—why, that would look tooty!"

Nancy's mother talked on, describing the expenses of the funeral, the arrangements, the relatives who had called. Nancy let her mother talk. Jack was still out on the beach, oblivious to the chill wind. The water dashed against clay-colored rocks that had been cracked into hundreds of slices by a powerful force, probably glaciers. The slices had not separated. They made Nancy think of Droste chocolate oranges, which fall apart into perfect slices when tapped on the top.

Mom said, "She's just beautiful—she looks thirty years younger! Her hair's fixed nice, and I bought her a pretty blue dress, a dress like she would have liked, with a Peter Pan collar and tucks."

"I thought she had a blue dress she'd been saving."

"Well, it was out of style, and they had these dresses at the funeral home, so I bought one, and bought beads. She always liked jewelry. And she has a corsage, and inside the casket lid is a blue spray. I hope somebody brings a camera. I want to get some pictures for you. She didn't want all that money spent on her, but it was *her* money, and I'm spending it on *her*, to send her out in style."

"Are you going to be all right, Mom?" asked Nancy.

"Well, they say you're never prepared for anybody to die. And it's true."

Nancy shifted the receiver to her other ear. She said, "Your life is going to be different from now on. You and Daddy can go somewhere together for the first time in years. You can come and visit me—at last."

"This morning he told me something that floored me," Mom said. "He said, 'Do you realize that last night was the first night we slept in a house alone together in forty years?' I said no, but it's true. Forty years! There was always somebody here to take care of. Oh, you should see all the food the neighbors brought."

Nancy's mother described the food—ham, chicken, steak patties, three pies, two cakes, baked beans, three-bean salad, Jell-O salads. As she listened, Nancy kept her eyes on Jack out on the fractured rocks, a frail silhouette against the sea.

Back at the reception, when Nancy finally cornered her old friend Laurie, who had once lived in a basement apartment below Nancy's and played Doors albums full blast, she felt glad she had stayed. Laurie's freckles danced around her smile.

"I've had so much champagne," she said. "And I've barely seen Ed since the ceremony. Is this what marriage is like?"

"It's a lovely wedding," said Nancy.

"Jack was so sweet to take those pictures."

"Are you going on a trip?"

"No. We took our honeymoon last week. But next week I'm going to Mexico with my brother. He's an archaeologist, and I have this fabulous chance to go on a dig. Ed can't go because he has to work."

Nancy felt like confiding in Laurie, the way she used to when they studied together for exams. She found herself blurting out the news about her grandmother. It seemed improper to mar the wedding, and when Laurie made sympathetic remarks, Nancy said hastily, "It was expected. And she was old as Methuselah."

"It feels strange not going home, but I'm glad I'm here," she added. "And I'm glad you're doing something affirmative."

"That's the way we looked at it," Laurie said. "Ed's best friend died this summer, and that led to our decision to get married. We realized how little time there is."

Laurie was holding Nancy's hand. Her flowers were askew.

Nancy said, "I'm sure my mother will flip out when it hits her that she's free at last. They've been tied down on the farm for *years,* taking care of my grandmother. They've never even left Kentucky to visit me."

"Did you say your grandmother was your dad's mother?"

"Yes."

Laurie said, "If Ed's dad were to die and his mother had to move in with us, I'd divorce him in a minute. I wouldn't take care of my mother-in-law like that. I'm not even sure I could do it for my own mother." Laurie was looking around cautiously as she spoke. Her mother-in-law was eating cake on the far side of the room, and her mother was out of sight.

"Do you know what my mother said on the phone?" Nancy said. "She said last night was the first night in forty years that she and my father had spent alone together."

Laurie's look of astonishment pleased Nancy. It was the best gesture of sympathy: to be amazed.

"Are you O.K., Nancy?" It was Jack, standing close, touching her. "You look off-balance."

"It's the champagne. I was O.K. until Mom started talking about how pretty Granny looked and telling about the dress. Now all I can think is this doll shut in a box in the ground with flowers in her face."

"You're not supposed to think about things like that."

"They really expected me to come home."

"I'm sorry I urged you not to go," Jack said.

Nancy drank some more champagne. "I couldn't go anyway in the fog," she said.

"You can go to Kentucky next week," Jack said.

"Yes. Oh, look! The musicians are packing up. I wish they wouldn't go. I loved that Gypsy violin."

On Sunday the ocean was calm and the sky was a transparent blue, reflecting in the water. Nancy and Jack were on a sightseeing boat, heading out from shore. About five times Jack said he wished Robert was along. When he saw whales on TV, Robert would yell out with breathless excitement. Nancy kept thinking of the time her mother mentioned in a letter a traveling exhibition that had come to the shopping center—a whale in a tank in a trailer truck. The whale couldn't even turn around.

"What do you feel?" Jack asked her as the shore disappeared.

"Confused," said Nancy, looking forward to the horizon. A barge lay in line with it.

"You've got to get your mom and dad up to visit us."

"Somehow I can't picture it. It would freak them out. They never went anywhere. I was the one who left, but they always expected me to keep running back."

The boat was passing close to a buoy, bobbing casually on the water. A seabird landed on it, like a spacecraft docking.

"They sent me out as an explorer," Nancy said. "Like Columbus."

"I read that Columbus brought syphilis back to Europe."

"That's what happens when you go out adventuring," Nancy said. "It's the nature of the game."

Jack tied the drawstring of her hood under her chin. She said, "I didn't wear my watch because I didn't want to get it wet. Do you have your pocket calculator?"

Jack patted his breast pocket and nodded.

"I want you to tell me when it's three o'clock," she said. "The funeral's at two. That's three, Eastern time. I want to know when it is, so I can think about it happening. At least I can be there in my imagination."

Jack punched tiny buttons on his calculator so that a beeper would sound at three. "I'm sorry I urged you not to go to Kentucky," he said. "It was selfish."

"No, I keep telling you, it's O.K."

"If I die, I don't want you to make a fuss. You can just throw me in the ocean."

Nancy could almost see Granny's face. The last time Nancy saw her, she had taken a kitten in to show her. On TV reports about pet therapy, children took puppies and kittens into nursing homes for old people to pet. Nancy had a vivid memory of an old woman's chalky face lighting up when she held a puppy in her lap. Nancy had offered the kitten to her grandmother, but Granny wouldn't touch it. Her face was grim and selfish. She didn't want the curtains opened either, and she didn't want a radio. No one read to her. Staring at the ocean, Nancy thought that its vast blankness and mystery were like her grandmother's mind in those final months—something private and deep she had saved for herself.

"Whale ahoy!" the captain cried suddenly.

Nancy did not pay attention when three o'clock came, for they were among the whales. A whale's back appeared like a large boulder out in the water, and then three or four, like stepping stones. As the boat drew nearer, a whale leaped up like a jack-in-the-box. The passengers were shouting and clumsily aiming their cameras. Water smacked their faces, and Jack and Nancy gasped with laughter. The whales began moving, making deep swirls and waves in the water, and then a humpback whale, barnacled like a circus elephant decorated with sequins, rose completely out of the water and seemed to fly. At that moment Nancy knew that this—not something quaint or cozy—was what she had come so far away from home to see. The engine stopped, and the boat started to rock in the wake of the whales. Jack's face was charged with delight. His camera hung loose on his chest. Another whale breached, close by, with a force that shot water up to the sky. As it plunged downward, its tail flukes wiggled, like an airplane tipping its wings as a signal to someone below.

Lying Doggo

Grover Cleveland is growing feeble. His eyes are cloudy, and his muzzle is specked with white hairs. When he scoots along on the hardwood floors, he makes a sound like brushes on drums. He sleeps in front of the woodstove, and when he gets too hot he creeps across the floor.

When Nancy married Jack Cleveland, she felt, in a way, that she was marrying a divorced man with a child. Grover was a young dog then. Jack had gotten him at the humane society shelter. He had picked the shyest, most endearing puppy in a boisterous litter. Later, he told Nancy that someone said he should have chosen an energetic one, because quiet puppies often have something wrong with them. That chance remark bothered Nancy; it could have applied to her as well. But that was years ago. Nancy and Jack are still married, and Grover has lived to be old. Now his arthritis stiffens his legs so that on some days he cannot get up. Jack has been talking of having Grover put to sleep.

"Why do you say 'put to sleep'?" their son, Robert, asks. "I know what you mean." Robert is nine. He is a serious boy, quiet, like Nancy.

"No reason. It's just the way people say it."

"They don't say they put *people* to sleep."

"It doesn't usually happen to people," Jack says.

"Don't you dare take him to the vet unless you let me go along. I don't want any funny stuff behind my back."

"Don't worry, Robert," Nancy says.

Later, in Jack's studio, while developing photographs of broken snow fences on hillsides, Jack says to Nancy, "There's a first time for everything, I guess."

"What?"

"Death. I never really knew anybody who died."

"You're forgetting my grandmother."

"I didn't really know your grandmother." Jack looks down at Grover's face in the developing fluid. Grover looks like a wolf in the snow on the hill. Jack says, "The only people I ever cared about who died were rock heroes."

Jack has been buying special foods for the dog—pork chops and liver, vitamin supplements. All the arthritis literature he has been able to find concerns people, but he says the same rules must apply to all mammals. Until Grover's hind legs gave way, Jack and Robert took Grover out for long, slow walks through the woods. Recently, a neighbor who keeps Alaskan malamutes stopped Nancy in the Super Duper and inquired about Grover. The neighbor wanted to know which kind of arthritis Grover had: osteo- or rheumatoid? The neighbor said he had rheumatoid and held out knobbed fingers. The doctor told him to avoid zucchini and to drink lots of water. Grover doesn't like zucchini, Nancy said.

Jack and Nancy and Robert all deal with Grover outside. It doesn't help that the temperature is dropping below twenty degrees. It feels even colder because they are conscious of the dog's difficulty. Nancy holds his head and shoulders while Jack supports his hind legs. Robert holds up Grover's tail.

Robert says, "I have an idea."

"What, sweetheart?" asks Nancy. In her arms, Grover lurches. Nancy squeezes against him and he whimpers.

"We could put a diaper on him."

"How would we clean him up?"

"They do that with chimpanzees," says Jack, "but it must be messy."

"You mean I didn't have an original idea?" Robert cries. "Curses, foiled again!" Robert has been reading comic books about masked villains.

"There aren't many original ideas," Jack says, letting go of Grover. "They just look original when you're young." Jack lifts Grover's hind legs again and grasps him under the stomach. "Let's try one more time, boy."

Grover looks at Nancy, pleading.

Nancy has been feeling that the dying of Grover marks a milestone in her marriage to Jack, a marriage that has somehow lasted almost fifteen years. She is seized with an irrational dread—that when the dog is gone, Jack will be gone too. Whenever Nancy and Jack are apart—during Nancy's frequent trips to see her family in Kentucky, or when Jack has gone away "to think"—Grover remains with Jack. Actually, Nancy knew Grover before she knew Jack. When Jack and Nancy were students, in Massachusetts, the dog was a familiar figure around campus. Nancy was drawn to the dog long before she noticed the shaggy-haired student in the sheepskin-lined corduroy jacket who was usually with him. Once, in a seminar on the Federalist period that Nancy was auditing, Grover had walked in, circled the room, and then walked out, as if performing some routine investigation, like the man who sprayed Nancy's apartment building for silverfish. Grover was a beautiful dog, a German shepherd, gray, dusted with a sooty topcoat. After the seminar, Nancy followed the dog out of the building, and she met Jack then. Eventually, when Nancy and Jack made love in his apartment in Amherst, Grover lay sprawled by the bed, both protective and quietly participatory. Later, they moved into a house in the country, and Nancy felt that she had an instant family.

Once, for almost three months, Jack and Grover were gone. Jack left Nancy in California, pregnant and terrified, and went to stay at an Indian reservation in New Mexico. Nancy lived in a room on a street with palm trees. It was winter. It felt like a Kentucky October. She went to a park every day and watched people with their dogs, their children, and tried to comprehend that she was there, alone, a mile from the San Andreas Fault, reluctant to return to Kentucky. "We need to decide where we stand with each other," Jack had said when he left. "Just when I start to think I know where you're at, you seem to disappear." Jack always seemed to stand back and watch her, as though he expected her to do something excitingly original. He expected her to be herself, not someone she thought people wanted her to be. That was a twist: he expected the unexpected.

While Jack was away, Nancy indulged in crafts projects. At the Free University, she learned batik and macramé. On her own, she learned to crochet. She had never done anything like that before. She threw away her file folders of history notes for the article she had wanted to write. Suddenly, making things with her hands was the only endeavor that made sense. She crocheted a bulky, shapeless sweater in a shell stitch for Jack. She made baby things, using large hooks. She did not realize that such heavy blankets were unsuitable for a baby until she saw Robert—a tiny, warped-looking creature, like one of her clumsily made crafts. When Jack returned, she was in a sprawling adobe hospital, nursing a baby the color of scalded skin. The old song "In My Adobe Hacienda" was going through her head. Jack stood over her behind an unfamiliar beard, grinning in disbelief, stroking the baby as though he were a new pet. Nancy felt she had fooled Jack into thinking she had done something original at last.

"Grover's dying to see you," he said to her. "They wouldn't let him in here."

"I'll be glad to see Grover," said Nancy. "I missed him."

She had missed, she realized then, his various expressions: the staccato barks of joy, the forceful, menacing barks at strangers, the eerie howls when he heard cat fights at night.

Those early years together were confused and dislocated. After leaving graduate school, at the beginning of the seventies, they lived in a number of places—sometimes on the road, with Grover, in a van— but after Robert was born they settled in Pennsylvania. Their life is orderly. Jack is a free-lance photographer, with his own studio at home. Nancy, unable to find a use for her degree in history, returned to school, taking education and administration courses. Now she is assistant principal of a small private elementary school, which Robert attends. Now and then Jack frets about becoming too middle-class. He has become semipolitical about energy, sometimes attending anti-nuclear power rallies. He has been building a sun space for his studio and has been insulating the house. "Retrofitting" is the term he uses for making the house energy-efficient.

"Insulation is his hobby," Nancy told an old friend from graduate school, Tom Green, who telephoned unexpectedly one day recently. "He insulates on weekends."

"Maybe he'll turn into a butterfly—he could insulate himself into a cocoon," said Tom, who Nancy always thought was funny. She had not seen him in ten years. He called to say he was sending a novel he had written—"about all the crazy stuff we did back then."

The dog is forcing Nancy to think of how Jack has changed in the years since then. He is losing his hair, but he doesn't seem concerned. Jack was always fanatical about being honest. He used to be insensitive about his directness. "I'm just being honest," he would say pleasantly, boyishly, when he hurt people's feelings. He told Nancy she was uptight, that no one ever knew what she thought, that she should be more expressive. He said she "played games" with people, hiding her feelings behind her coy Southern smile. He is more tolerant now, less judgmental. He used to criticize her for drinking Cokes and eating pastries. He didn't like her lipstick, and she stopped wearing it. But Nancy has changed too. She is too sophisticated now to eat fried foods and rich pies and cakes, indulging in them only when she goes to Kentucky. She uses makeup now—so sparingly that Jack does not notice. Her cool reserve, her shyness, has changed to cool assurance, with only the slightest shift. Inwardly, she has reorganized. "It's like retrofitting," she said to Jack once, but he didn't notice any irony.

It wasn't until two years ago that Nancy learned that he had lied to her when he told her he had been at the Beatles' Shea Stadium concert in 1966, just as she had, only two months before they met. When he confessed his lie, he claimed he had wanted to identify with her and impress her because he thought of her as someone so mysterious and aloof that he could not hold her attention. Nancy, who had in fact been intimidated by Jack's directness, was troubled to learn about his peculiar deception. It was out of character. She felt a part of her past had been ripped away. More recently, when John Lennon died, Nancy and Jack watched the silent vigil from Central Park on TV and cried in each other's arms. Everybody that week was saying that they had lost their youth.

Jack was right. That was the only sort of death they had known.

Grover lies on his side, stretched out near the fire, his head flat on one ear. His eyes are open, expressionless, and when Nancy speaks to him he doesn't respond.

"Come on, Grover!" cries Robert, tugging the dog's leg. "Are you dead?"

"Don't pull at him," Nancy says.

"He's lying doggo," says Jack.

"That's funny," says Robert. "What does that mean?"

"Dogs do that in the heat," Jack explains. "They save energy that way."

"But it's winter," says Robert. "I'm freezing." He is wearing a wool pullover and a goose-down vest. Jack has the thermostat set on fifty-five, relying mainly on the woodstove to warm the house.

"I'm cold too," says Nancy. "I've been freezing since 1965, when I came North."

Jack crouches down beside the dog. "Grover, old boy. Please. Just give a little sign."

"If you don't get up, I won't give you your treat tonight," says Robert, wagging his finger at Grover.

"Let him rest," says Jack, who is twiddling some of Grover's fur between his fingers.

"Are you sure he's not dead?" Robert asks. He runs the zipper of his vest up and down.

"He's just pretending," says Nancy.

The tip of Grover's tail twitches, and Jack catches it, the way he might grab at a fluff of milkweed in the air.

Later, in the kitchen, Jack and Nancy are preparing for a dinner party. Jack is sipping whiskey. The woodstove has been burning all day, and the house is comfortably warm now. In the next room,

Robert is lying on the rug in front of the stove with Grover. He is playing with a computer football game and watching *Mork and Mindy* at the same time. Robert likes to do several things at once, and lately he has included Grover in his multiple activities.

Jack says, "I think the only thing to do is just feed Grover pork chops and steaks and pet him a lot, and then when we can stand it, take him to the vet and get it over with."

"When can we stand it?"

"If I were in Grover's shape, I'd just want to be put out of my misery."

"Even if you were still conscious and could use your mind?"

"I guess so."

"I couldn't pull the plug on you," says Nancy, pointing a carrot at Jack. "You'd have to be screaming in agony."

"Would you want me to do it to you?"

"No. I can see right now that I'd be the type to hang on. I'd be just like Granny. I think she just clung to life, long after her body was ready to die."

"Would you really be like that?"

"You said once I was just like her—repressed, uptight."

"I didn't mean that."

"You've been right about me before," Nancy says, reaching across Jack for a paring knife. "Look, all I mean is that it shouldn't be a matter of *our* convenience. If Grover needs assistance, then it's our problem. We're responsible."

"I'd want to be put out of my misery," Jack says.

During that evening, Nancy has the impression that Jack is talking more than usual. He does not notice the food. She has made chicken Marengo and is startled to realize how much it resembles chicken cacciatore, which she served the last time she had the same people over. The recipes are side by side in the cookbook, gradations on a theme. The dinner is for Stewart and Jan, who are going to Italy on a teaching exchange.

"Maybe I shouldn't even have made Italian," Nancy tells them apologetically. "You'll get enough of that in Italy. And it will be real."

Both Stewart and Jan say the chicken Marengo is wonderful. The olives are the right touch, Jan says. Ted and Laurie nod agreement. Jack pours more wine. The sound of a log falling in the woodstove reminds Nancy of the dog in the other room by the stove, and in her mind she stages a scene: finding the dog dead in the middle of the dinner party.

Afterwards, they sit in the living room, with Grover lying there like a log too large for the stove. The guests talk idly. Ted has been sandblasting old paint off a brick fireplace, and Laurie complains about the gritty dust. Jack stokes the fire. The stove, hooked up through the fireplace, looks like a robot from an old science fiction movie. Nancy and Jack used to sit by the fireplace in Massachusetts, stoned, watching the blue frills of the flames, imagining that they were musical notes, visual textures of sounds on the stereo. Nobody they know smokes grass anymore. Now people sit around and talk about investments and proper flue linings. When Jack passes around the Grand Marnier, Nancy says, "In my grandparents' house years ago, we used to sit by their fireplace. They burned coal. They didn't call it a fireplace, though. They called it a grate."

"Coal burns more efficiently than wood," Jack says.

"Coal's a lot cheaper in this area," says Ted. "I wish I could switch."

"My grandparents had big stone fireplaces in their country house," says Jan, who comes from Connecticut. "They were so pleasant. I always looked forward to going there. Sometimes in the summer the evenings were cool and we'd have a fire. It was lovely."

"I remember being cold," says Nancy. "It was always very cold, even in the South."

"The heat just goes up the chimney in a fireplace," says Jack.

Nancy stares at Jack. She says, "I would stand in front of the fire until I was roasted. Then I would turn and roast the other side. In the evenings, my grandparents sat on the hearth and read the Bible. There wasn't anything *lovely* about it. They were trying to keep warm. Of course, nobody had heard of insulation."

"There goes Nancy, talking about her deprived childhood," Jack says with a laugh.

Nancy says, "Jack is so concerned about wasting energy. But when he goes out he never wears a hat." She looks at Jack. "Don't you know your body heat just flies out the top of your head? It's a chimney."

Surprised by her tone, she almost breaks into tears.

It is the following evening, and Jack is flipping through some contact sheets of a series on solar hot-water heaters he is doing for a magazine. Robert sheds his goose-down vest, and he and Grover, on the floor, simultaneously inch away from the fire. Nancy is trying to read the novel written by the friend from Amherst, but the book is boring. She would not have recognized her witty friend from the past in the turgid prose she is reading.

"It's a dump on the sixties," she tells Jack when he asks. "A really cynical look. All the characters are types."

"Are we in it?"

"No. I hope not. I think it's based on that Phil Baxter who cracked up at that party."

Grover raises his head, his eyes alert, and Robert jumps up, saying, "It's time for Grover's treat."

He shakes a Pet-Tab from a plastic bottle and holds it before Grover's nose. Grover bangs his tail against the rug as he crunches the pill.

Jack turns on the porch light and steps outside for a moment, returning with a shroud of cold air. "It's starting to snow," he says. "Come on out, Grover."

Grover struggles to stand, and Jack heaves the dog's hind legs over the threshold.

Later, in bed, Jack turns on his side and watches Nancy, reading her book, until she looks up at him.

"You read so much," he says. "You're always reading."

"Hmm."

"We used to have more fun. We used to be silly together."

"What do you want to do?"

"Just something silly."

"I can't think of anything silly." Nancy flips the page back, rereading. "God, this guy can't write. I used to think he was so clever."

In the dark, touching Jack tentatively, she says, "We've changed. We used to lie awake all night, thrilled just to touch each other."

"We've been busy. That's what happens. People get busy."

"That scares me," says Nancy. "Do you want to have another baby?"

"No. I want a dog." Jack rolls away from her, and Nancy can hear him breathing into his pillow. She waits to hear if he will cry. She recalls Jack returning to her in California after Robert was born. He brought a God's-eye, which he hung from the ceiling above Robert's crib, to protect him. Jack never wore the sweater Nancy made for him. Instead, Grover slept on it. Nancy gave the dog her granny-square afghan too, and eventually, when they moved back East, she got rid of the pathetic evidence of her creative period—the crochet hooks, the piles of yarn, some splotchy batik tapestries. Now most of the objects in the house are Jack's. He made the oak counters and the dining room table; he remodeled the studio; he chose the draperies; he photographed the pictures on the wall. If Jack were to leave again, there would be no way to remove his presence, the way the dog can disappear completely, with his sounds. Nancy revises the scene in her mind. The house is still there, but Nancy is not in it.

In the morning, there is a four-inch snow, with a drift blowing up the back-porch steps. From the kitchen window, Nancy watches her son float silently down the hill behind the house. At the end, he tumbles off his sled deliberately, wallowing in the snow, before standing up to wave, trying to catch her attention.

On the back porch, Nancy and Jack hold Grover over newspapers. Grover performs unselfconsciously now. Nancy says, "Maybe he can hang on, as long as we can do this."

"But look at him, Nancy," Jack says. "He's in misery."

Jack holds Grover's collar and helps him slide over the threshold. Grover aims for his place by the fire.

After the snowplow passes, late in the morning, Nancy drives Robert to the school on slushy roads, all the while lecturing him on the absurdity of raising money to buy official Boy Scout equipment, especially on a snowy Saturday. The Boy Scouts are selling water-savers for toilet tanks in order to earn money for camping gear.

"I thought Boy Scouts spent their time earning badges," says Nancy. "I thought you were supposed to learn about nature, instead of spending money on official Boy Scout pots and pans."

"This is nature," Robert says solemnly. "It's ecology. Saving water when you flush is ecology."

Later, Nancy and Jack walk in the woods together. Nancy walks behind Jack, stepping in his boot tracks. He shields her from the wind. Her hair is blowing. They walk briskly up a hill and emerge on a ridge that overlooks a valley. In the distance they can see a housing development, a radio tower, a winding road. House trailers dot the hillsides. A snowplow is going up a road, like a zipper in the landscape.

Jack says, "I'm going to call the vet Monday."

Nancy gasps in cold air. She says, "Robert made us promise you won't do anything without letting him in on it. That goes for me too." When Jack doesn't respond, she says, "I'd want to hang on, even if I was in a coma. There must be some spark, in the deep recesses of the mind, some twitch, a flicker of a dream—"

"A twitch that could make life worth living?" Jack laughs bitterly.

"Yes." She points to the brilliantly colored sparkles the sun is making on the snow. "Those are the sparks I mean," she says. "In the brain somewhere, something like that. That would be beautiful."

"You're weird, Nancy."

"I learned it from you. I never would have noticed anything like that if I hadn't known you, if you hadn't got me stoned and made me look at your photographs." She stomps her feet in the snow. Her toes are cold. "You educated me. I was so out of it when I met you. One day I was listening to Hank Williams and shelling corn for the chickens and the next day I was expected to know what wines went with what. Talk about weird."

"You're exaggerating. That was years ago. You always exaggerate your background." He adds in a teasing tone, "Your humble origins."

"We've been together fifteen years," says Nancy. She stops him, holding his arm. Jack is squinting, looking at something in the distance. She goes on, "You said we didn't do anything silly anymore. What should we do, Jack? Should we make angels in the snow?"

Jack touches his rough glove to her face. "We shouldn't unless we really feel like it."

It was the same as Jack chiding her to be honest, to be expressive. The same old Jack, she thought, relieved.

"Come and look," Robert cries, bursting in the back door. He and Jack have been outside making a snowman. Nancy is rolling dough for a quiche. Jack will eat a quiche but not a custard pie, although they are virtually the same. She wipes her hands and goes to the door of the porch. She sees Grover swinging from the lower branch of the maple tree. Jack has rigged up a sling, so that the dog is supported in a harness, with the canvas from the back of a deck chair holding his stomach. His legs dangle free.

"Oh, Jack," Nancy calls. "The poor thing."

"I thought this might work," Jack explains. "A support for his hind legs." His arms cradle the dog's head. "I did it for you," he adds, looking at Nancy. "Don't push him, Robert. I don't think he wants to swing."

Grover looks amazingly patient, like a cat in a doll bonnet.

"He hates it," says Jack, unbuckling the harness.

"He can learn to like it," Robert says, his voice rising shrilly.

On the day that Jack has planned to take Grover to the veterinarian, Nancy runs into a crisis at work. One of the children has been exposed to hepatitis, and it is necessary to vaccinate all of them. Nancy has to arrange the details, which means staying late. She telephones Jack to ask him to pick up Robert after school.

"I don't know when I'll be home," she says. "This is an administrative nightmare. I have to call all the parents, get permissions, make arrangements with family doctors."

"What will we do about Grover?"

"Please postpone it. I want to be with you then."

"I want to get it over with," says Jack impatiently. "I hate to put Robert through another day of this."

"Robert will be glad of the extra time," Nancy insists. "So will I."

"I just want to face things," Jack says. "Don't you understand? I don't want to cling to the past like you're doing."

"Please wait for us," Nancy says, her voice calm and controlled.

On the telephone, Nancy is authoritative, a quick decision-maker. The problem at work is a reprieve. She feels free, on her own. During the afternoon, she works rapidly and efficiently, filing reports, consulting health authorities, notifying parents. She talks with the disease-control center in Atlanta, inquiring about guidelines. She checks on supplies of gamma globulin. She is so preoccupied that in the middle of the afternoon, when Robert suddenly appears in her office, she is startled, for a fleeting instant not recognizing him.

He says, "Kevin has a sore throat. Is that hepatitis?"

"It's probably just a cold. I'll talk to his mother." Nancy is holding Robert's arm, partly to keep him still, partly to steady herself.

"When do I have to get a shot?" Robert asks.

"Tomorrow."

"Do I have to?"

"Yes. It won't hurt, though."

"I guess it's a good thing this happened," Robert says bravely. "Now we get to have Grover another day." Robert spills his books on the floor and bends to pick them up. When he looks up, he says, "Daddy doesn't care about him. He just wants to get rid of him. He wants to kill him."

"Oh, Robert, that's not true," says Nancy. "He just doesn't want Grover to suffer."

"But Grover still has half a bottle of Pet-Tabs," Robert says. "What will we do with them?"

"I don't know," Nancy says. She hands Robert his numbers workbook. Like a tape loop, the face of her child as a stranger replays in her mind. Robert has her plain brown hair, her coloring, but his eyes are Jack's—demanding and eerily penetrating, eyes that could pin her to the wall.

After Robert leaves, Nancy lowers the venetian blinds. Her office is brilliantly lighted by the sun, through south-facing windows. The design was accidental, nothing to do with solar energy. It is an old building. Bars of light slant across her desk, like a formidable scene in a forties movie. Nancy's secretary goes home, but Nancy works on, contacting all the parents she couldn't get during working hours. One parent anxiously reports that her child has a swollen lymph node on his neck.

"No," Nancy says firmly. "That is *not* a symptom of hepatitis. But you should ask the doctor about that when you go in for the gamma globulin."

Gamma globulin. The phrase rolls off her tongue. She tries to remember an odd title of a movie about gamma rays. It comes to her as she is dialing the telephone: *The Effect of Gamma Rays on Man-in-the-Moon Marigolds*. She has never known what that title meant.

The office grows dim, and Nancy turns on the lights. The school is quiet, as though the threat of an infectious disease has emptied the corridors, leaving her in charge. She recalls another movie, *The Andromeda Strain*. Her work is like the thrill of watching drama, a threat held safely at a distance. Historians have to be detached, Nancy once said, defensively, to Jack, when he accused her of being unfriendly to shopkeepers and waiters. Where was all that Southern hospitality he had heard so much about? he wanted to know. It hits her now that historians are detached about the past, not the present. Jack has learned some of this detachment; he wants to let Grover go. Nancy thinks of the stark images in his recent photographs—snow, icicles, fences, the long shot of Grover on the hill like a stray wolf. Nancy had always liked Jack's pictures simply for what they were, but Jack didn't see the people or the objects in them. He saw illusions. The vulnerability of the image, he once said, was what he was after. The image was meant to evoke its own death, he told her.

By the time Nancy finishes the scheduling, the night maintenance crew has arrived, and the coffeepot they keep in a closet is perking. Nancy removes her contact lenses and changes into her fleece-lined boots. In the parking lot, she maneuvers cautiously along a path past a mountain of black-stained snow. It is so cold that she makes sparks on the vinyl car seat. The engine is cold, slow to turn over.

At home, Nancy is surprised to see balloons in the living room. The stove is blazing and Robert's face is red from the heat.

"We're having a party," he says. "For Grover."

"There's a surprise for you in the oven," says Jack, handing Nancy a glass of sherry. "Because you worked so hard."

"Grover had ice cream," Robert says. "We got Häagen-Dazs."

"He looks cheerful," Nancy says, sinking onto the couch next to Jack. Her glasses are fogged up. She removes them and wipes them with a Kleenex. When she puts them back on, she sees Grover looking at her, his head on his paws. His tail thumps. For the first time, Nancy feels ready to let the dog die.

When Nancy tells about the gamma globulin, the phrase has stopped rolling off her tongue so trippingly. She laughs. She is so tired she throbs with relief. She drinks the sherry too fast. Suddenly, she sits up straight and announces, "I've got a clue. I'm thinking of a parking lot."

"East or West?" Jack says. This is a game they used to play.

"West."

"Aha, I've got you," says Jack. "You're thinking of the parking lot at that hospital in Tucson."

"Hey, that's not fair going too fast," cries Robert. "I didn't get a chance to play."

"This was before you were born," Nancy says, running her fingers through Robert's hair. He is on the floor, leaning against her knees. "We were lying in the van for a week, thinking we were going to die. Oh, God!" Nancy laughs and covers her mouth with her hands.

"Why were you going to die?" Robert asks.

"We weren't really going to die." Both Nancy and Jack are laughing now at the memory, and Jack is pulling off his sweater. The hospital in Tucson wouldn't accept them because they weren't sick enough to hospitalize, but they were too sick to travel. They had nowhere to go. They had been on a month's trip through the West, then had stopped in Tucson and gotten jobs at a restaurant to make enough money to get home.

"Do you remember that doctor?" Jack says.

"I remember the look he gave us, like he didn't want us to pollute his hospital." Nancy laughs harder. She feels silly and relieved. Her hand, on Jack's knee, feels the fold of the long johns beneath his jeans. She cries, "I'll never forget how we stayed around that parking lot, thinking we were going to die."

"I couldn't have driven a block, I was so weak," Jack gasps.

"You were yellow. *I* didn't get yellow."

"All we could do was pee and drink orange juice."

"And throw the pee out the window."

"Grover was so bored with us!"

Nancy says, "It's a good thing we couldn't eat. We would have spent all our money."

"Then we would have had to work at that filthy restaurant again. And get sick again."

"And on and on, forever. We would still be there, like Charley on the MTA. Oh, Jack, do you *remember* that crazy restaurant? You had to wear a ten-gallon hat—"

Abruptly, Robert jerks away from Nancy and crawls on his knees across the room to examine Grover, who is stretched out on his side, his legs sticking out stiffly. Robert, his straight hair falling, bends his head to the dog's heart.

"He's not dead," Robert says, looking up at Nancy. "He's lying doggo."

"Passed out at his own party," Jack says, raising his glass. "Way to go, Grover!"

1985

Spence + Lila

1

On the way to the hospital in Paducah, Spence notices the row of signs along the highway: WHERE WILL YOU BE IN ETERNITY? Each word is on a white cross. The message reminds him of the old Burma-Shave signs. His wife, Lila, beside him, has been quiet during the trip, which takes forty minutes in his Rabbit. He didn't take her car because it has a hole in the muffler, but she has complained about his car ever since he cut the seat belts off to deactivate the annoying warning buzzer.

As they pass the Lone Oak shopping center, on the outskirts of Paducah, Lila says fretfully, "I don't know if the girls will get here."

"They're supposed to be here by night," Spence reminds her. Ahead, a gas station marquee advertises a free case of Coke with a tune-up.

Catherine, their younger daughter, has gone to pick up Nancy at the airport in Nashville. Although Lila objected to the trouble and expense, Nancy is flying all the way from Boston. Cat lives nearby, and Nancy will stay with her. Nancy offered to stay with Spence, so he wouldn't be alone, but he insisted he would be all right.

When Cat brought Lila home from the doctor the day before and Lila said, "They think it's cancer," the words ran through him like electricity. She didn't cry all evening, and when he tried to hold her, he couldn't speak. They sat in the living room in their recliner chairs, silent and scared, watching TV just as they usually did. Before she sat down for the evening, she worked busily in the kitchen, freezing vegetables from the garden and cooking food for him to eat during her stay in the hospital. He couldn't eat any supper except a bowl of cereal, and she picked at some ham and green beans.

He knew she had not been feeling well for months; she'd had dizzy spells and she had lost weight. The doctor at the local clinic told her to come back in three months if she kept losing weight, but Cat insisted on taking her mother to Paducah. The doctors were better there, Cat insisted, in that know-it-all manner both his daughters had. Cat, who was careless with money, didn't even think to ask what the specialists would charge. When she brought Lila home, it was late—feeding time. Spence was at the pond feeding the ducks, with Oscar, the dog. When Oscar saw the car turn into the driveway, he tore through the soybean field toward the house, as if he, too, were anxious for a verdict.

They had told Lila that her dizzy spells were tiny strokes. They also found a knot in her right breast. They wanted to take the knot out and do a test on it, and if it was cancer they would take her whole breast off, right then. It was an emergency, Lila explained. They couldn't deal with the strokes until they got the knot out. Spence imagined the knot growing so fast it would eat her breast up if she waited another day or two.

They're crawling through the traffic on the edge of Paducah. When he was younger, Spence used to come and watch the barges on the river. They glided by confidently, like miniature flattops putting out to sea. He has wanted to take Lila for a cruise on the *Delta Queen,* the luxury steamboat that paddles all the way to New Orleans, but he hasn't been able to bring himself to do it.

He turns on the radio and a Rod Stewart song blares out.

"Turn that thing off!" Lila yells.

"I thought you needed a little entertainment," he says, turning the sound down.

She rummages in her purse for a cigarette, her third on the trip.

"They won't let me have any cigarettes tonight, so I better smoke while I got a chance."

"I'll take them things and throw 'em away," he says.

"You better not."

She cracks the window open at the top to let the smoke out. Her face is the color of cigarette ashes. She looks bad.

"I guess it's really cancer," she says, blowing out smoke. "The X-ray man said it was cancer."

"How would he know? He ain't even a doctor."

"He's seen so many, he would know."

"He ain't paid to draw that conclusion," Spence says. "Why did he want to scare you like that? Didn't the doctor say he'd have to wait till they take the knot out and look at it?"

"Yeah, but—" She fidgets with her purse, wadding her cigarette package back into one of the zipper pockets. "The X-ray man sees those X-rays all day long. He knows more about X-rays than a doctor does."

Spence turns into the hospital parking lot, unsure where to go. The eight-story hospital cuts through the humid, hazy sky, like a stray sprig of milo growing up in a bean field. A car pulls out in front of him. Spence's reactions are slow today, but he hits the brakes in time.

"I think I'll feel safer in the hospital," Lila says.

Walking from the parking lot, he carries the small bag she packed. He suspects there is a carton of cigarettes in it. Cat keeps trying to get Lila to quit, but Lila has no willpower. Once Cat gave her a cassette tape on how to quit smoking, but Lila accidentally ran it through the washing machine. It was in a shirt pocket. "Accidentally on purpose," Cat accused her. Cat even told Lila once that cigarettes caused breast cancer. But Spence believes worry causes it. She worries about Cat, the way she has been running around with men she hardly knows since her divorce last year. It's a bad example for her two small children, and Lila is afraid the men aren't serious about Cat. Lila keeps saying no one will want to marry a woman with two extra mouths to feed.

Now Lila says, "I want you to supervise that garden. The girls won't know how to take care of it. That corn needs to be froze, and the beans are still coming in."

"Don't worry about your old garden," he says impatiently. "Maybe I'll mow it down."

"Spence!" Lila cries, grabbing his arm tightly. "Don't you go and mow down my garden!"

"You work too hard on it," he says. "We don't need all that grub anymore for just us two."

"The beans is about to begin a second round of blooming," she says. "I want to let most of them make into shellies and save some for seed. And I don't want the corn to get too old."

The huge glass doors of the hospital swing open, and a nurse pushes out an old woman in a wheelchair. The woman is bony and pale, with a cluster of kinfolks in bluejeans around her. Her aged hands, folded in her lap, are spotted like little bird dogs. The air-conditioning blasts Spence and Lila as they enter, and he feels as though they are walking into a meat locker.

2

She felt that lump weeks ago, but she didn't mention it then. When she and Spence returned from a trip to Florida recently, she told Cat about it, and Cat started pestering her to see a specialist. The knot did feel unusual, like a piece of gristle. The magazines said you would know it was different. Lila never examined her breasts the way they said to do, because her breasts were always full of lumps anyway—from mastitis, which she had had several times. Her breasts are so enormous she cannot expect to find a little knot. Spence says her breasts are like cow bags. He has funny names for them, like the affectionate names he had for his cows when they used to keep milk cows. Names like Daisy and Bossy. Petunia. Primrose. It will be harder on him if she loses one of her breasts than it will be on her. Women can stand so much more than men can.

She makes him leave the hospital early, wanting to be alone so she can smoke a cigarette in peace. After he brought her in, he paced around, then went downstairs for a Coke. Now he leaves to go home, and she watches him from behind as he trudges down the corridor, hugging himself in the cold. Lila is glad she brought her housecoat, but even with it she is afraid she will take pneumonia.

In the lounge, she smokes and plays with a picture puzzle laid out on a card table. Someone has pieced most of the red barn and pasture, and a vast blue sky remains to be done. Lila loves puzzles. When she was little, growing up at her uncle's, she had a puzzle of a lake scene with a castle. She worked that puzzle until the design was almost worn away. The older folks always kidded her, but she kept working the puzzle devotedly. She always loved the satisfying snap of two pieces going together. It was like knowing something for sure.

Her son, Lee, towers in the doorway of the lounge. She stands up, surprised.

"Did you get off work early?" He works at Ingersoll-Rand.

"No. I just took off an hour, and I have to go back and work till nine. They're working me overtime this month." He has lines on his face and he is only thirty.

He hugs her silently. He's so tall her head pokes his armpit, where he has always been ticklish.

"I didn't know you were that sick in Florida," he says. "We shouldn't have dragged you through Disney World."

"I knew something was wrong, but I didn't know what." She explains the details of the X-rays and the operation, then says, "I'm going to lose my breast, Lee."

"You are?" The lines on his face freeze. He needs a shave.

"They won't know till they get in there, but if it's cancer they'll go ahead and take it out."

"Which one?"

"This one," she says, cupping her right breast.

A woman with frizzy red hair hobbles into the lounge, her hospital gown exposing her fat, doughy knees. "I was looking for my husband," she says, "but I reckon he ain't here."

Lila waits for the woman to leave, then laughs. She's still holding her breast. "You don't remember sucking on these, do you, Lee?" She loves to tease her son. "You sucked me dry and I had to put you on a bottle after two months. I couldn't make enough milk to feed you."

With an embarrassed grin, Lee looks out the window. "I believe you're making that up."

"You want one last tug?" She reaches up and tousles his hair. His eyes are her eyes—the same vacant blue, filled with specks, like markings on a baby bird. They both laugh, and she takes a cigarette from her housecoat pocket. Lee lights it for her, then lights his own cigarette. They share a Coke from a cooler filled with ice and free cold drinks in cans for visitors in the lounge. Lila's proud of her son. He has such a pretty wife and two smart kids, but he has to work too hard to keep up his house and car payments.

"Spence didn't know about these drinks," she says. "He went all the way down to the basement to the machine."

"He didn't stick around five minutes, I bet," Lee says, handing her the can.

"Lord, no. These places give him the heebie-jeebies."

"They do me too." Lee is playing with his lighter, flicking the flame on and off. "When's Nancy coming in?"

"I don't know. Cat called from the airport before we left home and said Nancy's airplane was late. They was supposed to get here by about four o'clock." She sips from the Coke and hands it back to Lee.

"Did Cat take off from work?"

Lila nods. "I told the girls they didn't have to go to all this trouble, but I guess they're scared I'm going to kick the bucket."

"No, you won't," Lee says. He hesitates, trying to say something, but he's exactly like Spence, bashful and silent at all the wrong moments. "What caused this?" he asks. "Do the doctors know what they're doing?"

"They're specialists," Lila says. "The woman that runs the dress store where Cat works recommended the doctor I went to yesterday. He's supposed to be good." Touching her son's knee, she says, "Promise me one thing, Lee."

He flicks ash off his cigarette by tapping it from beneath with his little finger. "What?"

"That you and Cat will start talking to one another. I can't believe my own children would hate each other."

"We don't hate each other!"

"Well, you could be nice to each other—it wouldn't hurt."

Lee stubs out his cigarette in the ashtray and nods his head thoughtfully. "I'll try," he says. "But it's up to her." He stands. "I have to get back to work."

"Are you going home for supper?"

"No. I'll grab a Big Mac or something."

Lee walks her back to her room and gives her another hug. His belt buckle presses under her breasts. When he was about fourteen, he started shooting up like a cornstalk and she thought he'd never stop. He was named after Lila's father, who abandoned her when she was four and went off to Alaska—long before it was a state. Lila was never sure it was appropriate to name her only son after him, but it's Christian to forgive. Now, as he leaves, she suddenly feels the fear she felt when Nancy left home for the first time—certain she won't see her child again.

After experimenting with the remote-control device, Lila watches television for a while. The news doesn't make any sense. The commercials are about digestion. Her digestion has always been good. Spence has heartburn and can't eat much for supper. Sometimes he has chest pains, but he says it's just heartburns. On the news, a couple about her age have won over three million dollars in a lottery. "We'll pay off the bills, I guess," the man says. "And get a new living room suit," the woman adds.

A nurse trots in with some forms for Lila to fill out.

"I can't see good enough," Lila says, searching for her glasses in her purse. "My glasses don't fit anymore, but my daughter says that's what I get for buying them at the dime store." She laughs and holds the forms at arm's length. Pointing to the blurred fine print, she asks, "What's this say?"

"It's just routine, ma'am," says the nurse. "Tonight when the doctor comes he'll give you a release form and read it to you and make sure you understand everything that's going on."

"What's going to happen to me?"

Before the nurse can answer, a girl walks in and plunks down Lila's supper tray without comment.

"My, you're getting a feast tonight," says the nurse, sending the tray toward Lila on a roller platform that fits over the bed. On the tray are dark broth, red Jell-O, black coffee.

"Couldn't I have ice-tea?" Lila asks. "Coffee makes me prowl all night."

"Don't worry. We'll give you a sleeping pill."

Lila watches the sports news, something she would never do at home. When the weather comes on, she pays careful attention. The radar map shows rain everywhere in the adjoining states, but none in western Kentucky. They need rain bad. They had too much rain back in the spring. The high today was eighty-nine.

The liquid supper splashes in her stomach. From behind the curtain partition, a woman is groaning. A nurse coaxes her out of bed and helps her walk out of the room. The patient is old, her face distorted with pain as she clutches a pillow to her belly.

Lila hasn't felt so alone since Spence was in the Navy. Nancy was two, and they were still living with Spence's parents. Rosie and Amp were so quiet, their faces set like concrete as they lost themselves in their chores. Lila was awkward in Rosie's kitchen, with Rosie hovering over her. When Lila wanted to warm food for Nancy, Rosie insisted that Lila had to use a certain small aluminum pan, so they wouldn't have to wash a large one. But the food always stuck to the little pan, and it was hard to scrape clean. Rosie washed dishes in an enamel pan set on a gas ring and scalded them in another pan on another ring. The scum of the slippery lye soap never really washed off the dishes. Rosie added the dirty dishwater to the slop bucket for the hogs. Hogs liked the taste, she said. That fall, a neighbor helped Amp butcher a hog and Rosie made lye soap from the fat. Lila sewed sausage casings from flour sacks. She added flecks of dried red peppers to the ground sausage. She added more than she should have, because she knew Spence liked it extra hot, and she wanted it to be spicy for him when he came home. She knew he would come home.

Lila had to talk to somebody, so she chattered away to Nancy in their room. She was still stunned by the new experience of having a baby. Nancy kept on nursing, and Lila let her, even though her teeth made the nipples sore. She read Spence's letters aloud to her. Nancy couldn't understand the words, but Lila knew she needed her daddy, and that was the best Lila could do to help her feel his existence. Nancy listened, serious and focused, like a curious bird. There was not much to see out there, he wrote—a few birds resting on the waves like setting hens, and now and then playful porpoises that seemed to do circus tricks in the water. Spence wrote about a storm at sea, in which the boat rocked like a tire swing, the waves washing the deck. The ship stopped at an island in the Philippines and he got a twelve-hour shore leave. He wrote messages to Nancy—had she learned to milk a cow yet? was she shedding her baby teeth? Silly things, to be funny. Not until he got home did he tell about the deafening noises of the war, a racket like the end of the world.

Their room was unheated and they had a hard winter. Nancy caught cold after cold, and Lila huddled her close in the bed, under the weight of half a dozen quilts. She was afraid of rolling over on her, the way a sow sometimes mashed her pigs. One night Lila woke up and found Nancy uncovered, wet and shivering. After that, the cold went into pneumonia. Lila wanted to take her to the doctor, but Amp protested, "Why, he would charge! We can doctor her." Rosie baked onions in ashes and squeezed the juice into a spoon and fed it to her. At night Lila warmed the bed with heated bricks wrapped in newspaper, and she hardly slept, making sure she kept the child covered up; in the daytime she made a bed for her in a box close to the fireplace. She wrapped her chest in greased rags. One frightening night, when Lila prayed so hard she was almost screaming, Nancy's fever finally broke, and gradually her breathing improved. Over the following weeks, as Nancy grew stronger, Lila kept talking to her, singing and reading Spence's letters aloud, trying to find new meaning and hope in each one. Finally, there was a warm spell, when the north wind didn't blow through the cracks around the windows of their room. The yellow bushes in front of the house put out some blooms, and some geese flew over.

Uneasily, Lila and Rosie sat by the fire and pieced quilt blocks, tuning in the war news on the radio at intervals. Their shared silent worry about Spence gradually drew them together, and eventually Lila loved Spence's parents as though they were her own. That spring, during a fierce electrical storm, they gathered in Amp and Rosie's bedroom and wrapped feather bolsters around themselves. Amp said lightning wouldn't strike feathers. "Did you ever see a chicken get hit by lightning?" Rosie asked.

Suddenly Lila's daughters are there, rushing to hug her. They're smiling too much. Nancy's eyes have that deep, private look Lila has often seen in them. She drops her backpack and tote bag on the bed and buries her head on Lila's shoulder. Lila's face is full of Nancy's hair, smelling faintly of shampoo. Nancy always washed her hair too much. Lila was forever warning Nancy not to go outside with a wet head or she would catch cold, but Nancy wouldn't listen, determined to do things her own way.

Cat smells like perfume, maybe the scent of irises. Lila rarely gets hugs from her, even though they are closer in some ways, because she hasn't moved away like Nancy and her comings and goings aren't such big events. Cat came running home in tears when she began having trouble with Dan, but Nancy never mentions anything wrong in her life. Nancy analyzes everything closely, passing judgment on it, the way her grandmother would have examined someone's quilt—studying and evaluating the stitching for evenness and smallness. Nancy would never make a quilt, though. But Cat would.

"My plane got fog-delayed in Boston," Nancy says, pulling back from Lila. "And instead of landing in Nashville, we flew all the way to Birmingham and then back to Nashville. How are you feeling, Mom?"

"Well, I ain't ready to go out and pick cotton," says Lila. "But you didn't have to come all this way."

"I wanted to come."

Cat says, "I ate lunch twice while I was waiting for the plane. And read two whole magazines from cover to cover. And watched people. I saw a lot of weirdos."

Nancy plops on the side of the bed. "When Cat's nervous she eats, and when I'm nervous I can't eat."

Cat, her car keys still in her hand, has on a long skirt with a flounce, from the boutique where she works. Nancy dresses like a boy most of the time and has worn the same belt on her bluejeans for

years, but Cat has always been a fashion plate. In high school she was
Miss Sorghum at a festival. Cat used to get exasperated with Nancy
and say she didn't want to be seen in public with her, but she's finally
given up on her sister. Cat always said, "Be fancy, Nancy!"

The girls run through a million questions they want to ask the doctor, but Lila cannot remember what she wants to ask. She meant to tell
the doctor yesterday about her mastitis and to ask whether it causes
cancer. The main thing is the cost. Cat assured her everything would
be covered, but Lila doesn't believe insurance covers everything. She
heard that if it was cancer, it wouldn't be covered. Now Cat is investigating the drawers and closets in the room, checking things. Cat has
always been particular. She's a fine housekeeper, something Lila never
had time to be. Cat won dozens of ribbons in 4-H.

"Look what I hatched out," Lila says proudly to the nurse who
comes in to take her temperature. "My little girls."

"They don't look a thing alike," the nurse says, then glances at her
watch.

After the nurse removes the thermometer and leaves, Nancy says,
"Robert wanted me to tell you he misses you and he's sorry he
couldn't come."

Lila smiles. Her grandson is a thoughtful boy, always sending her
cards on Mother's Day and her birthday.

"Jack too," Nancy says.

"Jack's awful good to let you come traipsing down here."

Nancy flinches in protest. "He didn't *let* me! He had nothing to do
with it. You're my mom and I came to see you."

The bed is loaded with Nancy's things, blue pouches with zipper
pockets. Lila thrives on such confusion. She teases Nancy, "I swear,
with all that stuff you tote around you're just like old Aunt Hattie
Cross. Aunt Hattie always carried her wash pan and her toothbrush
everywhere she went. We kidded her about packing her potty around.
We'd say she brushed her teeth in her pot."

"I've got my toothbrush right here—somewhere," Nancy says,
grinning. "I didn't bring my pot, though."

"Well, you can use mine," Lila says with a laugh. "There's one in
the bathroom with my name on it!"

She tousles Nancy's hair lovingly. Lila's children are all grown, with their own families. This is what life comes down to, she realizes—replacing your own life with new ones. It's just like raising a crop. Somehow, this makes her think of prize-winning vegetables at the fair. It always made her sad to see the largest and prettiest vegetables on display. The best tomatoes and corn and broccoli sat there and ruined just so people could look at them.

"Lee was here," Lila says. "He said he'd talk to you, Cat, but it was up to you. I wish y'all would stop fussing over that air conditioner."

"It wasn't the air conditioner. It was that dumb three-wheeler!" Cat says angrily. "He never should have let Scott ride it. He was too little, and he didn't have a helmet. Those things are dangerous!"

"Where are Scott and Krystal?" Lila asks, shifting the subject.

"With Dan. They went to Hopkinsville yesterday to stay two weeks with him. I thought you knew that."

"No." Lila is puzzled. She says, "I can't keep things straight anymore. I thought Lee was mad at you over that air conditioner you gave him. I didn't know it was the three-wheeler."

Cat pats Lila's hair. "Let's don't worry about this stuff, O.K.?"

Nancy says, "The main thing right now is you."

"I think they're going to take this breast off," Lila says, placing her hand under her right breast.

"You've always been so proud of those," Cat says, reaching to touch the top of Lila's breast lightly.

"My big jugs," Lila says, smiling. "I raised three younguns on these. I guess they're give out now." She can't say what she feels—that the last thing she would have expected was to be attacked by disease in the very place she felt strongest. It seemed to suggest some basic failing, like the rotten core of a dying tree.

Nancy rests her hand on her mother's shoulder. "Is all this too fast?" she asks.

"Well, I have to get it done."

"It's up to you—if you feel it's going too far, or if you want to wait." Nancy removes her hand to smooth her hair. Lila spots a gray hair on Nancy's head and almost bursts into tears.

"No, I want to get it over with."

"We hate to see you pushed around," Cat says. "They're your breasts, and if they're worth more to you than all this—"

"It's your decision," says Nancy.

"I know what you mean," says Lila, cradling her breasts like babies. "But they ain't worth more than living."

"I think it's going to be all right, Mom," says Nancy, taking Lila's hand. "The lump isn't big and you found it early."

"I wouldn't have found it if it hadn't been for Cat." Lila starts to cry. "Don't y'all stare at me. I don't like to be stared at."

The old woman in the other bed, behind a curtain, yells at a nurse, "You can just take that thing and ram it up your butt."

Cat and Nancy start snickering. "I'll be like that tomorrow!" says Lila, laughing back her tears. "Oh, me!"

3

Spence can't sleep. With the frenzied urgency of a hunting dog, Oscar is barking at an animal out in the field. Spence wonders if it could be the wildcat that had screamed out by the barn one night. Wildcats scavenged at the dump beyond the industrial park, and a man had shot one there not long ago. Spence was heartsick when he heard about that. Some people would shoot anything, just to see how it killed. Last year, he saw, for perhaps ten seconds, a wildcat at the pond. It was small and scrawny, with a short, black-tipped tail and long, tufted ears. It disappeared into the scrub along the creek.

He jams pillows under his neck. They are soft like her breasts, but he doesn't want to let himself think about her body. She has been looking bad for a long time, losing weight, not eating. She kept making excuses, saying she wasn't hungry, or that she was more active than usual. In early June, when they were in Florida, she was sick. They went with Lee and his wife, Joy, and the kids, all crammed in Lee's station wagon. It was the wrong season. When Lee planned the trip, they didn't think about the season because they could only go in the summer, after Joy finished the school year. She teaches the second grade. In Florida, the temperature was already in the high nineties. They stayed in a cabin at Flamingo, the southernmost point on the U.S. mainland. When they entered the cabin, clouds of mosquitoes swarmed in through the door with them. Afterwards, they laughed at the way they had frantically slapped at the insects and sprayed each other down with insect repellent. It reminded Spence of spraying cows for flies. After they wiped out the mosquito invasion, he and Lee sat in the air-conditioning and watched TV while Lila and Joy cooked supper. The children, Jennifer and Greg, scratched their bites until they were raw. Through the night mosquitoes whined only occasionally, and then the next day the hot sun burned them off. Spence loved the heat. As they rode along the main highway, he told Lila, "I wouldn't mind having a job mowing the shoulders along the road down here."

It was his first real trip since he was in the Navy. He was surprised at how much he loved the swamp. On a lookout point, they gazed out over the endless sea of saw grass. It was studded with little rises, like islands. The Indians called them hummocks. He felt free. The sun blazed down on them, and he thought he could live there always. Lee kept apologizing for bringing them to Florida in the wrong season. Most of the migrating birds had gone north. In the winter, thousands of herons and egrets and storks and ibises gathered in the Everglades, but in the late spring the swamp was bare, with only a few birds, and the alligator hole was quiet, the alligators lying still like rotting logs in the murky water. Once, they spotted an alligator crossing the road, sluggish and lizard-like. They saw a blue racer. And several long-necked white birds. A few blue herons.

Lila didn't like Florida. Earlier in the trip, when she started having the dizzy spells and the numbness in her arm, they took her to a hospital in Orlando. The doctor—who charged sixty-five dollars for an emergency-room visit and spent only five minutes with Lila—said she had an irritated nerve and suggested she go to her own doctor when she returned home. They spent two miserable days at Disney World— the purpose of the whole trip, for the kids. Spence didn't care for it. He wanted to see snakes and birds and alligators, so Lee drove them on down to the Everglades. They had insisted Lila didn't have to go, but she said she didn't mind, that she felt better. But when they explored the trails, she stayed in the car, with the air conditioner blowing, and smoked and napped, while Spence and the others explored the boardwalk trails through the swamps. He was fascinated by the mahogany hummocks, and he read all the plaques that told about the wildlife. He liked to imagine when the Indians lived there in the swamp, venturing from hummock to hummock in their canoes, exploring. Back in the stuffy, smoky car, she was quiet and her face was pale, but she said she was all right. "It's the heat," she said. "I'm hotter than a she-wolf in a pepper patch!"

Those dizzy spells turned out to be little strokes—TIAs, the doctor in Paducah called them. The blood wasn't feeding to her brain. Now Spence shudders in the night, imagining a scene in Florida—Lila having a major stroke on one of those lonely trails. The nearest hospital was fifty miles away, and they would not have known how to find it. If something had happened to her then, he would have been to blame.

Dawn is creeping under the shades. The sheets are wadded, the quilt is lying on the rug, the cat scratching at the back door. Lila is crazy about the cat, Abraham. Spence has never seen her so crazy about a cat, the way she baby-talks to him. The morning after Spence heard that wildcat, Abraham's fur was ruffled, as though something had been chewing on him and rolling him in the dirt. Abraham has long hair and is spotted like a Guernsey. Stiff and aching, Spence gets up and watches the sun rise over the soybean fields. Oscar is out there, walking slowly, sniffing close to the ground.

While CNN blares out the latest on Iran-Iraq, Iran-contra, Nicaragua, South Africa, something in Idaho, Spence makes breakfast in the microwave. He watches the strips of bacon curl up and ooze grease down the ridges of the bacon rack. When the bacon is done, he makes scrambled eggs. He sets the dish in for twenty-five seconds, then stirs the eggs with a fork and cooks them for twenty-five more seconds. Spence bought the microwave so he could fix his meals while Lila was away on her trips with the senior citizens. She has been to Hawaii, the Badlands, Savannah and New Orleans.

He bought the microwave at a flea market, almost new. At first, he set it on top of the refrigerator, but Lila couldn't reach it. So he found a wobbly metal table at a sale and set the oven on it next to the kitchen table. The first time he tried the microwave, he cracked an egg in a dish and the egg exploded in the oven with a sound like a shotgun. He learned to punch the yolk with a fork to let the pressure out. "Crazy thing," Lila said on the telephone to one of her friends. "He never reads the directions to anything." The oven came with an incomplete set of instructions, and he had to learn how to use it by trial and error. Once, he exploded a potato, for fun.

After eating, he and Oscar head for the barn to feed the calves, five little Holsteins he is raising for beef in a pasture between the barn and the woods. The fencing is makeshift—boards and an electric wire.

"Oscar, you sure are smart," Spence says. "You learned about that electric fence in one easy lesson."

Oscar wags his tail. The calves flick flies with their tails. They amble forward, rubbing each other and gazing at Spence with liquid eyes the texture and size of fried eggs. A horrifying image flashes through his mind—jabbing their eyes with a fork. Once he tried raising a veal calf, and every time he remembers it he hates himself. The little thing stayed in the dark stall alone, and whenever Spence came to bottle-feed him, the calf cried. When after only a few weeks Spence took him to the slaughterhouse, the calf couldn't stand up. The meat was tender and pale. He and Lila couldn't talk about it. The packages languished in the freezer, and by the time she cooked the last ones, the meat had lost its freshness.

He steadies himself against the barn door for a moment, then enters the barn, the calves following. He distributes cups of feed into the troughs, and the calves dig their heads in. He fastens their necks to the stanchions, and while they feed he talks to them.

"Sunflower," he says. "You're too skinny. Whoa, there, Mudpuddle. Watch what you're doing, Dexter. Delbert. Boss Hogg, don't get crazy now."

Always, when Spence feeds his calves, he goes through their names.

4

Lila says, "They sure don't let you get lonesome here—all the traipsing in and out they do at all hours."

Cat and Nancy are hovering over the bed, staring at her with an unnatural sort of eagerness. "Did you sleep?" Cat asks.

"Off and on," says Lila. She tries to sit up against the pillow, but she feels woozy from this morning's medicine. "That coffee last night made me jumpy, but they give me some pills and a shot."

Nancy says, "That's outrageous! There was no good reason to give you coffee. You should have refused it."

Cat's earrings dangle in Lila's face. Lila's mind feels fuzzy, far away. She is afraid the operating room will be cold.

"Are you scared?" Nancy asks, holding Lila's hand.

"They work you over too much for you to be scared. I haven't had time to think." Lila squeezes Nancy's hand and reaches for Cat's. "You girls are being good to me," she says. "I sure am lucky."

"Well, we care about you," Cat says.

"You're going to be just fine, Mom," says Nancy. "You're tough."

"I guess I better say goodbye to my jug," Lila says, laughing and looking down at herself. "If Spence don't hurry on here, he's going to miss his chance."

Just then Spence appears, still in short sleeves. Yesterday she tried to tell him to wear long sleeves, but he wouldn't listen to her. After giving Nancy a hug, he steps back and eyes her up and down to see how much older she seems.

"You look poor as a snake," he says. "Why didn't you bring Robert?"

"He's going off to camp tomorrow. Jack's taking him up to New Hampshire. It's the same place he went last year, where they go on treks into the mountains."

"Bring him down here. I'll see that he communes with nature." Spence grins at Nancy.

"I'm sure you will. You'll have him out planting soybeans." Nancy twists out of a nurse's way.

"It would be good for him," Lila says sleepily. "Working out in the fields would teach him something."

She closes her eyes, vaguely listening to Spence and the girls talk. If this is her time to go, she should be ready. And she has her family with her, except for Lee, who had to work. She feels she is looking over her whole life, holding it up to see how it has turned out—like a piece of sewing. She can see Cat trying on a dress Lila has made for her, and Lila checks to see whether it needs taking up. She turns up the hem, jerks the top to see how it fits across the shoulders, considers an extra tuck in the waist. In a recurrent dream she has had for years, she is trying to finish a garment, sewing fast against the clock.

They are still chattering nervously around her when the surgeon appears. He's young, with sensitive hands that look skilled at delicate finger work. Lila always notices people's fingers. Nancy and Cat keep asking questions, but Lila is sleepy and can't follow all that he is saying. Then he moves closer to her and says, "If the biopsy shows a malignancy, I'm going to recommend a modified radical mastectomy. I'll remove the breast tissue and the lymph nodes under the arm. But I'll leave the chest muscles. If you follow the physical therapy, then you'll have full use of your arm and you'll be just fine." He smiles reassuringly. He resembles a cousin of Lila's—Whip Stanton, a little man with a lisp and a wife with palsy.

"How small would the lump have to be for you to recommend a lumpectomy instead?" Nancy asks the doctor.

"Infinitesimal," he says. "It's better to get it all out and be sure. This way is more certain."

"Well, more and more doctors are recommending lumpectomies instead of mastectomies," Nancy argues. "What I'm asking is, what is the dividing line? How large should the lump be for the mastectomy to be preferable?"

Lila sees Spence cringe. Nancy has always asked questions and done things differently, just to be contrary. "Nancy, Nancy, quite contrary," they used to tease her.

The doctor shrugs and leans against the wall. "It depends on a number of factors," he says. "You can't reduce it to a question of size. If it's an aggressive tumor, a fast-growing one, then a smaller lump might be more dangerous than one that has grown slowly over a longer period of time. And my suspicion is that this is an aggressive tumor. You can get a second opinion if you want to, but we've got her prepped, and if the second opinion was in favor of a lumpectomy, then wouldn't you have to go for a third opinion, so you could take two out of three? But in this case, time is of the essence." The doctor grins at Lila. "What do you think, Mrs. Culpepper? You look like a pretty smart lady."

"Why, you're just a little whippersnapper," Lila says. "All the big words make me bumfuzzled. I guess you know your stuff, but I got you beat when it comes to producing pretty daughters." She has heard he is single, and she heard the nurses joking with him. She can't keep her mind on the conversation. It's as though she's floating around the room, dipping in and out of the situation, the way the nurses do.

"That's for certain," he says, twirling his stethoscope like a toy.

"My daughters are curious, though," Lila says apologetically. Even the outfits they are wearing are curious—layers of dark, wrinkled cotton.

"They're weird," Spence says.

"No, we're not," says Cat indignantly. She's dressed up in one of her man-catching outfits, with heavy jewelry, but what man would like that getup? Cat claims women actually dress for women. Nancy was always too impatient to fool with her appearance. She's like Lila that way, wearing any old thing handy. When Nancy moved up North she stopped wearing lipstick and curling her hair, and for a while she didn't even wear a brassiere. Lila was afraid Nancy's breasts would be damaged.

"Do you have any questions, Mr. Culpepper?" the doctor asks. "Is there anything I can clarify?"

Lila senses Spence's embarrassment as he shakes his head no. The nurses are whizzing around, and the woman in the other bed is arguing with her doctor.

"What about them strokes?" Spence pipes up then.

"Well, the first priority is to deal with this lump in her breast, and later we'll check the obstructions in the carotid arteries." The doctor touches his neck, indicating the main blood vessels. He says, "It's possible that I'll recommend further surgery next week to clean out the plaque in those arteries."

"I was having strokes in Florida," Lila says. She touches her arm, where the numbness spreads a few times a day. As they talk, she feels one of her dizzy spells coming on. She longs for a cigarette.

"How risky is that second operation?" Cat demands.

"Well, there's always the risk of death," the doctor says bluntly. He's not looking at anyone. His eyes are fixed on the doorframe. "And a carotid endarterectomy is tricky because there's always the chance the patient will have a stroke on the table. But the benefits outweigh the risks. Increase the blood supply to the brain and she'll stop having those transient ischemic attacks, and we'll prevent the big stroke down the road."

"The big stroke down the road," Nancy repeats, after he leaves. "It sounds like the title of a children's book."

Spence seems frozen in his position in the corner chair. His eyes stare vacantly as a nurse comes in with a syringe in her hand like a weapon. "Are you ready, Mrs. Culpepper?"

"Oh, must I?"

"It'll all be over with before you know it."

"Y'all messed up my fishing trip," Lila says crossly, trying to manage a smile. "I was aiming to go fishing this week."

"That's why we call you patients—because you have to be patient," the nurse says cheerfully. "Now you want to lie back for me? And make a fist."

From out of nowhere, Lila can hear Spence telling about the war, about a guy on his ship who went ashore one night on one of the Pacific islands and got himself tattooed. Spence wrote in his letter, "He had his whole butt tattooed with a picture of two beagles in a field—a pretty field, with green grass. And the dogs were after a rabbit that was disappearing into his crack. The next day the bos'n made him chip paint all day, and he hurt so bad he cried. It was a pretty picture, though, the grass was just as green! But I sure bet that hurt. He's a big guy too." She's about to laugh, remembering that letter.

She sees the girls whispering. The patient in the other bed is up walking again, but she refused her breakfast. Lila's breakfast was ice water. She wasn't hungry anyway. Food doesn't taste right to her anymore. The food on her trip to New Orleans back in March was unappetizing. The gumbo even had shells in it. Now Nancy is bending over her, hugging her, followed by Cat, her face close to Lila's. Cat whispers, "Hang in there, Mom." Spence is edging out the door as the orderlies appear with a bed on wheels. In their green outfits, they are leprechauns. Or men from Mars. "Are you going to give me some sugar or not?" Lila calls to Spence.

"I reckon," he says, clutching her hand and bending down to kiss her. He's self-conscious, but the nurse is busy filling out a chart and doesn't notice them.

"Take care of my babies," she says, meaning the cat and dog. "And don't forget them beans."

"I won't forget your old beans!" He chokes on his laugh.

As the leprechauns wheel her away, she sees Spence gazing after her helplessly. She has forgotten to tell Nancy and Cat something, something important she meant to say about Spence. His face disappears and she is in an elevator, with music playing, the kind of music they play in heaven.

5

Spence can't stand hospitals. The smells make him sick. The sounds of pain hurt. In an hour, the doctor will telephone Lila's room with the biopsy report, which will determine how he should proceed with the surgery. Spence hates waiting.

He drives to a gas station that has a mini-market. There, he buys two baked potatoes with cheese topping and eats them in the car with a can of Coke. He plays the radio, his rock station. The potatoes need more pepper. Nancy and Cat urged him to eat in the cafeteria with them, but he had little appetite in a building with so many sick people and their germs. In the corridor when he arrived at the hospital that morning, Spence saw a man with a hole in his face where his nose had been. Spence knows a man who went to the cancer specialists in Memphis and had a new nose grafted on. His face doesn't look bad with the new nose, considering it came from a dead man. When Spence told Nancy about it, she didn't believe him. Nancy always believes what she wants to believe. He smiles, thinking of how the doctor outsmarted her when she tried to challenge him. Spence is proud of his daughter, though. She has an important job—something to do with computers—with a company that requires her to travel all over the United States. When Nancy married Jack Cleveland, a Yankee, Spence was sure she was making a mistake. He was afraid there wasn't a living in photography—more of a hobby than work—but the marriage has lasted, and Robert is a smart, good-looking boy. It pains Spence that Nancy lives so far away. She went up there right after college. She was always restless and adventurous, because of the books she read. When she was little, she would read the same book over and over, as if she could make it come true.

Spence finishes the potatoes, gasses up the car, then drives to an auto-supply store to buy a windshield-wiper blade refill, but he can't find the right length and he doesn't want to buy a whole new wiper. He needs to get a tune-up, but he forgot to bring the coupon he clipped from the newspaper for a free one. He tries to calculate whether he would come out ahead if he went instead to that filling station offering the free case of Coke with a tune-up. But he doesn't have time to fool with the car today anyway. Impatiently, he drives back to the hospital, the radio blasting out rock-and-roll. The music fits the urgency of his life. The music seems to organize all the noises of public places into something he can tolerate. The rhythm of driving blends with the music on the radio and the beat in his nervous system. Before the children were born, he and Lila used to go dancing at little places out in the country that people called "nigger juke joints." They went to one across the country line where they could get beer. Lila never liked beer, but she loved to dance. He can imagine her long legs now, flashing white in the dark of the dance floor. He remembers a saxophone player and a blues singer as good as Joe Williams. The real music is always hidden somewhere, off in the country, back in his head, in his memory. There are occasional echoes of that raunchy old music he always loved in some of the rock songs on the radio.

At the hospital, he is forced to park in the last row. "Midnight Rambler" by the Rolling Stones comes on the radio then, and he sits there and listens until it is finished. His family is busting out at the seams—like the music. He can't keep track of what they are up to. When a plane crash is on the news, he's afraid Nancy was on the plane. And Cat's life is a mess. She married too young, and her husband had big ideas he couldn't follow through on. He managed a hardware store, then opened his own waterbed outlet, but it failed. Spence told Cat the day Dan leased the store that waterbeds were filled with snake oil, not water, and she was mad at him for a long time for saying that. Lila tried to talk Cat into staying with Dan, but Spence is glad she got rid of him. Lila worries about Cat and the kids alone at night, with no man around the house, but Lila isn't afraid to go gallivanting around the world herself.

When Spence's mother died a few years ago, they were free to travel. By then, they had sold off the cows and weren't tied down on the farm. Spence told Lila he was going to send her around the world. She begged him to go too, but he refused to go traveling with a bunch of old people, yammering about their ailments. "I ain't that old," he protested.

"But we couldn't light out by ourselves," she said. "We'd get knocked in the head and robbed. We'd get lost. On these tours, they take care of you."

He was afraid for her to go off, but he wanted her to have the chance. Her first trip was to Hawaii, and at home alone he imagined her out on the Pacific, in a cruise boat that stopped at Pearl Harbor. When she came home from Hawaii, she brought a certificate for a hula-dancing course (three lessons) and some ceramic pineapples. "Did you get scared?" he asked. "Not a bit," she said. "I slept good, had the biggest time of my life." The airplane, she said, was big enough to play ball in. On her second trip, a bus tour out to the Badlands, she brought him a toy rabbit with antlers—a jackelope. It was a joke present, but she wouldn't admit it, insisting she saw a jackelope cross the highway. After that, she went on two more trips, and when relatives commented snidely about how his wife was running around on him and spending all his money, it made him furious. He told them, "She took care of my mother for ten years, and she deserves to get out and have fun. If she wants to go to the moon, I'll let her. I don't care how much it costs."

While she was away in Hawaii, his memories of the Pacific grew louder, more insistent. The sounds of the antiaircraft guns echoed and reverberated below deck, where he was an ammunition passer. Storms battled the ship relentlessly, slopping the decks and plunging and hurtling the ship like a carnival ride. In the dark, cramped quarters—stinking with B.O. and puke—he tried to sleep, but he thought about Lila, nursing the baby and helping his parents get the crops in. He could see her milking the few cows they had during the war, washing the milk cans. One calm, sunny day, he carried buckets of water to swab the deck and forgot momentarily where he was, imagining he was carrying buckets of milk from the barn to the house. Then a fighter plane zoomed down low over the destroyer to land on the aircraft carrier a few hundred yards off the port bow.

When Spence enters Lila's room, the girls are reading magazines. The air-conditioning is cold. He's in a short-sleeved shirt, but they are wrapped up in layers of clothes.

"We stole her cigarettes," Cat says. "She had five packs at the bottom of her bag."

Nancy seems smaller each time he sees her, while Cat fattens up like a Butterball turkey. Cat has on a wrinkled jumpsuit with buttons and zippers all over it, and a wide belt with three buckles, and several pounds of beads. Nancy has on a sweater and a jacket and baggy pants with buttons at the ankles. This is July.

"Where did y'all get them clothes?" he says. "The rag barrel?"

Cat lets out a giggle. "One of the doctors called us 'honky Shiite terrorists.' "

Spence's daughters have never acted their age, but in a way he doesn't mind—they are still his little girls. He may burst into tears. Feeling a pang of heartburn, he sits down and grabs a section of the *Courier-Journal* from the floor. Too late, he thinks about the germs on the floor.

A nurse flies in and says to Nancy, "I'll have to ask you to get off the bed, hon. It's for the patient."

"I was warming it up for her," Nancy grumbles. She folds her reading glasses and slips them into a case.

"Y'all are always arguing with the doctors and nurses," Spence says to his daughters after the nurse leaves. "Talking back to them."

"Well, if we left it up to you, who knows what could happen to Mom!" Nancy says, sitting up on the edge of the bed and reaching for her shoes. "She could get mutilated. A lot of doctors just want to operate because they're enamored with their equipment." Nancy situates herself on a spread-out newspaper on the floor. "Let me ask you one thing, Dad. If you were in the hospital hooked up to tubes and you weren't even conscious, or maybe you were in excruciating pain—what would you want us to do?"

"I'm afraid of what y'all might have them doctors do to me." Spence shudders.

"Well, maybe you ought to think about it," Nancy says. "While you're still in charge."

"I'll solve that one," he says. "I just won't go to doctors. You're right about them anyway. They just want to work you over and take your money." He folds the newspaper and drops it to the floor. He says to Cat, "I believe your mama is more worried about you than she is about this operation."

"Well, I don't know what to do about it. She didn't see Scott laying on the ground that time. I thought he was dead!"

"He wasn't hurt."

"But Lee never should have let Scott ride that dumb three-wheeler. He was too little, and he didn't have a helmet. Those things are dangerous, the way kids ride them all over creation."

For a moment Spence sees Lila in his daughter. Lila swinging in a porch swing the night they married, her shoulder pads sticking out like scaffolding.

Cat goes on, "When I took Scott to the hospital, his fingers were numb—that's a sign of concussion. There was a kid killed just last week on a three-wheeler. Didn't you see that in the paper?"

Spence shakes his head in despair. It was an accident, and Lee was scared too. He says, "That's not what I meant. Lila's just worried about you—staying by yourself at night."

"What does she want me to do—bring some guy home with me?"

The telephone trills just then and Cat snatches it up. "Yes. Yes." She listens grimly.

"What is it?" Nancy says, motioning anxiously to Cat. "Is she O.K.?"

Cat nods. When she hangs up, she says, "The biopsy showed it was malignant, and he's going ahead with the mastectomy."

Spence's stomach lurches. "Oh, no," he says faintly. His heart is racing. Nancy says nothing. Cat picks at her nails.

"They won't have her back up here till she gets out of the recovery room," Cat says. "It could be hours."

"Let's get out of here," Nancy says. "Let's go do something." She rolls her magazine and plunges it into her tote bag.

Cat, feeling for something in her purse, says, "I knew she had cancer when I saw her after she came back from Florida. I could see it in her face."

Later, in the lounge, Spence spins through all the TV channels, but there are no ball games on today. The Cards are having a good season, especially with Joe Magrane, a Kentucky boy, pitching. Spence settles on a game show, but in his mind he sees her garden, with the corn growing full, and he sees her coming to the house early in the morning with buckets of vegetables. Her straw hat is set cockeyed on her head, and her blouse is damp. She bends over in the shade of the big oak and sorts through handfuls of shell beans, picking out some dried ones to save for seed. The cat twines himself around her ankles and she talks to him softly and sweetly, praising him for his morning's exploits. Behind her, the soybeans stretch out like a dusty green rug. The soybeans have been invaded by grasshoppers, and Spence is afraid of losing the crop. He never had a problem with grasshoppers before he switched to one-crop farming. His neighbor, Bill Belton, promised to spray the beans soon. Bill has a little cropduster plane and won't charge Spence much. He has been kidding Spence about going up in the plane with him, but Lila won't hear of Spence going up. Spence has thought about it, though, imagining what it would be like to see the fields from up high, with the pond like a glass eye and the buildings like dollhouses. He has never been up in an airplane.

He goes to the rest room and washes his teeth. Some of the potato is under the upper plate and starting to irritate the roof of his mouth. Earlier, he was in such a hurry to get back to Lila's room he didn't wash his teeth. On the commode, he smokes half a cigarette. For the last several years, he has limited himself to two cigarettes a day. But he can't stop Lila. She puffs away like the smokestack in the industrial park beyond the soybean fields. Sometimes he watches her puffing and sees the smokestack puffing simultaneously, and they are like coordinated events in his life, events he has no control over. He runs water at the sink over the cigarette butt and drops it in the waste can.

In the hall, he runs into Guy Samson, a man he sees often at the feed mill. Spence used to rent Guy's bulls.

"Spence, have you got somebody here?" Guy asks.

"My wife," Spence says, feeling himself tremble. "She's being operated on. Breast cancer."

"That's tough, Spence," Guy says, shaking his head worriedly. "My mother-in-law's here now with cancer, and she's real bad. She's hooked up to them machines in intensive care."

"They're hooking everybody up these days."

"Ain't that the truth. Does your wife have to have cobalt?"

Spence shudders. "They haven't said." He knows that with cancer they will give her cobalt treatments, and he has tried to put this out of his mind.

"That cobalt is what I'd be afraid of," Guy says, nodding his head sympathetically.

Spence is shivering in the cold.

"Take it easy, Spence," says Guy as they part.

The word "cobalt" stung Spence to the quick. He has known people who had cobalt. Claudine Turrell lost her hair and was sick from radiation poisoning, like the Japanese after the bomb. Claudine finally died, after suffering for weeks. The same thing happened to Bob Miller and Clancy Stone. And Lila's friend Reba died only last year, after several rounds of cobalt treatments. It occurs to Spence now that Lila has not even mentioned Reba, as if it would be bad luck to say her name. Lila visited Reba in the hospital and came home describing Reba's bald head and skinny neck—a picked chicken, Lila said sadly.

The doctors would say, "These cobalt treatments might give her a little time." There is no choice about it, really. There are no significant choices most of the time. You always have to do what has to be done. It's like milking cows. When their bags are full, they have to be milked.

6

Lila feels a twitching on the back of her hand, like a fly that has landed, but she is unable to swat at it. Then she feels the tube hanging out of her hand. She eases open her eyes, sees blurred faces and machines with hoses—like the electric milkers they used to have for the cows. Her eyes close and she sees green beans setting on blooms again and okra poking up like hitchhikers' thumbs. A volunteer sunflower has sprung up amidst the peppers. There is a burning in her chest, a smoldering fire in a woodstove. Something bulky is there, a heavy weight holding her down. She is too weak to bring her hand up to touch it. A TV set, somewhere near, seems to be playing a story about a woman's best friend dying of cancer. The friend's name is Reba, and they play cards and go fishing together. Reba is smart and has a giggle like a little girl. One day Reba finds a lump the size of a golf ball in her breast. She claims it came there overnight, but she is lying. Reba kept it a secret, hadn't wanted to admit it was there. She had such tiny breasts, not like Lila's large, knotty breasts. A golf ball could hide in Lila's unnoticed. Reba's hair falls out and she wastes away to nothing and disappears beyond the garden.

Someone wheels a cart into the room. Lila hears tinkling glass, the sucking of rubber soles, voices bubbling. The sound of the TV story has faded away. Outlines of people grow sharper, faces peering quizzically at her. Lila does not want them staring at her. She must look awful.

7

All the way to the hospital the next day, Spence listens to tapes of the Blasters and Fleetwood Mac that Nancy brought for him. The Fleetwood Mac tape doesn't even sound like Fleetwood Mac. He wouldn't have recognized the group. The Blasters remind him of Jerry Lee Lewis. Spence saw Jerry Lee Lewis on a special recently. He looked bad—old and worn out.

He dreads seeing Lila, so he has fooled around half the morning, delaying the trip to Paducah. In Paducah, before going to the hospital, he looks for a gallon of windshield-washer fluid and has to go to a couple of places to compare prices. He pays four dollars for it. Later, in the Wal-Mart, where he stops to look for that wiper-blade replacement, he spots the same brand of washer fluid on sale for two dollars. He has blown two bucks. It makes him mad. All the coffee makers and video games and electric ice-cream parlors in the Wal-Mart are depressing. People are buying so much junk, thinking it will make them happy. And then when they can't even make a path across the floor through their possessions, they have a yard sale. Spence can't stand to waste anything. His parents never wasted a scrap. "Always be saving," Pap told his grandchildren. "Hard times might come." Cat fought him, pitching a fit once over two shelly beans left on her plate. These days, with all the new money, everyone has gone wild. Around here, there is nowhere to go, so people either get drunk or go crazy—sometimes both. Spence knows a guy whose wife left him and ran off to Biloxi, Mississippi, with a prefab-home builder whom she later shot dead. After that, the guy had a nervous breakdown and was sent off to the asylum. The children went to foster homes. Spence can't imagine what the world is coming to. Yesterday, the newspaper reported two burglaries in town—a holdup at an all-night food store and a break-in at an old widow's house.

In the Wal-Mart parking lot, he has a sudden queasy feeling. He can't remember where he is. He sees rows and rows of cars. His brain reels. He must have a car here, but he can't remember what car. He sees a Camaro, an Oldsmobile, rows of shiny silver and white cars,

lined up like teeth. The vertical lines of street lamps tower in the landscape like defoliated trees. The parking lot seems slightly familiar, but
he can't place it. He may be thinking of one he has seen on TV. He
stumbles onward and suddenly spots his car—the Rabbit that needs
a tune-up. The little car seems to have aged ten years overnight. It is
parked next to a black van with round windows and a pink-and-blue
mural of an angel and a Jesus with a halo. Spence wonders what
loony drives such a vehicle. Spence has never been comfortable in
church. He is suspicious of most preachers and believes all the evan-
gelists on the radio and TV are con artists. The night before, when
Lila came out of the recovery room and was wheeled back into Room
301, she said to him, "Did you pray for me?" Her question startled
him. They never spoke of prayer, or heaven, but Spence knew she
prayed for him, frequently, because she went to church and was
afraid that because he didn't they wouldn't end up in heaven together.
When he answered her, he felt a chill up his spine. "Sure," he said,
joking. "You know how good I am at saying grace." She got tickled
at him then but had to stop laughing because she hurt. "I've got a
long row to hoe," she said. She wasn't fully awake.

8

Lila feels as though she has been left out in a field for the buzzards.
The nurses are in at all hours, making no special effort to be quiet—
a nurse who checks dressings, another one who changes dressings, a
nurse with blood-thinner shots three times a day, a nurse with breath-
ing-machine treatments, various nurse's aides who check temperature
and blood pressure, the cleaning woman, the mail lady, the priest and
nuns from the hospital, the girls who fill the water jugs, the woman
who brings the meal trays, the candy stripers selling toiletries and
candy and magazines from a cart. Lila can't keep track of all the
nurses who come to check her drainage tube—squirting the murky
fluid out of the plastic collection bottle, measuring the fluid intake
and output, writing on charts. The nurses walk her around the entire
third floor twice a day, accompanied by her I.V. bag, wheeling on a

stand. Spence is nervous, bursting in anxiously, unable to stick around. And the girls are in and out, bringing her little things—a basket of flowers from the gift shop downstairs and some perfume. Lee and Joy brought a rose in a milk-glass bud vase. The church sent pink daisies. The old woman in the other bed has no flowers.

The surgeon told Lila she could live without a breast. "You couldn't live without a head, or a liver, or a heart," he said when he informed her in the recovery room that he had removed her breast. "But you can live without a breast. You'll be surprised."

"It would be like living without balls," Lila replied. "You'd find that surprising too, but you could probably get along without them."

Lila is not sure she said that aloud, and remembering it now, she is embarrassed that she might have, under the influence of the drugs. She's surprised Nancy hasn't said the same thing to the doctor's face.

Lila hears the old woman in the other bed grunting and complaining. "I'll not leave here alive!" she shouted when a nurse gave her a bath. "You're wasting your time fooling with me."

By the second day after her surgery, Lila is no longer hooked to the I.V. She plucks at the hospital gown in front where her bandage itches. The drainage tubes irritate her skin. She feels weak, but restless. "I'm afraid my blood's too thin already," she tells the nurse who comes with the blood-thinner shot.

"No, this is what the doctor wanted," the nurse says.

"I'm getting poked so full of holes I'm like a sifter bottom."

Besides the shots, there are the tests. They have wheeled her into the cold basement three times to run her through their machines. They have scanned her bones, her liver, her whole body, looking for loose cancer cells. Now the cancer doctor comes in to tell Lila the results of the tests: The cancer has spread to two out of the seventeen lymph nodes that were removed. Spence isn't there yet, but Cat and Nancy fire questions at him. Lila's head spins as the doctor explains that once the cancer has reached the lymph nodes, it has gone into the bloodstream, and then it can end up anywhere. The news doesn't quite register.

"I'm recommending chemotherapy," the doctor says.

"Is that cobalt?" Lila asks weakly. The doctor is young and reminds her of the odd-looking preacher who led the revival at church last year. The preacher had a long nose and wore a gold shiny suit.

The doctor says, "No. This will be a combination of three drugs—Cytoxan, methotrexate and 5FU." He explains that she will have a chart showing two weeks of treatments, then a three-week rest period, then two weeks of treatments, and so on. She will get both pills and shots. Like dogs teaming up on a rabbit, Cat and Nancy jump on him about side effects.

"This particular treatment is tolerated very well," he says. "That's not to say there won't be side effects. A little hair loss, a little nausea. Some people react more adversely than others."

Lila can't keep her mind on what he's saying. "I've got plenty of hair," she says, tugging at her curls. "And it's coarse, like horse hair." The last permanent she got didn't take on top.

"You're going to have to lay off the smoking too," the doctor says, consulting his clipboard.

"They won't let me smoke here," Lila says. She bummed a cigarette from a visitor in the lounge the night before, but it burned her lungs and tasted bitter. She couldn't finish it.

The cancer doctor says now, "Cigarettes will interfere with the chemotherapy."

"See!" Nancy says triumphantly. "Doctor's orders. And you wouldn't listen to us."

"These girls snitched my cigarettes," Lila says to the doctor. "Is that any way to treat an old woman that's stove up in the hospital?"

"Best thing for you," the doctor says with a slight grin.

"And they're telling me I can't eat what I'm used to," Lila goes on.

"She eats a high-fat diet," Nancy says.

"Don't listen to them," the doctor says to Lila. "You eat anything you want to. If I was your age, I'd eat anything I wanted to."

Lila sees Nancy bristle. Nancy says, "She's eaten bacon and eggs every morning of her life and she has clogged arteries. What are you saying?"

"It's too late for her to do anything about her diet. Cutting back on cholesterol won't help at all. It's simply too late. And it's too late for you too," he says. "How old are you?"

"Forty-two."

"Too late." He nods at Cat. "How old are you?"

"Thirty-four."

"It might help you a little, but not much. They did autopsies on the soldiers who died in Vietnam, and those young boys—nineteen years old—already had plaque in their arteries."

"Not all doctors agree with you about cholesterol," Nancy says, shooting him a mean look.

As he scribbles on his chart, the doctor tells a complicated story about some experiments on Italian women conducted with the drugs he is prescribing. Nancy and Cat follow him out into the hall. Lila suspects they are keeping something from her. She doesn't know what to think. The doctor didn't say if she would be cured, and she was afraid to ask.

She can feel the wound draining, little drips that tickle. The nurses don't use any kind of ointment on it. When she was a child, she had an infected place where she had stuck a stob in her shin. Her aunt Dove bought some Rosebud salve from a peddler and it healed the sore. Lila remembers when they used to rub dirt in wounds; dirt was pure, what grew things. Good dirt was precious.

In the other bed, the old woman yells at the nurse bringing her lunch tray.

"You can just take that right back, because I don't want it."

"If you don't start eating for us, we'll have to put you back on the I.V., Mrs. Wright," the nurse says in a tone one would use to a child.

The nurse disappears into the hall and comes back with Lila's dinner.

"Oh, no, not more food," Lila says.

Spence, looking tired and cold, comes in a little later. She is still picking at her dinner.

"The doctor said it spread to two out of seventeen lymp' nodes," Lila tells him. Before she can respond to Spence's shocked expression, Cat and Nancy return and tell him what the doctor said.

"He's going to try chemotherapy," Cat says.

"Cobalt?"

"No."

Spence grins, the worry on his face lifting. "I was afraid they were going to do cobalt. I couldn't sleep none all night, thinking about it."

"No. Just shots and pills."

Spence says, "What'll it do?"

"He wouldn't say."

"He was optimistic," Nancy assures Spence.

Cat repeats what the doctor said about the treatment. Lila, amazed that anyone can remember all that, notices that Cat doesn't go into detail about the discussion on fat. Spence listens without comment.

Lila shoves her tray at Spence. "Here, does anybody want some of this turkey? I can't go another bite."

"That mess looks awful." He turns up his nose.

"We're going to the cafeteria," Nancy says. "Why don't you come with us, Daddy?"

He shakes his head. "I found this place with baked taters four for a dollar."

"*Four* baked potatoes?" Cat asks.

"I just get two," he says. "And a Coke and some peanuts."

"You better go down to the cafeteria," Lila says to him, "and get you some meat and vegetables. I can't say much for their cooking, though."

"You can say that again," Mrs. Wright in the other bed says, her voice calling through the curtain partition. "They call this turkey and dressing? It ain't even Thanksgiving. We had better grub at the poorhouse when I used to work in the kitchen."

Lila says, "You better eat it, though, to keep body and soul together."

"I told 'em I wasn't eating a bite and I won't. I'll not leave this hospital alive anyway."

Spence and Cat and Nancy grin at each other. Cat whispers to Spence, "She's been going on like that all morning."

A nurse says, "I'll be back to check your drainage when you're done eating."

"They never leave you alone," says Lila. "All night long they come in. 'Mrs. Culpepper? Time to take your temperature.' 'Mrs. Culpepper? Time to check the drainage.' They come in here and wake me up just to refill the water jug."

"They go by their rules," Nancy says. "They don't care about you as a person."

"There's one nurse that's cute as a bug's ear," Lila says. "She tickles me. She's got a cute disposition and the littlest feet."

"Isn't Mom doing great?" Cat says to Spence with a grin.

"She's got her fire back," Spence says, beaming at Lila.

"This place ain't seen nothing yet," says Lila. "I'm tough as nails and rough as a cob!" She laughs at herself and feels the bandage pull her skin. She wants to be cheerful, for the girls, but she doesn't feel cheerful.

In the afternoon, when the girls have gone, a nurse draws back the curtain partition, and the sunlight through the window next to Mrs. Wright's bed floods Lila's side of the room. The TV is playing a soap opera about a woman whose husband is having an affair with their adopted daughter.

"I hate them old stories," Mrs. Wright says. "The same thing ever' day, and it never does come to an end."

"They just want to keep you going on them," Lila says. The adopted daughter on TV is pregnant now. She has agreed to be a surrogate mother for her adoptive parents, who can't have children.

"My belly steeples is itching," says Mrs. Wright. "I feel like yanking 'em out."

"Don't you have any family close by to come and see you?" Lila asks. The woman has had no visitors.

"None except my brother, but he's in Tennessee. And he don't care a rat's behind what happens to me. There's a bunch of nieces and nephews and their littluns—just little tadpoles."

Lila says, "I've raised three fine younguns." She fumbles for the remote-control box by the bed and turns down the sound of the soap opera.

Mrs. Wright says, "I've farmed all my life except for a year when I went to Detroit and worked during the war. I've gone out in the morning when the dew was dried off and cut hay and baled it and got it in before it rained. We'd work till ten or eleven at night."

"I always helped hay too," Lila says. "You ain't got nothing on me."

"I lifted the bales right into the truck just like a man. Did you lift bales into the truck?"

"Well, I *drove* the truck," says Lila. "They wouldn't let me lift like that—in case my insides might drop."

"That could be the cause of my trouble," Mrs. Wright says. "I wouldn't have come to this place, but they bellyached and bellyached till they got me here. I could have got along fine without them cutting me open."

"Who bellyached?"

"Oh, them people I rent my trailer from."

The woman rattles on, but Lila pretends to be falling asleep. In the TV story, the adopted daughter is driving over a bridge. The bridge railing breaks. Debris scatters, gray water rolling with bits of wreckage. Then an instant soup is steaming in a cup and a bleached-blond woman in a shiny kitchen is smiling. Lila's kitchen is not that fancy, even though they remodeled a few years ago, but she remembers how proud she was to get out of Rosie's miserable, dark kitchen, with the dishwater simmering on the gas stove. By the time Cat was born, Lila and Spence had built their own house, a hundred yards away from his parents' house, through the woods. They had two dozen cows by then, and the dairy prospered. Rosie churned butter; Lila helped with the milking and bottling; Spence made the deliveries in town; Amp and Spence raised corn and hay. In her new house, a plain four-room square, Lila had her own kitchen, with running water. With her blackberry money, she bought a pressure cooker. Later, they bought a freezer and installed indoor plumbing, and eventually they added more rooms. Lila relaxed and let things go. She didn't yell at the kids for strewing their clothes and toys everywhere. She spoiled them. Before Easter Sunday, she often found herself staying up past midnight finishing their Easter outfits. And she made so many clothes for Cat over the years she could have stocked a store. Her children were always well fed and wore good clothes.

The house she grew up in had a sort of unfinished feeling to it. Some of the rooms upstairs were bare wood walls, with the studs showing, and the family itself felt unfinished. It shot off in different directions—in-laws, cousins, widows, a cousin with an illegitimate child, an aunt whose husband had abandoned her. Uncle Mose took in strays like Lila, anybody with a pair of hands to help him work his tobacco, but Lila always felt she was just an extra mouth to feed. When she married Spence and moved in with his parents, she felt out of place. Their house was dark and filled with silences. Rosie even shelled beans with great concentration, as if chatter would be inefficient. Lila tried to fit in, as she had learned to do in a large household of grownups, but when Amp and Rosie stepped on her feelings, or made her feel unworthy because she didn't know how to do things their way, there were no aunts or cousins to run to. At Uncle Mose's, in that big clumsy bunch, she was the youngest, and she had to play by herself. She tied doll bonnets on cats and packed them, squirming, from place to place. A cat drowned in the cistern once. The men drained the cistern, and her cousin Dulcie, who bossed everybody, made Lila descend a ladder into that dark pit to get the dead cat. "You're so crazy about cats, you're the right one to send," Dulcie said in a practical tone. Lila brought the cat up in her arms, slimy and already rotting, and for a long time after that the water wasn't fit to drink, but they washed in it. Even now, whenever Lila sees a dead cat she recalls that cat in the cistern.

As Lila is waking up, later in the afternoon, Nancy appears with a cup of coffee, and the old woman says to her, "You'll be high, wide and handsome about eleven o'clock tonight if you drink that."

"How are you doing, Mrs. Wright?" Nancy asks.

"I'm still swelled, but he looked at it and said I was doing good. But I'm not."

"Did you eat your lunch?"

"No. That hospital food ain't fitten to eat—no seasoning."

"You didn't touch a bite," Lila reminds her sleepily. "So how do you know it wasn't any good?"

"I could tell by looking." Mrs. Wright heaves her heavy blue-and-white legs over the edge of the bed and faces the window. "Nobody'll ever talk me into going in the hospital again."

Nancy sets her coffee on the night table and clasps Lila's hand.

Lila feels strength flowing into her arm from her daughter, and she holds Nancy's hand tightly.

"Do you want me to read to you?" Nancy asks. "Cat had to go to work. She said she'd be back at six."

"No, that's all right. I couldn't keep my mind on it."

"How do you feel?"

"There's too much commotion going on here to think," Lila says. She pulls at the front of her gown.

Nancy touches the limp curls that droop onto her mother's forehead. "I think it looks very promising," Nancy says. "They caught it early and they can do wonders nowadays."

A nurse, appearing suddenly, closes the curtain partition between the two beds. "Mrs. Culpepper? We need to check your dressing."

The nurse shoos Nancy out and pulls another curtain around the bed. She pokes at the bandage and peels it back. Lila doesn't want to look, but she glimpses a brown spot. She wonders if they saved her nipple. Cat mentioned earlier that if they saved her nipple they could rebuild her breast. The brown spot is far off center.

9

The way doctors throw their forty-dollar words around like weapons is infuriating. Spence knows big words, plenty of them. He prefers not to use his vocabulary in conversation, though, for fear of sounding pretentious. Using the right simple words at the right time requires courage enough. At times there is no way on earth he can say what he feels.

He knows what he *wants* to say, and he imagines saying it to Lila, but it takes guts to admit guilt and wrong, to express sorrow, to lavish loving feelings on someone. If only he could, he would say, "Lila, you and me have been together a long time, and we've been through a lot together." He laughs to himself. How phony that would be. It sounds like something on television. He has never said those things because he would feel as though he were speaking lines. Real love requires something else, something deeper. And sometimes a feeling just goes without saying.

Show her you love her, they say. Doesn't he show her? Everything he does is for her, even when he goes his own way and she is powerless to stop him—like the time he drove the tractor across the creek after it had washed out and she was afraid the tractor would turn over. As he headed out through the field to the creek, she called and called, but he wouldn't stop. He has always teased her about her habit of worrying herself sick over nothing. Teasing rattles her, but it would be out of character for him to behave any other way, and she would respect him less.

He could say to Lila, "It's all right. Your breast isn't your life. You can live without it, and I'll accept that." More lines. He has to show her another way, letting her know indirectly how much he still loves her. "Our love will never die." Words are so inadequate. Phony. Nobody he knows says things like that anyway. People either lie to be nice or they say what they think. The girls used to accuse Spence of being cruel when he spoke his mind, but that is not true. He is just honest. He hates hypocrites.

The morning after her operation, when he came in so late, afraid to see her, she was sitting up in bed, gabbing with a nurse as if nothing had happened. "Where in the world have you been?" she said to him accusingly. "I thought you'd forgot about me." She had on lipstick, and her hair was pretty, the color of straw. Later, he helped her walk down the corridor, pulling her I.V. along like a child's wagon, and she joked with him about her lost breast. She said, "I didn't realize how you depend on your jugs for balance. I feel all whopperjawed! And I have to go around holding the other one up till I can wear a brassiere." Spence told her he could rig her up a sling, like the one he fashioned for a hound dog once when she had an open wound on the bottom of her paw.

When they made a turn at the end of the hallway, Lila suddenly asked him, "Why do you think this happened to me?"

"No reason. Things just happen. What do you mean?"

"I don't know. It just don't seem right."

Spence wanders through the house now, seeing her things. The collection of dolls she laboriously sewed clothes for, the knickknacks she bought at yard sales, her closet stuffed with pants suits and flowered dresses she made for herself, the rack of quilts she spent so many winters constructing. A casserole she made for him is still in the refrigerator, as well as a ham and bowls of green beans and stock peas. Neighbors brought Spence an odd assortment of dishes—coconut pie, lima beans cooked with macaroni, stewed tomatoes, green Jell-O streaked with shredded cabbage. Spence doesn't eat much in the evenings because food at night gives him heartburn, and he is at the hospital during the day, so the food is spoiling. It is depressing. If it were Lila's funeral, the same people would bring the same food.

He is walking to the pond with Oscar, escaping the chaos in the house. Nancy and Cat have come to clean, and they're rearranging everything. They moved his outdoor clothes out of the living room— his boots, his jackets, the manure-stained pants he wore for feeding the animals. Lila always let him keep the clothes by the door, where they were handy, but Nancy and Cat dumped them all—including his boots and bootjack—in a corner of the bedroom. "Honestly, Daddy," said Cat in exasperation. She handed him a slop bucket to take to the ducks.

"What do you think, Oscar?" he says aloud. At that moment, Oscar sees the ducks and bounds forward merrily. Oscar is a small gray dog with shaggy hair down in his eyes. "Get back here. Don't chase them ducks!" Spence shouts. On the pond bank, the ducks skitter ahead of Oscar and splash into the water. Oscar tests the water, then gets distracted by a grasshopper. Spence empties the slop bucket on the bank—rotting lettuce and blackening radishes and rubbery break beans from the vegetable crisper that Cat cleaned out. The ducks paddle to the bank and dart their bills furtively at the garbage. Oscar has gone down into the creek. Spence scans the pond bank for the hoofprints of deer. Recently he saw three deer crossing the field to the pond—a doe and two young ones. Spence has never shot a deer and does not plan to.

From a rise near the pond Spence surveys the ocean of soybeans, with the dips and waves in the front fields and the stripe of corn edging the back ten. The farm has seventy-three acres. He remembers his father teaching him how to figure while they worked the fields. Pappy drilled him in the multiplication table as they cultivated the rows of corn with a mule. When Spence was eight, he realized that when he was thirty-three Pappy would be sixty-six, twice his age. Now Spence is almost sixty-six himself. His father has been dead for twenty-five years. Spence is glad Pappy did not live to see the milk cows sold off.

A grasshopper shoots through the air. The soybeans are thick with them. With no-till beans, he had to use a weed-killer a week after planting, and he suspects that it killed a certain weed the grasshoppers liked, so they are eating the new bean leaves instead. Bill Belton will have to spray soon. Besides the cropduster plane, Bill is deeply in debt for a combine and a planter. Spence has never gone into debt, but he knows a couple of farmers who have lost their land after over-borrowing. When he took a part-time job, driving a van during the school year for the high school, he was able to get medical benefits, which will help now with Lila's illness. But he worries about whether it is enough. He might have to cash in his certificate of deposit, which doesn't mature until October. In his worst moments, he can imagine losing his farm to doctors.

On the edge of the field, he steps across a ridge of dirt pushed up by a tractor tire. A few stray soybeans perch on the top, and the tire print beside it is dry like a scar. He thinks of the furrow the doctors may cut in Lila's neck.

When he was looking at her things, he ran across a postcard she had written him from Savannah. It showed a picture of a lighthouse. When he got home from the Navy, she seemed stronger, tougher, and he felt weaker, torn apart. After the Navy, Spence never wanted to travel again. Home was like that lighthouse. At night on the ocean, the exploding artillery shells kept him awake. The seasickness was worse below deck. Swinging in his hammock, slamming against metal walls and poles, he wanted to die. The sounds down there were magnified—whistles, loudspeakers, the big thumps bombs made hitting water, feet running on deck, metal doors clanging shut. It was deafening. He never saw any of the battles. He knew when there was a battle because the lights turned red. He threw up on a five-inch shell on its way up to the gun turret. He never knew if the shells he touched found their way to the heart of an enemy craft. Up on deck, it was calmer: the fighter planes coming and going from the flattop; the big ship protected in the huddle like a queen bee. It felt better out on deck, because he could see what was going on. He was where the weather was. The fighters landing on the carrier reminded him of snake doctors floating through the air, alighting on a weed, flitting off. A snake doctor touched down on his bare arm once when he was a child and left a blister as large as a nickel. In his nightmares out on the sea, the kamikazes made blisters on the deck of the destroyer and the ship exploded with fire. After he came home, he still couldn't sleep. He stayed up late and read about the battles, wanting to find out about the big battle he was in, but he couldn't find many books about the Pacific. Most of them were about Germany. He could see the battle in his mind's eye, from what he heard afterwards, but there wasn't enough information in the books. He wanted to know how his destroyer fit in the larger picture, a whole world at war. He had so many questions about the Japanese, the islands, the atom bomb. He wanted to know every detail of what happened, how it happened, why. But the more he read, the more confusing it became, the larger it grew. He couldn't keep up the reading at night because he always had to get up so early to milk, and after that he faced a long day in the fields. Eventually, his eyes went bad and reading gave him terrible headaches. "Forget about that war," Lila told him. "It's over."

Last night he had a nightmare about Godzilla invading his soybeans. Now he imagines his fields barren and swampy, like the Everglades. He has heard that when the big earthquake expected in the Mississippi River Valley hits, everything for miles will turn to liquid clay.

By the time Spence returns to the house, the girls have finished cleaning, and now they are freezing corn. Nancy is cutting corn off the cob, and Cat stirs corn in a skillet on the stove. Cookie pans spread with cooked corn are cooling in front of the air conditioner. The kitchen is steamy. Freezer bags litter the table.

"Ain't it too late in the day to pick corn?" he asks.

"We couldn't wait till tomorrow. It's getting too old," Cat says.

Nancy cuts the corn off the cob the way her mother taught her to do it years ago—first halfway through the kernels, then all the way, then scraping the cob for the juice. It has been years since Nancy has done this, and there is a frown on her face.

"Mom took the news about the chemotherapy real well," says Cat.

"She's more scared than she admits," Nancy says.

"She's really brave," Cat says. "But she's being extra brave for us."

"I'd go to pieces," Nancy says, viciously scraping the cob with the knife.

"I hope she stays off the cigarettes," Cat says.

"The cigarette tax is going up," Nancy says. "Reagan will just send the money to the contras."

Trying to stay busy, Spence collects the trash from the basement and starts burning it in the trash barrel behind the old milkhouse. The cloud of black smoke blows south, toward the smokestack of the industrial park. Spence likes that—he's sending the park a message, like Indians with smoke signals. Suddenly Nancy, the corn knife still in her hand, is standing there yelling at him.

"You're not supposed to burn those plastic Coke bottles!"

"But how am I going to get rid of them?"

"You'll have to dump them. You shouldn't buy that kind."

He throws some boxes on the fire, and angry, dark smoke boils up.

"Plastic releases polyvinyl chloride," she says. "It's a deadly pollutant."

"I don't want to dump too much trash in the creek."

Nancy runs inside the house, holding her nose, and he tosses the remaining plastic bottles onto the fire. The two-liter size is ninety-nine cents, a savings of a dollar-eleven over Coke in cans. He feels helpless. Nancy is so much like Lila. He remembers Lila chasing him with a mop all the way to the railroad track once. They were very young, and she was mad at him for tracking his muddy boots on the floor she had just mopped. He can still see her short, loose dress, her breasts swinging like fruit on a branch in a strong breeze.

10

Lila feels the arteries in her neck throbbing, heavy with blood trying to reach her brain. Nancy claimed the blood vessels were stopped up with bacon grease. The bacon that comes with the hospital breakfast is usually burned, and Lila still has no appetite, but she tries to eat because it is wrong to waste food. She hasn't smoked. The thought of cigarettes makes her gag.

She doesn't believe the cancer has spread. She can't feel it anywhere. The doctor said the knot was only the size of a lima bean. She is self-conscious about the emptiness on her right front. The bandage itches, and the drainage tube irritates her. The tube coils out of the wound and connects to the plastic drainage bottle taped to her stomach, close to her shaved groin. She does not know why they had to shave her there. With the bottle flapping as she walks down the hall, she imagines that this is what a man's balls must be like. She pulls at the hospital gown, filling it out with air so she won't appear so lopsided. With the drainage bottle and her flattened chest, she might have had a sex-change operation. Her mind still seems cloudy at times, and then sometimes all the recent events come at her in a rush. She probably shouldn't have gone to Florida. She recalls Cat saying, "Lee and Daddy never should have taken you to the Everglades when it was off-season—ninety-eight degrees and wall-to-wall mosquitoes." Lila told Cat, "That cloud of mosquitoes was purely black!"

Losing her breast feels something like giving birth. Part of her that used to bulge out is now vacant, the familiar growth gone. It's an empty sensation, but not exceptionally painful. Now that she has been thinking about it, it seems natural, after all, that disease should attack her there, that she should be most vulnerable there. Probably she strained her breasts; they were too large; and she has had so much mastitis. It makes sense. When Lee was born, she was tired and overworked. During the winter she had been working at the clothing factory, and that summer she made several premature trips to the hospital, returning home empty-handed. It was frustrating, and when

Lee was finally born, the other children stood beside her hospital bed accusingly, as if she had done something peculiar for her age. She was only thirty-two, but seeing Nancy, who was already twelve, made her feel old. Nancy pleaded, "Come home soon, because nobody will do what I say and I hate to cook." They didn't tell Lila until later about the scare with Cathy—as she was called then. She wasn't called Cat until that movie *Cat Ballou*. Cathy had disappeared, and they didn't find her for over two hours. She was walking down the railroad tracks, her face stained purple—probably from eating poisonous pokeberries. She was sick all night.

After Lila came home from the hospital with the baby, he cried so much at night that Spence started sleeping on his parents' screened-in porch. Lila realized Lee was hungry for solid food. She began feeding him baby food, as well as cow's milk in a bottle. For the only time in her life, Lila could barely manage. Vegetables from the garden were coming in, the blackberries were ripe, and Cat was still so little she had to be watched every minute. Nancy was becoming difficult—moody and resentful of her chores. She played loud music on the radio. Lila got no sleep those first few months. But a few years later, they bought their first television, and an unexpected harmony filled the house. They gathered in the living room with a dishpan full of popcorn. Their favorite show was *I Love Lucy*. When Lucy broke into one of her childish bawls, Lee would pucker up and pretend to bawl too. "A great sense of humor for a kid," Nancy said. Lila recalled long winter nights at Uncle Mose's, when there was no entertainment to work by. There was only the bickering of her older cousins over the ironing and sewing, with Uncle Mose in his rocking chair, reading the Bible and farting, seemingly at will. Behind his back, they called him Old Whistlebritches.

Nancy is waving a large envelope in Lila's face. "Mom, I have something wonderful to show you. Jack just sent some new pictures of Robert."

"He's going to be a lady-killer," Cat says. "Nancy, I wish you'd brought him with you!"

"Oh, let me get my glasses," says Lila eagerly. She doesn't see her oldest grandchild often, but in the pictures Nancy frequently sends,

Lila has watched him grow, like that kitten in the television commercial who changes into a grown cat in just a few seconds.

Nancy, removing the pictures from the envelope, says, "Jack sent them Federal Express to me at Cat's. He sent them last night and they got here this morning."

"I can't get over that," says Cat. "Anymore, everything's so fast."

Lila adjusts her glasses and examines the pictures as Nancy hands them to her one by one. They are large black-and-white pictures on thick paper, unlike the little snapshots the drugstore develops.

"He's filled out a lot," Lila says. "He don't look like a starved chicken anymore."

Robert seems confident and grown. In one picture, he's holding something, maybe keys, and in his sunglasses he's in a playful pose, pretending he's somebody famous. He's in dark pants and a T-shirt with faint writing on it.

"Isn't he darling?" Cat says. "I could just eat him up."

"He's about five-ten now," says Nancy. "Look at this one."

"That's my favorite," Cat says. "He looks like Daddy."

"Why, he does!" Lila studies the picture closely. She can see Spence hiding there—the firm lines of the jaw, the clenched teeth, the concealed beginning of a grin. Spence wasn't much older than Robert is now when she first saw him. He was riding a mule down Wolf Creek Road. His mother had cut his hair, causing his cowlick to shoot up like a tuft of grass on top of a stump, but it only accentuated his good looks. Lila gets tickled and laughs at Robert's hair. "I sure didn't know he had a cowlick," she says.

"It's not a cowlick. It's spiked," Nancy explains. "It's what kids do to their hair these days."

"Robert has your eyes," Lila says, noticing the dark glint in Nancy's eyes. "I always said he had your eyes."

Lila remembers the time Lee cut his foot on the jagged edge of a rusted coffee can that had been opened by one of those old-timey can openers. Lila knew from Nancy's scared eyes as she ran toward the house with Lee in her arms that something terrible had happened, even before she saw the blood from Lee's foot.

"And now for the prize." Nancy is hiding the last picture against her chest. "This is Robert at the end of the school year. They didn't have a prom. They had what they call a 'superlative.' It's an honors thing, where they celebrate their achievements."

"I can't believe this," says Cat as Nancy turns the picture face forward.

Robert, in a tuxedo, is standing against a doorway next to a pretty girl in a long dress with a ruffle around the neck. Both of them have that wild hair, standing up as if electrified.

"He's girlfriending already!" Lila cries. "Law, that hair."

"Her name is Amy," says Nancy. "Her mother is our accountant."

"I bet all the girls are crazy about him," says Cat. "Look at that sexy grin."

Nancy says, "They're just friends, or so I'm told. Amy's dress is pink, and he has a pink cummerbund to match."

"Everything is pink now," says Cat.

"Why don't Jack ever take anything in color?" Lila asks. "I have to use my imagination."

"I guess that's the idea," says Nancy. She laughs. "Jack didn't want to send this picture earlier, but I guess he changed his mind. He thought you might have a fit over the hair."

Smiling, Lila lays her glasses on the nightstand. "Well, I'm mighty proud," she says. "You sure did put out a fine youngun, and stayed married—for how long now?"

"It was twenty years ago today—"

"Today?"

"No, not today. That's a song allusion. Eighteen years."

"That's a record," Cat says in a flat tone.

Lila realizes the sadness in Cat's voice. She is certain Cat could have patched it up with Dan. Quickly, Lila says, with deep pride, "All of my children have given me some mighty fine grandchildren."

"Krystal and Scott both asked about you on the phone, Mom," Cat says. "Krystal hates it in Hopkinsville and wants to come home."

Nancy gathers up the photographs, promising to leave them for Lila to look at again later.

"Y'all don't have to be here every minute," Lila insists to Cat and Nancy.

"We're here because we care about you," says Cat.

"Well, you're showing it," Lila says. A sudden swell of emotion rises in her throat. The tugging sensation of nursing them as babies is as clear as yesterday. Nancy liked to bite. Cat was always hungry. Nancy wasn't weaned until she was two and a half. Rosie would say, "You're giving that youngun too much peezootie." That was a word of Rosie's Lila never heard anyone else use.

"Is there anything you want us to do?" Nancy asks.

With a little catch in her voice, Lila says, "There's something I wanted you to promise me. I didn't get to say it before."

They listen, like a pair of young cats fixed on a squirrel. Lila says, without her voice breaking, "I want you to take care of your daddy if something happens to me. He won't be able to take care of hisself."

"Don't worry, Mom. We'll take care of him." Cat caresses Lila's hand, picking at a cuticle where nail polish has smeared.

Lila says, "I don't want to be buried in that Spring Valley mausoleum. It's on the side of the road on a curve, and a truck could come along and bust it open."

"Don't think that way!" Nancy says.

Cat leans forward to give Lila a hug. "We'd never leave you by the side of the road. You know that."

"I wouldn't have found that knot if it hadn't been for you. In the old days, people didn't get breast cancer. Or they didn't know they had it. They just got sick and died."

"Well, science can do amazing things nowadays," Nancy says. "And the chemotherapy is going to work."

"You just don't realize how far we've come," says Lila, squeezing Nancy's hand.

"Yes, I do. I would have died at age ten of pneumonia if it hadn't been for penicillin."

Nancy always has an answer. But she seems not to realize she had survived pneumonia another time, when she was two. That was before penicillin. The memory jolts Lila.

"Times are better now," she insists to her daughters. "You don't know how good you've got it."

Nowadays, Lila thinks, young people expect to have everything right at the start. House and car, washer and dryer. They're not patient. When she worked at the clothing factory, she earned enough money to make life a little easier. In the few years she worked there, she bought a steam iron, an electric mixer, an electric stove, a set of steak knives, a dinette set. Spence never wanted her to go to work, but after Nancy started to school, and before Cat and Lee came along, the factory was hiring. Excitedly, Lila applied for the job, wearing a suit she had made. The hiring man admired her sewing and gave her the job. She sat at a large machine, stitching in collars or cuffing pants. She put on weight, sitting long hours on the high stool, but her arms grew strong from pushing and pulling the heavy suit material through her machine. The oiled wood floors were sticky with clumps of thread, and the air was stifling, despite the overhead fans. She carried her dinner—pimiento or tuna-fish sandwiches, with the lettuce wrapped separately; and sometimes a tomato, and salt and pepper folded in little pieces of waxed paper. She usually carried cake or cookies. On her breaks and lunch period, it was a deep pleasure to drink a cold, slippery bottle of Coca-Cola from the large cooler in the hallway. Lila loved the people, the talk that went on above the noise. She bragged on her child and listened to others brag on theirs; they swapped pictures and stories. The woman at the machine next to hers had asthma attacks from the wool dust in the air, and they had to carry her outside occasionally. A man working at the end of her row always entertained the hands with songs popular on the radio. She can still hear him singing "Slow Boat to China." Recently someone told her he had left his wife and died of a brain tumor in Arizona, alone. Another woman was always called "Miss Gregory" instead of her first name because she always dressed so elegantly for such rough work. They would say, "Miss Gregory sets on a pillow sewing a fine seam." Lila felt that way too, proud and alive. It was piecework, and sometimes she could make nearly ninety cents an hour, she was so fast.

Later, Cat has gone down the hall to the bathroom and Nancy is reading. Lila is telling Mrs. Wright she doesn't think her cancer has spread, when Cat returns, excited. "Did you see that prisoner on this floor? There's a guy with a guard from the state penitentiary. He's two rooms down the hall. He looks really sick, like he couldn't crawl an inch even if he tried to escape."

Lila shudders. "I hope that guard don't fall asleep. That's all I need, to be held hostage in the hospital!"

Mrs. Wright says, "It won't make me one bit of difference."

11

On Sunday Lila's half-sister, Glenda, and her husband, Bill, stop by the hospital with a basket of artificial violets. It has a little ceramic rabbit in it, nibbling at the leaves. Lila is wearing her good blue gown and a bed jacket. Cat put Lila's makeup on her that morning and fixed her hair. Lila's scalp itches, but she doesn't want to wash her hair for fear of catching cold.

"Well, Lila, are you going to have to have cobalt?" Glenda asks. Glenda is overweight, with baby-fine light hair that used to be a pretty blond.

"No, I'm not," says Lila happily. "Just shots and pills for six months, and then they do all the tests again to see if it spread."

"I told Bill I didn't think you'd have to have cobalt," says Glenda.

Bill is a red-faced, deliberate sort of man, a retired farmer. He says defensively, "Well, seems like they want to put everybody through that."

"I don't think it spread very much," Lila says. "I could feel it in those leaders under my arms, but they think they got it all out." She runs her hand down her arm, which is stiffening up. The physical therapist has been there, instructing her how to work her arm. Lila has to grasp a yardstick, one hand on each end, and slowly raise it above her head, then lower it and swing it from side to side.

Glenda says, "We heard you're going to be operated on again, Lila."

Lila nods. "Depends on what they find out with my neck." She scrapes her fingers down her throat. "The blood ain't going through good."

Glenda says brightly, "Bob Barber had *his* veins cleaned out and he said it was like getting new glasses. He could think better after they operated."

"Are they going to do that test where they shoot you with the dye?" asks Bill.

"Uh-huh. I purely dread it too."

"They say that really hurts," Bill says. "They shoot it in your leg and it works its way up to your head and burns."

"They told me I had to lay real still for eight hours after they do it," Lila says. "If I turn over it might be dangerous."

"A clot might go to your brain," Glenda says.

"How have y'all been?" Lila asks, changing the subject. If Spence were here, he would be furious at them.

"All right, I reckon," says Glenda. "Bill here has to go in for his checkup—he has sugar—and he has to have tests for that spasmatic colon he's got."

Bill, hacking at a cough, says, "I told them I wasn't going to have that test where you drank that drank again. I had that last year, and my bowels backed up and didn't move for three months. It made a knot as big as my fist. It stayed there and everything went around it. I liked to died."

Glenda laughs. "He sure was something to live with while that was going on."

"Lila, you look like a spring chicken," says Bill. "Why, your hide won't hold you when you get home!" He offers to get Cokes for everyone.

"You can get a free drink in the lounge," Lila says.

After he leaves, Lila says, "I'm so proud to see you, Glenda!"

Glenda was eight and Lila was four when their mother died. Lila has one memory of her: a chubby little woman with dark hair, saying "fried pies" out on a porch, with a dog running up from a field—somewhere Lila could never identify. Her mother was only about twenty-eight when she died, of childbed fever. Glenda, who remembered her better, told Lila once, "She was light-complected and had pretty teeth. She liked to ride horses, and they say that's why she died. She rode a horse when she shouldn't have." The baby died too. Lila had been told it was a girl. Lila's father left Lila at Uncle Mose's and disappeared. Glenda went to live with her real daddy and his second wife in a little place down below Wolf Creek.

Lila didn't see Glenda again until after she married Spence and the war was over. Lila and Spence visited Glenda one Sunday afternoon. They sat on Glenda and Bill's porch and watched the traffic go by. Lila remembers her happiness that day—Glenda's daughter, Laura Jean, teaching Nancy how to ride a little red scooter; a dusty driveway; a setting hen; a can of sorghum Bill gave them. She remembers Glenda shooing flies from the apple slices spread out on a screen door to dry in the sun. Glenda was fat. That day she told Lila the baby their mother died with was a boy, not a girl.

"Lila, how are those daughters of yours treating you?" Glenda asks now.

"Oh, they've been awful good to me. They've been here every minute." Lila laughs. "They froze my corn the other evening. They should have done it in the morning when the dew's wet."

"It won't be crisp," Glenda says, nodding. "It'll be tough."

"I hope I'm out of here in time to do all the pickles. They'll draw the line at pickles."

"Nobody can do dill pickles like you can, Lila. You've got a secret recipe, I believe. One of these days I'm going to get you down and mash that recipe out of you."

"I just do it by guess. Last year I got them too sour. They was sour enough to make a pig squeal!" Lila laughs, then hiccups.

The old woman's voice booms through the curtain. "Who's got the he-cups over there?"

"Me," says Lila. She can't get comfortable, and the little jolts hurt her incision.

"You're a-growing," Mrs. Wright says. "That's what that means."

"I hope so," Lila says, pulling at her gown. "I wish I could grow a new jug."

"You can't get no sleep around here to save your neck," Mrs. Wright says. "They come in here late last night and started burning the house down!"

Lila sees the prisoner trudging past the door, clinging to his uniformed guard. His gown gapes open in the back, exposing his hairy rear end. He shuffles along, his head bent. Lila feels a sudden fore-boding of death. This is all there is left to life: lying here in a hospital gown with her breast amputated, watching a bare-butt criminal go by and listening to a nutty old woman griping behind a curtain. Days ago, Lila told herself she was ready to go, that she had made her peace with the world, that she had had a good life and she was grate-ful. But now she revolts. She doesn't want to give up. She swings out of bed a little too quickly, and a pain shoots through her arm. But that's O.K. It will go away.

"Walk me down the hall," she says to Glenda. "I ain't ready to die yet."

12

"You're not eating for us, Mrs. Wright," the nurse says disapprov-ingly. This nurse is the cute one, with the tiny feet. She's the only nurse who bothers to chat with the old woman.

"She made a little sign on it," says Lila.

"I like broccoli cooked *done,*" says Mrs. Wright, sitting up against her pillows defiantly and pushing her tray trolley forward. "I like all kinds of greens. I could eat my weight in asparagus. But not raw."

It's time for Lila to breathe oxygen. The nurse's aide hauls the breathing contraption to Lila's bedside and pulls the curtain between the beds. She aims the blue mask at Lila's face.

"I believe my lungs is clearing up," Lila says to her.

"Well, they ought to be if you keep off them cigarettes," the girl says.

"Woman!" Mrs. Wright booms through the curtain. "I did some-thing for sixty-five years and then quit—and you can too."

"What's that—smoking?" asks Lila.

"Naw—chewing tobacco. I started in the first grade, but since I was operated on four days ago I haven't wanted a chew. Got a bad taste in my mouth."

Lila can't reply because she is holding her breath. The girl says, "You're doing good. Just hold it two more seconds. There."

Lila says, rubbing her neck, "These veins need oxygen."

"That smoking was closing them down," the girl says.

"I'm worried about that test they're going to run on my neck. They don't want to operate on both sides at once. They need to keep one vein open to feed the brain in case I have a stroke on the operating table." The words rush out. Lila can talk to the nurses about her fears, but doctors make her flustered.

"I'm sure they know what's best for you," the nurse's aide says. "Now breathe in again. The test will tell them which way to go."

"I'm more scared of that test than I am of the operation," Lila says. She sucks in air, feeling her face go red, her stitches tickling.

As the girl leaves, she rips open the curtain again, and Mrs. Wright says, "I'll be glad when I get back to my cat."

"Well, that's the first I heard you were going to leave the hospital!" says Lila. "I thought you wasn't aiming to leave here alive."

Mrs. Wright grumbles and works at her short-tailed gown, which has ridden up. "The doctor didn't say nothing about going home, but he said something about getting these belly steeples out. I feel like jerking 'em out myself. They put a screw in and some plastic. I had this herny for five or six years, and I was doing just fine with it till they started in bellyaching about it."

"Is somebody feeding your cat?" Lila misses Abraham. Spence won't give him enough attention.

Mrs. Wright shakes her head. "I guess she'll find something. That cat—she's a beautiful cat. Calico. She has the prettiest face. Where she's white she's *white,* and where she's black she's *black,* and where she's red she's *red!* She ain't got no tail. When she was a kitten she got in the hay baler and got her tail cut off. And she got her ears snipped off too somehow. She's crippled up in one paw. But she can catch mice. She catches 'em with one paw and stuffs 'em in her mouth and reaches out and hooks another one. That cat sleeps with me in the house every night in the world!"

"My cat doesn't come in the house," Lila says. "Spence never did like cats in the house."

"I'd tease the menfolks and offer 'em a chaw of tobacco straight out of the tobacco barn. I'd say you ain't a man if you can't chew that." Mrs. Wright laughs, a man's grunt. "If you chew tobacco, you won't never have worms. Lands, I ain't worked tobacco in ten years! That's how I ruptured myself, lifting a ten-by-twenty-five presser of tobacco."

"We never raised tobacco. I've got corn coming in and my girls don't know how to do it right."

"Honey, there ain't a soul to tend to my garden. I've got bell peppers and okry and Kentucky Wonders. Everything will ruin."

The TV news comes on, and the old woman says, "The politicians send all our money overseas, where all they do is fight and all they ever *will* do is fight."

The hospital routines are becoming too familiar—the florist's delivery cart passing by the door, the physical therapist who comes in each morning to help Lila work her arm to keep it from freezing up, the boy who sweeps the floors every afternoon, the night nurse with the cold hands and the way she has of popping the thermometer in Lila's mouth just as though she were using a dipstick to check the oil level in a car engine. When Lila asked the night nurse about the prisoner, she said, "I don't know what happened to him, but I sure wouldn't want to meet him in a dark alley."

Lila tries to read recipes in *Family Circle,* but her eyes blur and her glasses don't help. She would like to read from the Bible in the drawer of the nightstand, but the print is too fine. The preacher is supposed to come by, but he hasn't.

13

Sitting in the lounge while Lila naps, Spence is surrounded by worried-looking strangers, most of them overweight. Human beings come in such freakish forms, it always surprises him to be in a crowd of them. His nerves are bad. He can't sit still. Downstairs, he saw a woman in a wheelchair; evidently she was too fat to walk. She was the fattest woman he'd ever seen outside a circus. He works a Coke out of the ice in the cooler and lifts the tab. He takes a long drink and belches. Heartburn. The night before, it woke him up at two-thirty and he

couldn't go back to sleep. His head whirled, catching memories of recent events until he was brought up to date, to the awful present. If
Lila didn't make it through the second operation, her funeral could be
as early as next weekend. In the dark, tossing in bed, he imagined her
funeral. He couldn't stop whole scenes from playing in his head, like
a TV documentary. The sermon, the flowers, perfunctory conversations with the kinfolks at the funeral home, coming home with his
children and solemnly feasting on that food the neighbors brought.

If this is going to be her time, then what he and Lila should do is
have a last fling together. But he can't go in her room and make love
to her. He can't even talk to her or tell her how he feels while she's
lying there in that white-cold bed with the nurses bumbling around
the room like doodlebugs working on a cowpile. And now it seems
likely that the doctors will get hold of her again, with their knives and
scissors, probing violently in another place precious to him—her
rugged throat, always tanned and healthy. The surgeons in masks will
probably laugh and joke while they work, probably because they're
making so much money. They must feel immense power, like presi-
dents and TV executives. Spence's stomach turns over as a cloud of
cigarette smoke fills the room. Someone switches the TV from a fishing show to the Nashville channel. Spence hates hillbilly music.

Lee and the kids came to see Lila earlier that afternoon. Now Lee
joins Spence in the lounge, drinking a Sprite and gazing vacantly at
the TV while Jennifer and Greg explore the hospital. Lee always
seems tired. He didn't want to learn farming because he didn't want
to get up at four to milk, but he has to work even harder at his factory job. He owes the bank almost four hundred dollars a month for
a squatty little brick ranch house on a hundred-foot lot in town with
no trees. It makes Spence sick.

The prisoner enters the lounge with the guard, who walks him
around the room as if on an inspection tour. He is huge and young,
with short blond hair and freckles. He looks as though he might have
been a nice boy who turned bad. His dark eyes somehow don't fit his
physique—a clue, Spence thinks, to why he turned bad. Something
about his body isn't quite right. The sight of him is jarring. The guy
has probably known that all his life, and the conflict made him mean.

The criminal's I.V. rolls along with him like an obedient dog on a rope.

"I bet he got stabbed," Lee says. "All those prisoners want to do is cut on each other when they get the chance."

Spence says, "When the guard has to go to the bathroom, he chains that guy to the bed. I saw him."

"He don't look strong enough to get very far."

Spence asks, "How does she seem to you?"

"Mom? Oh, she's bearing up. She almost seems like her old self." Lee stares at his lap. "I feel terrible that we dragged her to Florida."

"She worries," Spence says. "She gets something in her head. Like that deal with you and Cat over the air conditioner."

"Mom didn't have anything to do with that."

Spence rubs his hands against his jeans. "I thought Cat give you that air conditioner."

"I told you how it was." Lee takes his time lighting a cigarette. "Cat said I could have the air conditioner, so I went and got it and installed it, and then she changed her mind and wanted it back, but I already had it in the window. I had to rework the frame to get it set right. It would have been easier for her to get a secondhand air conditioner than to fool with this one. She got mad because I wouldn't let her have it back."

"She claims she just meant to let you borrow it."

"She said I could have it, and I took her at her word."

Words. Lila's kinfolks deliberately tried to hurt her with words. They put him in a sour mood. And her friends chattered about diseases. Lila ate it up. His daughters embarrassed him. They even complained to the doctors about the hospital food, but the doctors had nothing to do with it. When Lila's first meal after surgery was a hamburger with pickles and potato chips, Nancy said it wasn't nutritious, especially for someone with carotid-artery disease. "A greasy old hamburger!" Nancy snapped at the doctor. Spence wanted to spank her. He can remember when he and Lila were courting, and they went out for hamburgers. A hamburger and Coke at Fred and Sue's Drive-in was the most delicious meal they had ever had. Even after they were married, they looked forward to going out for hamburgers al-

most as much as they looked forward to making love. His mother
was stingy with meat and cooked the same plain grub day in and day
out.

Lee is speaking to him about subdivisions. Lee brings up subdivisions about once a month, trying to convince Spence that since his
land is close to town it will be worth something someday.

"Why don't you sell off some frontage and get a start on a development?" Lee asks.

"What would I want to do that for?"

"You're setting on a gold mine."

"Good. You can come over and dig in it."

"You could sell one lot and get enough to build a house on another lot and then sell it at a profit."

"Why didn't Joy come today?" Spence asks.

"She went to Mister Sun. Her and her sister go to the tanning
booth every chance they get. I gave her a membership for her birthday." Lee stands to go, as Jennifer and Greg appear in the lounge. "I
have to get home and finish paneling the den. The wallpaper's peeling
off, and Joy's having a fit."

"You're going to do that on Sunday?" asks Spence, surprised. "I
thought your mama taught you not to work on Sunday."

"I don't have time during the week, with overtime."

"Why don't you repaper? Ain't that cheaper?"

"No. I'd have to put up some new gypsum board, and by the time
you get gypsum board and tape it and paint an undercoat, it's cheaper
to panel." Lee clutches his Sprite can, crumpling it, left-handed.

"Paneling's got formaldehyde in it," says Spence. "It causes cancer. Ask Nancy. Nancy can explain it to you."

"Nancy's got an explanation for everything," Lee says with a
laugh. "What does she say caused Mom to get cancer?"

"Bacon grease. She says them veins in her neck is stopped up with
bacon grease."

"Bacon grease in her neck?" asks Jennifer, Lee's seven-year-old.

"Come on, Goofus," says Lee to Greg, who is punching on Lee,
trying to get his attention. "Let me know if there's anything I can
do," Lee says to Spence.

After Lee leaves, Spence goes to check on Lila one more time before he heads home for the evening. He runs into Cat in the hall. She's wearing some kind of pink getup with a green-flowered ruffle at the bottom.

"Hi, kid," he says. "Where you been all day?"

"I went to the River Days Festival. They had a flea market and a fiddle contest."

"Fiddles ought to be outlawed."

"Why?"

"They make too much noise. The way they screak gives me a rigor."

She ignores him. "Did you see how pretty Mom looked? I fixed her hair and painted her fingernails this morning before her company came."

He nods. "You look pretty too. Except your ears look like some tobacco worms are sucking on 'em." Her earrings are fat and pale green and hang down past her chin line.

Cat slaps at his arm playfully. "I don't know how Mom put up with you all these years," she says.

"Where are you going?" he asks when Cat turns toward the elevator.

"I have a date to go out to eat."

"With that guy that took you up to Carbondale and left you that time?"

"No. He was a jerk."

"I thought you had more sense than that."

"Well, sometimes you just get in a fix and you don't know how you got there."

The elevator doors open and she steps on, waving goodbye. As the doors close, he remembers the time Cat was coming down the lane to meet him in the field. She was only about three. She crawled under the fence and started across the pasture toward him when a bull saw her and headed her way. "Go back, Cathy," he cried. "Get under the fence!" He never saw such a calm, smart child. She purposefully turned and sped toward the fence and crawled under. He was always proud of that, of how smart she was.

14

A woman from the mastectomy support group arrives the next afternoon, bringing Lila a temporary pad to stuff in her brassiere until she can be measured for a permanent one. Lila feels embarrassed because both her daughters and Spence are right there. Spence is reading the newspaper noisily, rattling the pages and jerking them out smooth. Lila worries about his nerves.

"It's called a prosthesis," the woman explains. Lila did not catch her name. Cheerful and little, pert as a wren, she stands beside the bed, speaking to Lila like a schoolteacher. She presents Lila with the object, which is in a plastic bag.

"Law," says Lila. "That weighs a ton." It reminds her of those sandbags used to hold down temporary signs on the highway.

"I can tell you're surprised," the woman chirps. "We don't realize the weight we're carrying around. You can put a strain on your back if you don't get properly fitted. So don't just stuff your bra with any old thing to make it look right. It's got to feel right and it's got to be the right weight, or you can run into serious problems."

The woman says she has had a mastectomy herself, and presumably she is wearing one of these sandbags in her brassiere. Lila notices Spence squirming. Nancy and Cat don't jump on this woman the way they did on the doctors. Cat is playing solitaire and Nancy is reading a book. Mrs. Wright is asleep.

The woman tells a long tale about her own mastectomy. "I was worried about recurrence," she says. "And I did have a lump to come in the other breast. It was tested and it was benign, but I made the decision to have the second breast removed too. I just didn't want to take the chance of having cancer again. Now, that may sound extreme to you, but it was just the way I felt. So I'm free from worry, and the prosthesis works just fine."

The woman's little points are as perky as her personality. If the originals were that small, she probably doesn't miss them, Lila thinks. The woman talks awhile about balance, and then she talks about understanding. She has a packet of materials for Lila to read. "You may get depressed over losing part of your femininity," she says. "And we want you to know we're available to help." Lila listens carefully, but she can't think of anything to say.

"The doctors were skeptical when we started our organization," the woman says, leaning toward Lila and speaking in a confidential half-whisper. "But after we advertised, we had fifty women come to the first meeting. There was a great need for this, and we want you to know that we're there to serve you."

"Would I have to come all the way to Paducah?"

"Yes. That's where we hold our meetings, on the first Monday night of each month."

"Well, I don't get out much at night. And I don't like to drive on that Paducah highway."

"Let me urge you just to try it and see what it does for you. I'll give you the names of some people to contact." She talks on and on, about how the family should be understanding. In the packet are letters to daughters and sons and husbands. Spence and the girls are pretending they aren't there. "The letters say things that you may be uncomfortable saying, things you might be afraid to say, but they will explain your feelings at this delicate time when you need emotional support. All you have to do is send the appropriate letter to your daughters and your husband and to your sons, if you have any. It will be a nice surprise for them if you just send them in the mail. It's a much easier way for you to communicate your feelings."

"My girls have stood by me," Lila says, nodding proudly at Cat and Nancy. "And my boy works long hours and can't come as often, but he does when he can. Nancy flew all the way down here from New York."

"Boston," Nancy says, peering over her reading glasses.

"That's the same thing to us down here," the woman says with an apologetic smile.

"How much will this thing cost?" Lila asks. "If you charge by the pound, it might be high." She laughs at herself. She wonders why the woman didn't replace her breasts with big ones. Small-breasted women were always envious of Lila.

"The important thing is to get the proper fitting. With your fitting, and the bra and the prosthesis, the package comes to about a hundred and fifty dollars."

"Good night!" Lila and Spence cry simultaneously.

"But it's an important investment."

After the woman has gone, Spence says, "Will insurance cover that?"

"I doubt it," Lila says. "I failed to ask her. Law, I hope I don't have to have false teeth anytime soon! I won't be able to keep track of that much stuff."

"You don't need that thing. We can rig you up something."

"Why, shoot, yes," Lila says. "I ain't spending a hundred and fifty dollars for a falsie."

Nancy laughs. "I read about a woman who stuffed her bra with buckshot, and she got stopped at the airport by the metal detector."

Cat says, "I heard about a woman who had an inflatable bra, and she went up in an airplane, and with the change in air pressure they exploded!"

They're all laughing, and Lila spontaneously tosses the prosthesis to Spence. "Catch!" she cries. Spence snatches it out of the air and flings it to Nancy and Nancy tosses it to Cat. Cat starts to throw it to Lila but stops herself, probably realizing Lila's right arm is weak. Lila is laughing so much her stitches hurt. Cat hands her the little sandbag and Lila says, "Well, it'll make a good pincushion."

They all laugh even harder then because Lila is in the habit of keeping stray straight pins and safety pins fastened to her blouse, and more than once in her life she has accidentally jabbed her breast with a pin.

15

"Well, so long," says Lila to Mrs. Wright, who is riding out the door in a wheelchair. She's going home.

The old woman crouches, her eyes aimed at her belly. She's in a print dress, lavender and green. She doesn't look up, but grunts faintly. Lila hopes she never develops such an attitude.

"I bet she can't wait till she gets back to her trailer so she can fix her up a mess of hog jaws and turnip greens," she says to her friends Mattie and Eunice, who are visiting. "She wouldn't eat a bite here."

Mattie and Eunice are in Lila's card-playing group. Last year, Reba was the fourth, and this year the fourth is Addie Mae Smith. But now Addie Mae is visiting her daughter in Florida and doesn't know Lila is in the hospital. "The flowers are from all of us, though," Mattie says, giving Lila a bowl of houseplants. "Addie Mae can go in on them when she gets back."

"I had a big crowd Sunday," says Lila. "Cat fixed my hair, but the curl's fell out now." She tugs at some stray sprigs. Cat took such care with her, fluffing her hair expertly with the plastic pick, like a hen pecking fondly at her chicks. When Cat was fussing with her, she said, out of the blue, "Mom, I know I didn't do the right things the right way. I should have gone to college and not married so young. But everything's different now, and you don't know how hard it is to work it all out. Things aren't the way they used to be—if they ever *were*." She sounded bitter, but then she said, "It's not your fault I didn't turn out right. You're the sweetest mother in the world, and I'll never be as good as you." They had cried together for a moment, until they were interrupted by a nurse with a blood-thinner shot.

Mattie and Eunice won't let Lila say anything bad about herself. They tell her how good she looks. They chatter about their families and events at church. The conversation works around to the weather occasionally, and that prompts them to tell her again how good she's looking. They bring her a nightgown—store-wrapped in pink flowered paper. Lila can tell that it won't hang right over her new bustline, but it's the thought that counts. Mattie and Eunice haven't mentioned her breast. No one mentions Reba and her months of suffering. It's as though Reba never existed. Lila folds the gown and places it inside the tissue in the box. She smooths out the wrapping paper and folds it to save.

"It's freezing in here," Mattie says.

"I've been cold as a frog," Lila says. "Nancy and Cat had to bring me an undershirt and this sweater." She has on a blue cardigan of Cat's. "In here, I can't tell what the weather is."

Mattie has to get up and stir for her circulation. She sets the gift box on a shelf in the closet. Restlessly, she pokes in Lila's things, while Eunice flips through one of Cat's magazines. Mattie pats her little gray curls, flashing her rainbow of rings. Her rings and brooches and beads overwhelm her small frame. She has a whole houseful of doodads she collects from yard sales, and she spends half her time dusting. Lila wouldn't have the patience.

Eunice is sitting close to the bed so Lila can see the pictures in the magazine. Eunice pauses over a picture of a handsome young man in his underwear.

"Look at all that going to waste," Lila says to Eunice.

"Are you sure that ain't stuffing?" says Eunice, examining the picture carefully.

"No, that ain't stuffing! That's the real thing!"

Eunice begins giggling and then Lila starts. Her breast jiggles and pulls across at her stitches. Eunice's face is red.

"I'm liable to say anything," Lila says. "This place is making me goofy. The nurses think I'm nuts."

Mattie looks disapproving, but Lila loves to watch Eunice laugh at a sexy joke. Eunice is a widow. Her husband, Herbert Wall, was big and fat, and Eunice once said he had such a load of "equipment" that it gave him a hernia. That remark made Lila think of a sheep, its swinging sack the size of a mushmelon. The boy in the underwear ad is young enough to be Lila's grandson, but he makes her feel a twinge of desire. She wishes she could go home right now and get in bed with Spence. One of the magazines Cat brought mentioned that men lose their desire for women who have had mastectomies. The thought hurt her and made her feel an anxiety like the urges she used to feel when she was working tobacco and she first knew Spence. He lived five miles down the road, and he would walk past the field where she worked after school and dawdle there. Lila's uncle found out he was hanging around and tried to scare him away, but Spence was daresome and he flirted openly with her, slowing down her work. Whenever she broke a tobacco plant by mistake she buried it so Uncle Mose wouldn't find out. She used to meet Spence at the edge of the tobacco field, down in the creek. They chewed gum from the black gum tree. It made their teeth black and their breath fresh, and when they kissed it was like a cool, sweet breeze.

Mattie walks over to the bed and stares closely at Lila. "When are they going to operate on your neck?"

"I have that test tomorrow, and they'll operate a-Thursday, depending on what they find out." She closes her fist and opens it. It feels slightly numb.

"Are you scared, dear?" Eunice asks.

"I didn't have time to get scared the first operation, and now there's so much going on I can't think. My brain was addled anyway." Lila laughs. "Probably from being out in the hot sun."

"All that gardening you do, Lila," says Mattie kindly.

"I've never seen anybody do as much yard work as you do," says Eunice. "You've got a lot to be proud of. You've got the prettiest yard."

"Well, I sure am lucky, with my children, my family, the things I've done. All the trips I got to go on." Lila is growing sleepy. Her arm feels numb, the way it did in Florida.

"That's something to be thankful for, Lila," says Mattie, and Eunice nods.

"Spence would hate all the noise and waiting in line. He'd rather be home digging taters!" Lila laughs at the thought of Spence on a bus tour with the senior citizens. Abruptly, she says, "The doctor said I could live without a breast. He said I'd be surprised."

"My sister told me about a woman she works with who had her breast takened out," says Mattie, who has been standing by the crucifix on the wall, studying it as if it were for sale. "She was a terminal case. The cancer had spread to ninety percent of her lymp' nodes."

"It just spread to two of mine, but they takened them out," Lila says, touching her right armpit.

Mattie doesn't seem to hear Lila. She's wound up, like the musical doll Cat gave Lila once for Mother's Day. "But come to find out—this woman lived!" Mattie continues. "She had chemotherapy five years and she had cobalt, but the cobalt burned a hole in her heart and gave her heart trouble, and so she had to have her chest wall replaced. She

waited too late to sue, because her husband thought she was going to
die and he didn't think they could do anything. But she got better and
then all of a sudden her husband died of a brain tumor, and then six
months after that her son was killed in a car wreck! But *she's* still a-
kicking."

"I never heard of so many things happening to one woman," says
Eunice.

"It's a miracle she bore up under all that," Lila says.

"Well, Lila, the Lord never gives us more than we can bear," says
Mattie.

"Yes," Lila says, gazing at the underwear ad.

One summer night shortly before her eighteenth birthday, she ran
away with Spence and they were married. She brought her few possessions in a bag she had sewed out of sacking. She didn't even have
a Bible. They drove across the state line, not really knowing if they
would go through with the plan. It seemed outrageous, like something the old folks told about in one of their stories of the pioneers.
Spence promised her a good life. He already had a start, on his father's farm. "I don't ask for much," he said. "Just to have my clothes
kept up and food on the table." He drove an old Ford with a door
that rattled and headlights that sometimes blinked out. While searching for the justice of the peace, they got lost on a back road, which
ended in a woods across from a cornfield. Spence persuaded her to
have the honeymoon first and then look for the justice of the peace
later, arguing that they'd never find this perfect, peaceful place again.
Lila was always a practical person and she could see his line of rea-
soning. When they finally arrived at the justice of the peace, the man
had already gone to bed, but he obligingly got up, tied his barking
dog, and performed the service for them on his front porch. In the
dim porch light, neither he nor his wife, who acted as the witness, in
her curlers and housecoat, could tell how wrinkled Lila's clothes
were. She had on a new suit she had made, with shoulder pads, and
Spence told her she was the most beautiful girl in the world. They
sneaked into his house before daylight, and at milking time he
brought her out of his room to meet his astonished parents. She was

tall and thin, but even then her breasts were large, and they jutted forward into the surprised line of sight of her new mother-in-law.

The artificial breast is in the drawer. The pamphlets are hard to read, and the letters don't say the right things—not the things she would say to her husband, her daughters, her son. The girls have read through the packet, and Lila thinks it would be even more embarrassing to send letters than to say what she felt. The letters wouldn't sound like her. One of the pamphlets says, "Women usually go through periods of depression after a mastectomy. They equate their femininity and their sexuality with the lost breast." Lila is so confused, with so many people telling her what to think, that she can't quite grasp her own thoughts.

Last week, the day she was operated on, she remembers waking up in a fog, wanting to turn over onto her side, but something held her flat. The room was extremely cold. Her feet were numb. And then she felt her habitual cough grab her and shake her out like a dust mop. She wondered, even then, before she was sure they had removed her breast, how they disposed of it: Did it all come out in one hunk, or did they hack it out? She thought about dressing a chicken, the way she cut out the extra fat and pulled out the entrails. She thought of how it was so easy to rip raw chicken breasts.

16

Bill Belton's brick ranch house, just down the road from Spence, is only a few years old, but the plastic shutters are warped and one of the downspouts is crooked. In the backyard, a wash line runs between the house and Bill's dish antenna. The dish has a happy-face painted on it. Bill's tobacco barn sags, the paint worn off years ago. Bill hasn't grown tobacco since the bottom fell out of the burley market. Now he has a hundred acres in soybeans and a crop-dusting plane. Spence often sees Bill's plane above the countryside—flying low, aggravating cows and horses.

"Ho, there, Spence," says Bill, who is down by his dilapidated barn, working on his tractor. The airplane is parked under a makeshift carport shelter on the side of the barn.

"When do you aim to dust my beans?" asks Spence. "The grasshoppers is eating 'em up. In the middle of the night I can hear 'em gnawing. I'm afraid I'll wake up one morning and the fields will be bare."

"I been meaning to get over there, Spence," says Bill, picking up an oilcan from a rickety table of rusted tools.

The outside wall of the barn is decorated with squirrel tails, snake-skins, and a coon skin. Memories of dead animals jam Spence's mind: a butchered hog, a cat smashed under the car's tire, a crippled dog slowly dying of a festering wound, a cow that was down and had to be shot, a bird with a wing shot to shreds.

"How's Lila doing?" Bill asks.

"She's fussing at me, as usual." Spence grins. "But she's getting some tests done today, and I'm afraid she'll have to be operated on again tomorrow—this time on her neck." He touches his neck and can almost feel it being slashed.

"The one where they go in and clean out your veins?"

Spence nods.

"Seems like everybody and his dog's having that one. Is your in-surance going to cover all that, Spence?"

Spence shakes his head worriedly. "I doubt it. I heard if it's cancer they won't pay it all."

"Well, at least you've got some benefits from driving that van for the school. Me, I don't got nothing. I was in a mess here while back when Mozelle had colon trouble." He toys with the oilcan, as if he has forgotten what he meant to do with it. "They come at me to the tune of three thousand dollars. And I already owed fifty thousand on this machinery."

"So how did you manage? How'd you buy that airplane?" A few years ago, Bill had splurged on his combine—soon after building his house.

Bill just gazes off over the barn roof at some blackbirds wheeling around in the sky. Nothing but blackbirds swarm over anymore, Spence has noticed. Most of the songbirds have disappeared since the industrial park was built. Bill says, "You want some coffee, Spence? Want to come on in the house? Mozelle's gone to get her hair fixed, but I think I know how to run that coffee machine."

"No, I ain't got time. And coffee jags me out." Spence doesn't want to start in on his coffee spiel, about imports versus domestic crops. He thinks the coffee habit is a conspiracy—to get people addicted to a luxury that comes from a foreign country.

"Since when do you drink coffee?" asks Spence as they walk toward the car.

Bill shrugs. "I got to be nearly this old before I found out it can keep you awake when you need to be awake. All that business about how you don't need as much sleep when you get old ain't true. It was just a story they told." He opens the screen to the porch and says, "Come on indoors. I want to show you something."

Bill's den wall is covered with what Spence calls "gimme caps"—caps with ads on them. Massey Ferguson, Budweiser, John Deere, Black & Decker, Strong Feed Co. The wall is full of colors, reminding Spence of a game at a carnival where you throw darts at a wall of balloons. Bill shows Spence a green cap that says, HICKMAN COUNTY STUD. Bill laughs. "A guy had this made up special for me, just for a joke."

Bill takes out a coffee can from a cabinet under the TV set. Spence remembers the rusty coffee-can lid that Lee stepped on when he was little. He was running in the grass and cut his foot open. Nancy panicked. She ran to the house packing him in her arms, her words streaming out incoherently, like the blood from Lee's foot. Nancy panics easily; that's why she thinks the world is going to be ruined by poisons and nuclear bombs and fat, anything she hears on the news.

"I don't want no coffee," Spence says.

"Hold your horses, Spence. This ain't coffee." Bill removes the plastic top from the can and pulls out a handful of pale, round seeds—like mustard seeds. "I'll sell you these babies for ten dollars a teaspoon," he says.

"Where'd you get those?" Spence knows what they are—marijuana seeds. He recognizes them from something he has seen on TV.

"A guy gave 'em to me and I planted some of them." Bill dribbles the seeds back into the can. "You know how many I set out last year?"

"How would I know? I don't come over and count your crops."

"Twenty. Guess what I made off of 'em."

"I don't know. A thousand dollars?" Spence always exaggerates guesses like this to undercut the other guy's joke.

Bill laughs. "I set out about twenty slips, back in the cornfield. I had twenty acres in corn last year, so I strewed 'em out." He flings his arm toward his south fields. "These things grow like weeds, but you need to water 'em good. They need a lot of water the first two weeks. After that, they just grow like burdock. They do better if you sucker 'em. At the end of the summer, when they started turning, I cut the stalks off and packed 'em to the barn in a gunnysack and cured 'em. Then I put 'em in a big bed sheet and rolled it with a rolling pin and pounded the stalks good. I didn't want to take a chance on losing a smidgen of that leaf. Then I took the stalks out and packaged up the leaves in those little plastic zipper bags. And I took 'em up to the truck stop in Newton and sold 'em to a fellow I know. Them suckers brought twenty thousand dollars."

"Gah!" says Spence, his mouth open.

"A thousand bucks *apiece,* Spence." He shook the coffee can. "Look at these babies," he says gleefully. "My millions."

"Pretty soon you'll be sowing an acre of this stuff and then you'll get caught."

"Hell, Spence, I ain't talking acres. This is the small farmer you're talking to. I ain't no goddamn corporation."

Spence turns to go, and Bill says, "I figure there ain't nothing wrong with it. I don't sell it to kids."

"Yeah, but you sold it to truckers, and then they get out on the road, high on dope."

"Nah! They take it home. It ain't like tobacco, Spence. You don't smoke it all the time. You wait till you're setting around watching television or something."

"Sounds like you know what you're talking about."

"I'm just being a good farmer, Spence. Knowing my product. Now

I'm ahead on my payments and I've got that airplane that can pull in the cash."

"Then I reckon you can give me a cut rate."

Bill grins. "For you, Spence, good buddy. I'll come early in the morning if it ain't windy. Better fasten up your calves tonight." He returns the coffee can to the cabinet under the TV. Jokingly, he says, "Why don't we go sow some of these seeds up along the railroad track?"

"I don't have time to get involved in organized crime," Spence says with a grin.

"You know what, Spence? You ought to go take a walk back to your back fencerow and see what's growing there."

"Why?"

"Those boys on the old Folsom place are liable to be growing something on your side of the line and you not know it. And then if the law was to find out—why, it's on your property, not theirs."

"I hadn't thought of that," Spence says, alarmed. "You reckon?"

"I wouldn't put it past 'em. They've got that new truck and I didn't see soybeans doing that good last year, and they've got that combine to pay for and they had a new pond bulldozed. They're really turning it on over there."

The Frost brothers—a bachelor and a widower—bought out the old Folsom farm, the property behind Spence's, but they don't know how to farm it. They came from down in Mississippi and aren't used to Kentucky soil. Lila was upset with them once for running over her petunias when they came to bring some firewood from a dead post-oak tree they had sawed down on the fence line. Spence was surprised they had let him have the wood.

As Spence opens his car door, Bill calls after him, "Let me take you up for a ride in the airplane, Spence."

"I don't even like to ride in your truck with you, Bill. You're too reckless."

"Got to live dangerously, Spence!"

"Well, you seem to be doing that. You'll get cancer breathing them bug-killer fumes."

"Oh, go up with me sometime just for a ride. We don't have to spray when we go. I'll show you what your place looks like from the air."

Spence starts up his Rabbit. He would like to fly. He wishes he could just get in that flimsy little plane and fly off somewhere.

17

Spence hates the familiar smells, the cold temperature, the sounds of the scurrying nurses. The sight of the old people being led for their walks down the corridor bothers him most. They clutch pillows to hold their insides in.

That morning Lila had the test she dreaded, and now she has to lie quietly all day, without turning or raising her legs. "It wasn't as bad as they said it would be," she says when Spence comes in. "It felt warm in my head, like it was going to blow up, but it didn't hurt that awful much."

"All that worry for nothing," he says, squeezing her hand. "That's the way you always do. You listen to them old women talk."

"The doctor says he wants to operate on the left side."

"Tomorrow?"

"Tomorrow about one o'clock." Her new roommate is staggering out the door with a nurse. "She had her gall bladder takened out," Lila explains to Spence.

"Where's the girls?"

"Cat had to go to work and Nancy's gone to see about the garden. Didn't you pass her on the road?"

"I didn't notice." Nancy has been driving Lila's car, even though the muffler is growing louder.

"All those machines they've got in the basement for the tests—it was the space age down there! I felt like I was on television, with all those gadgets they used." Lila shivers. "I'm taking cold. They tried to tell me they keep it cold to keep the germs down, but I always take cold when my neck gets chilled."

Her hand works away from his and grabs at the air. "Reach me some water," she says.

He pours water from her water jug into a paper cup and holds it close to her face. She can't raise her head and he has to bend the flexi-neck straw and aim it at her mouth. This is the extent of his ability to deal with the sick.

She says, "If I don't make it, I don't want to be stuck in that mausoleum. A truck could come along and bust that thing open."

"Don't worry about that," Spence says with a grin. "We'll put you back in the field where you can keep an eye on the corn crop."

She starts to laugh and is stopped by her cough. A pretty but snaggle-toothed nurse materializes beside the bed. "How are we doing?" she asks.

"We're doing fine," says Spence.

"Let me sleep," Lila says. "I've had enough torture for one day."

"Honey, I just have to check one thing," the nurse says.

"Won't y'all ever leave me alone?"

"You're being so good we just don't want to let you go home," says the nurse cheerfully. "We're just trying to keep you here 'cause we like you so much. Sir, would you step outside?"

Spence waits in the hall, lost in a memory of Lila feeding a calf formula from a bucket with a nipple. The cow, Honey Bunch, had calved down near the creek, below the pond. When Spence brought the calf to the barn, the cow tagged along, nudging his elbow, making soft noises. The next day, Lila noticed her returning to the creek, confused. Lila followed her and found a second calf there, nestled beneath a hickory tree on the creek bank, too weak to follow its mother to the house. Lila said the cow had strained her milk by running back to the creek, trying to nurse both calves. Patiently, Lila hand-fed the calves and talked to them, even getting up in the night to go to the barn to tend them. She would do the same with wild rabbits, kittens, anything. Spence feels helpless. What if he had to feed her? Change her bed?

The surgeon arrives, in his green garb. Spence is relieved that Cat and Nancy aren't there to pounce on him.

"We have the results of the angiogram," the doctor says, glancing at his clipboard. "She's sixty percent blocked on the left side and forty percent on the other one. My recommendation is to open up that artery on the left side and pull out that plaque, and then see how she does. I don't want to do them both at once because of her weakened condition. And there's a chance she'll do so well she won't need the other one done."

The thought of opening an artery makes Spence picture skinning a snake. He tries to think of what to ask. "She complained about that dizziness down in Florida," he says.

"The blood flow was impaired," the doctor says. He has a complexion like canned wienies and seems as delicate as a woman. He says, "We have to be careful removing the plaque, because if a fragment gets into the bloodstream it could flow to the brain and cause damage. And of course the angiogram doesn't show us everything. It doesn't show if there's blockage around her heart, for example."

Nancy and Cat would have thrown questions at him about her heart, but Spence doesn't want to ask about that. He says goodbye to the doctor, sees that Lila is trying to sleep, and leaves the hospital, glad to be out in the hot July sun. He spends the afternoon running errands—picking up bulk feed from the feed mill, paying the electric bill, gassing up his Rabbit. He has that coupon for the free tune-up, but the line at the gas station is too long, and he'd rather do it himself anyway.

When he gets home, Nancy is there, bringing a bucket of cucumbers and tomatoes from the garden. She's in shorts and a T-shirt, looking sixteen. He remembers her at that age, sitting on the corn planter behind him as he drove the tractor. She complained because she got so bored, sitting there all day in order to close up the seed bins at the end of each row while he turned the tractor. As they worked, she kept coming up with schemes for mechanical inventions to eliminate her job. "You're just not paying attention," he insisted to her. "There's everything here if you just notice." Weeds, the patterns of the rows, the language of the birds overhead, moisture levels inside the soil the harrow turned up. He felt free on his tractor. He could

ride a tractor from now to the end of the world, rejoicing in the pleasure of his independence.

Now Nancy sets the bucket under a shade tree and he tells her
what the doctor said.

"I know," she says, pulling her long bangs out of her eyes. "I
talked to him before I left."

"The test wasn't as bad as she expected."

"No. She was scared of it, but it wasn't bad."

Indoors, he changes clothes and puts on his boots. He can't get
used to keeping his clothes in the bedroom, instead of near the door,
where they were handy.

"Where are you going?" she asks when he goes out again.

"Back in the field."

"I'll come with you."

They walk down the lane to the pond, Oscar bounding ahead,
then occasionally racing back. Abraham follows them, his fluffy tail
held high. At the pond, the ducks swim away from Oscar. Spence
stoops to pet Abraham's head, but he slinks away from him and leaps
into the soybeans after a grasshopper. The grasshoppers are jumping
among the beans like giddy children on trampolines.

"Mom really loves that cat," says Nancy, who is playing with a
sprig of dried grass, trying to get Abraham interested.

Spence says, "Do you know what old Cousin Dulcie said to Lila?"

"No, what?"

"She told Lila about some woman who had that operation and
then went home and died."

"Dulcie has the sensitivity of a turnip."

Spence nods. "Do you think she's too weak to go through with another operation?"

"I don't know. She was always so strong it's hard to tell."

"Oscar!" Spence calls. The dog is onto a trail, his nose to the
ground. "Oscar, don't you go scaring up them rabbits."

Nancy says, "Mom doesn't want us to think she's not strong and
positive. It's her maternal instinct. She can't stop protecting us, even
when she has been violated in the worst way—" She breaks off, as if

she thinks Spence might not understand her words. He's embarrassed. She tosses the sprig of grass toward the pond and the ducks look up. "Is the water O.K. now?" she asks.

When the tobacco warehouse up on the highway caught fire last fall, the blackened, tar-stained water from the fire hoses ran down into the creek and emptied into the pond. The water was hot, and the heat killed the fish. The tobacco company official who investigated assured them the tar was harmless and offered them two thousand dollars compensation. It was twice as much money as they had invested bulldozing and stocking the pond, so they had to accept it, but Spence and Lila grieved, seeing the fish floating in the water, then massing on the bank. They had to bury them.

"It seems all right now," he says. "When it happened, the frogs was as thick as them grasshoppers on the beans out here. So all the frogs died, and all the fish. I even found a big mud turtle in with all them fish."

"Did you have the water tested?"

He shakes his head no. "It's O.K. There's a runoff, and the water keeps running in from the creek."

He can feel Nancy tense up, wanting to lecture him on how he should have sued. But Spence doesn't trust lawyers any more than he trusts the company officials. The two thousand was a good deal. Kicking at a shampoo bottle that has washed out of the creek, he says, "She's worried herself sick over first one thing and then another. The pond and losing them fish. And she worries about Cat being by herself at night and what it's doing to the kids. And then that business with Cat and Lee."

"I think Cat's sorry about that," Nancy says.

"Have you talked to her about it?"

"Not much."

"Have you seen Lee?"

"A couple of times, but we didn't talk about it. Cat was mad at Lee for taking Mom to Florida when she wasn't feeling well."

I can't live without Lila, Spence thinks suddenly. Somewhere from the depths of his memory sprouts an old scene of her milking a cow named Turnipseed. The flies were bad. Lila tied Turnipseed's tail to the stanchion to keep it from switching her in the face as she milked. He can even remember the polka-dotted dress she was wearing on that particular day. There she is, sitting on the milk stool, splotches of lime on her heavy brown shoes. When the cows were all milked and turned out, she scraped the manure off the floor and scattered lime all over the concrete. That scene happened thousands of times; it is strange that one stands out—Turnipseed's tail, the spots on her shoes like the dots on the dress.

"What's going to happen to this farm?" Nancy is asking.

Spence is struck by how old he is, so old even his children are aging. "I'll leave it for you kids to fight over," he says. "I can't keep up this place much longer—I'm about give out. I can't keep the gullies filled up. The whole farm's going to wash away if I don't keep at it."

"It'll become a subdivision like that monstrosity down the road," Nancy says. "It makes me sad that we can't carry it on."

"Well, we had two strikes against us," Spence says. "Starting out with two girls." He grins at her, imagining Nancy as a farm wife instead of an adventurer.

"Why didn't you teach Lee how to farm?" she asks. "It's a shame he has to work such long hours at that factory."

"He makes a better living at what he's doing than he ever would on a farm these days."

"It still would have been good for him to know," Nancy argues. Back when she was in college, she would have argued the opposite. He remembers a time when she tried to persuade them to move to town and open a grocery store.

"I always made good, and we never had to do without," Spence says. "But nowadays a young couple would have to borrow too much to start out. There wouldn't be a living in it anymore—not in a place this size."

They head down the lane into the creek below the pond. A gap in the bank is stopped up with layers of rusted car parts, old bedsprings, chair frames—all filled in with piles of leaves. An enamel coffeepot and some rubber tubing have washed out of the trash. Oscar paddles in the creek, slopping his big paws through the shallow puddles.

Nancy skips across on some flat rocks and Spence strides right through the mud and gravel. On the other side, Nancy stops and turns to face Spence.

"Daddy, do you remember one day when we rode the hay wagon across the creek? You were driving the tractor and Mom and I rode on top of the hay all the way back to the house."

Spence shook his head. "We did that every year."

"It felt like riding an elephant when the wagon bobbed down into the creek. Granny sent back our dinner at noon and we ate on the creek bank at the back field. She sent fried chicken and biscuits and ham and those white peas I like and slaw and sliced tomatoes and onions and a jug of iced tea."

"How do you remember all that?"

"I don't know. I just remember being happy that day."

A car horn sounds in the driveway, across the field. "That's Cat," Nancy says. "We've got to do corn again." But she doesn't leave immediately. She says, "That day Mom was so pretty. It was before she got worn down taking care of Granny. I thought then that she'd live forever." Nancy, suddenly fighting back tears, says, "When I was little, I don't think it ever once occurred to me that I might lose one of you."

Spence is too choked up to speak. Nancy crosses the flat rocks again, her shoe sinking into some soft gravel, and when she reaches the other side, she says, "Cat came back here that day with the hired hand and the dinner, and she rode back with us. I remember that now. We found a bird's nest in a cedar tree, and down in the creek we saw some footprints of a raccoon. Cat tore her dress on the fence and cried. That was the summer you bought me a cowboy hat."

Nancy leaves, following the path along the upper creek, which feeds the pond. He's not sure he remembers that day, but he can see Lila riding on top of the load of hay as clearly in his imagination as he could in memory. Lila and the girls in straw hats, Lila in some of his old pants and a long-sleeved shirt with a rip in the sleeve. As the picture grows clearer in his mind, Nancy's straw hat changes to a cowboy hat, Cat's dress to a robin's-egg blue—the same as her car in the driveway now. He smiles, remembering the cowboy hat. He had to hunt all over town to find one Nancy's size.

He follows the creek line down toward the back fields. In the center of one of the middle fields is a rise with a large, brooding old oak tree surrounded by a thicket of blackberry briers. From the rise, he looks out over his place. This is it. This is all there is in the world—it contains everything there is to know or possess, yet everywhere people are knocking their brains out trying to find something different, something better. His kids all scattered, looking for it. Everyone always wants a way out of something like this, but what he has here is the main thing there is—just the way things grow and die, the way the sun comes up and goes down every day. These are the facts of life. They are so simple they are almost impossible to grasp. It's like looking up at the stars at night, seeing them strung out like seed corn, sprinkled randomly across the sky. Stars seem simple, even monotonous, because there's no way to understand them. The ocean was like that too, blank and deep and easy.

Spence moves on. Above, a jet plane flies over, leaving a white scar. At the back of the farm the creek joins another creek, a twisted gully that cuts through several farms before joining Wolf Creek. Oscar has strayed momentarily, but comes rushing up to lap at the water in the creek. The water is very clear, the pebbles shining. It is rarely deeper than Spence's knees, and in summer it is just patchy puddles, but sometimes Spence has dreams about swimming in this clear, shallow water. He dreams of the knock and dash of waves high as buildings.

The back field holds the ten acres of corn. It's tall, and the ears are fattening up. Oscar threads his way through the rows of corn, and Spence follows the narrow edge next to the fencerow. He reaches the back line just as Oscar rouses a cottontail, which bounds erratically along the path, then disappears into the blackberry briers. Perplexed, Oscar roots around, then gives up, coming to Spence as if to win approval for his restraint.

"Oscar, you know I don't want you catching them rabbits."

In Spence's opinion, dogs and cats should have amusing, old-fashioned names—Buford, Brutus, Nebuchadnezzar, Abraham. He doesn't like names like Fluffy and Fifi or names from television, like Mr. T. He knows a man with two Boston bull terriers named Cagney and Lacey. Spence never watches that show because Lacey's New York accent grates on his nerves.

There they are. It is true. A scattering of marijuana plants, thriving on the fertilizer he used on his corn. The plants grow in amongst the cornstalks of the first three rows, like inseparable companions. He wouldn't have guessed what pretty plants they are. The lacy leaves are almost tropical, like the vegetation he vaguely recalls from the islands in the Pacific. These plants are strong, with the unmistakable nature of weeds—hardy, tenacious, stubborn.

He counts thirteen of the plants. He suspects Bill knows about them, because it is odd that Bill mentioned the possibility. Bill's land joins Spence's on one edge, across the creek. Spence figures that Bill, not the Frost boys, planted them himself and decided to let Spence in on the joke, before Spence either got in trouble or missed out on the harvest. Bill and Spence have always played tricks on each other. Once some puppies showed up at the house. They had been dropped on the road. But Spence recognized the puppies—a litter from Bill's hound. Spence packed up the puppies in a box and dropped them back at Bill's house. The next time he saw Bill, the subject of the puppies didn't come up.

Lila often teased Spence about the way his pranks sometimes backfired—such as the time he got his eyes tested, part of the physical exam he had to take in order to drive the school van. The doctor positioned him in the chair but then left the room and jabbered with another patient about some designer glasses frames for such a long time that Spence grew irritated. He walked over to the eye chart across the room and memorized the last line, the finest print. Later, during the eye examination, Spence reeled off the last line. "That's amazing," the eye doctor said. "Read that again." Spence repeated the line of meaningless letters. "That's truly amazing," the eye doctor said. "For a man your age! Now, let's see you read it backwards."

A sound in the creek startles him. It's just a bird squabble. A blue jay soars out of a scaly-bark hickory. Spence gazes back over the field, taking in where he has been.

He can visualize that battle he was in as clearly as if it's happening now. He was below deck, frantically passing the five-inch shells to the main guns above, and then he could hear the one-point-ones—the dive-bombers were closer, heading for the capital ships. He could hear the antiaircraft guns going faster, sharper, the boom-boom-boom overlaid with bah-bah-bah-bop, then the rat-tat-tat chatter of machine guns. Sailors who had been on duty above deck told him later that radar had picked up six Japanese dive-bombers heading toward the carrier. The fleet shot down three of them, but the other three were closing in on their target. Suddenly several American fighter planes appeared, to finish up the job the ships failed to do. Like sparrows teasing a hawk, the fighters began swirling up and down and over and around each of the bombers. They shot down two of them, but the remaining bomber penetrated the defenses and was closing in on the big ship. The fighters swirled in all directions and then one fighter got on the bomber's tail, in the right position to shoot it down. The Japanese plane was already swooping toward the carrier, and the American fighter flew straight at him, like a mad bumblebee. Instead of shooting him down, the fighter rammed him from above and behind, just as crazily and fearlessly as the kamikazes nose-dived into the American decks. The explosion sent both planes cartwheeling, on fire, into the sea. It was impossible to believe, the crew said. He flew right up the Jap's ass. His guns must have jammed. They were sure his guns jammed, and there were just a couple of seconds to go before the enemy plane would have released the bomb. The fighter, in position, made an on-the-spot decision to die, to save the carrier. It was a moment frozen forever. The sailors talked about it all the way to Guam. They knew their ship might have to do something like that. At any moment their captain could whip the ship into the path of a torpedo. They might have to take a torpedo, the same way that fighter rammed the bomber. That's what they were there for.

Spence was sure the pilot's name would be in all the books he read later, but he couldn't find it. He was just another anonymous hero.

18

Her head is clearing and she can turn over now and stir her limbs. She feels warmer. It is night, and a glow from the hall shines on the crucifix, highlighting it like a Christmas display.

The woman in the other bed has four visitors. Her family has paraded past the foot of Lila's bed all day: kids of all ages, uncles, aunts, parents, in-laws. The smallest child, the patient's little boy, seems to feel neglected and confused by his mother's illness. He slams the plastic bedpan on the bathroom floor deliberately, and when he's scolded he bursts into tears and says everybody's picking on him. His aunt takes his side. Lila would hate to have to cook for that bunch. They seem helpless without the woman at home to take care of them. They had gone to eat at the Cracker Barrel, reporting back to the sick woman every single thing they ate and how much it cost. Several times they got a laugh out of how the oldest boy spilled iced tea in his pie and ruined it. The little boy's grandmother said she had to cut up his ham for him and then he refused to eat it. She said she hated to waste ham, hogs were so high. The woman in bed is barely awake after her surgery, and the kinfolks are talking, talking, talking, laughing, telling stories. The noise competes with the television. Lila tries to watch *Family Feud*, but she has *Family Feud* right here, live.

She might die tomorrow.

Spence left soon after they brought her supper—broth and Jell-O and coffee, the same meal she had the night before her mastectomy. She didn't drink the coffee. When he left, abruptly, she felt so much was left unsaid. Lee and Joy and their children were there, as well as the crowd by the other bed, and Lila knew Spence's nerves couldn't bear the commotion for long. She imagined him going home, feeding the calves and the ducks, talking to Oscar, fixing some cereal, maybe eating a tomato, watching TV all evening—mumbling to himself the way he had started doing the last few years. She imagined that routine continuing. Tonight, tomorrow night, more nights, alone, for years.

When Spence's father died, Lila and Spence had talked about what each would do if the other went first. Spence was only forty then, but he said he had just realized he would die someday, had never believed it before. But Amp was so old. His passing seemed natural. Much later, after Rosie had gone too, and Spence and Lila were alone together for the first time in their marriage, they felt as though they would live forever. They could never imagine one of them without the other.

If Spence went first, her life would change as much as it changed when she was eighteen and married him. She would be afraid to stay on the farm alone, with all the crime spreading out from town into the country these days. But she wouldn't want to have to move in with Cat or Lee and be a burden to them, the way Rosie was to her. Rosie lived on for twenty years after Amp died, moving in with Spence and Lila toward the end. She was unhappy in their house. She would get up from a nap in the afternoon and eat breakfast, swearing the sun came up at three-thirty that morning. She thought the people on TV were in the room with them. "I want to go home," she'd say repeatedly, and sometimes she would go back, wandering up to the old house in her gown. But strangers lived in her house; they had rented the place. She gave up her sewing and spent her days playing with scraps of material and pieces of paper, sorting them in boxes like a half-witted child. When she died, Lila found boxes and boxes of nothing but smaller boxes, and plastic bags stuffed with more bags and twist ties. She found strings and a lifetime's collection of greeting cards. Rosie even saved name tags from Christmas in a hosiery box. To Granny from Catherine. To Granddaddy from Lee.

Lila can't sleep. Random scenes pass before her eyes. The strong, comfortable smells of cows in the barn waiting to be milked, the steamy air in winter. Gathering in tomatoes before a frost. Sprinkling lime on the potatoes spread out on the ground in a stall of the barn. Laying the onions on screen-door racks above. An electrical storm scattering black tree limbs across the yard. Rosie's foot clamping down on the step-pedal of her slop bucket. Life has turned out so differently from anything she could have imagined at Uncle Mose's. The world has changed so much: cars, airplanes, television. She can't complain. She tries to go along with anything new, but she is afraid that inside she hasn't changed at all. It still hurts her to see liquor kept in a house where there are children, to see farmers out spreading manure on their fields on Sundays, to see young people fall away from the church.

Her innocence has always embarrassed her. Her children went away and came back with such strange knowledge she can't fathom. Nancy makes her feel dumb, with that bossy way she's always had of bringing home new ideas—cholesterol, women's rights. What Nancy knows is from books, but Cat knows people. She knows instinctively what looks good on her customers and knows how to compliment them. Cat can make people feel beautiful. But Cat would rather spend money on expensive outfits than take the time to sew. Cat is never satisfied. Lila always says, "The more you get, the more you want." Lila never wanted much. But on Waikiki Beach, she felt thrilled and grateful for the chance to see what was out there. And she thought she would never get enough. She was seeing what Spence saw in the Navy, and maybe seeing what Nancy was looking for when she left home.

Growing into old age toward death is like shifting gears in a car; now she's going into high gear, plowing out onto one of those interstates, racing into the future, where all her complicated thoughts that she has never been able to express will be clear and understandable. Her mind cannot grasp these thoughts exactly, but there is something important about movement that she wants to tell. The way corn will shoot up after a rain. The way a baby chicken's feathers start showing. The way a pair of wrens will worry and worry with a pile of sticks, determined that the place they have chosen is the right one for a nest—the ledge over the door that gets disturbed every morning at milking time, or a pocket in a pair of overalls hanging on the wash line. A baby's tooth appearing like a shining jewel.

When her children were babies, Lila used to powder their bottoms and then kiss them right between the legs before she pinned on the diapers. They would squeal with pleasure. Nancy saw her do that to Cat and Lee when they were babies, and she was appalled. Lila said, "You don't see how I can do that, do you?" It was such overwhelming, simple love, there was nothing wrong with it. As they grew bigger and bigger, Lila couldn't tear herself away from them. She always wanted to pet them, though it embarrassed them. Even now she likes to kiss them on their lips. Lee turns red. Nancy is stiff, Cat more receptive. Cat is more like Lila, with the need to keep hugging her children, touching and holding.

After Spence came home from the Navy and began to build up the dairy again, they were happy, beginning to get a little ahead. One morning Spence had gone into town to deliver the milk and Lila was scrubbing overalls on the washboard out in the wash house. Rosie was adding coal to the fire under the wash kettle. Suddenly they heard Nancy crying indoors. When Lila rushed up the steps to the porch and to the kitchen to see if Nancy had fallen, she found Amp with the razor strop, whipping Nancy on the legs. Lila screamed at him to stop, but he kept on, aiming the strop precisely and fiercely. Nancy was howling, her legs already black with bruises. Like someone rushing into a jump-rope game, Lila ran through the flailing razor strop and snatched up Nancy, fleeing with her to their bedroom. "She climbed up on the table after I told her not to," Amp explained, following them. "She wouldn't *mind*. She has to learn to mind."

"Don't you never do that again!" Lila shouted. Her rage against his authority shocked her. She slammed the door and clung to Nancy on the bed, both of them crying until Nancy's sobs finally subsided into hiccups. Lila bathed the poor legs in Epsom salts, soaking the bruises. When Spence found out, he threatened his father, saying he would leave the farm, leave him without any hands to work it. But Spence was immobilized. There was nowhere to go, no way to get their own land. Lila doesn't believe Nancy remembers. She always loved her grandfather, and he never hurt her again. But she always clung to Lila for protection. Strangers frightened her, and she would look up at Lila, waiting for her mother to speak for her. Lila felt like an old mother hen holding out her wing. Even now, Nancy's strange, frightened expressions remind Lila of that incident, and she doesn't have the heart to bring it up again. She never understood why Amp did that to Nancy. Men, Lila believed, had a secret, awful power. She was always taught not to hang around the men when they got together, when one came to visit and they would talk out at the stable. Rosie cautioned her about that.

A nurse interrupts Lila's thoughts, bringing her a pill. Lila doesn't ask what it is. She swallows it with a sip of water. The new roommate is getting some kind of midnight treatment, and she gives out a burst of little pup yelps.

There are loose ends: things Lila can't get out of her mind. The yellow bushes by the house that would bloom so pretty in the spring, with their sweeping arms. Spence cut them back so he could paint the side of the house and they grew bigger the next year, even more beautiful. Eventually, they died back, and for many years Lila longed to see those bushes again, but they were in the past. As you grow older, you give up things, hand things over to the younger generation. You plant a smaller garden. Instead of accumulating, you start giving away, having a yard sale. But Lila never felt she was growing old, until just a few months ago, when she started getting so tired. When she had babies she never slept. She remembers the years at the factory, when she worked from eight until six and still managed to cook, wash, iron, clean, sew, garden, can, even help with the crops and cows. She never knew when to stop.

When she eloped with Spence, she brought something with her that has lasted to this day—a handful of dried field peas, a special variety that her cousins told her that her mother had raised. Lila kept the peas going in the garden year after year, always saving out some seed. They weren't brown and ordinary. They were white, plumper than most field peas, and she never saw that kind anywhere else. She always called them "our peas."

You grow older, you start reversing direction. Old people draw up in a knot like a baby in the womb. Rosie died curled like a grubworm. Tell Nancy about the peas.

Her mind fights the tranquilizer. She'll fight to the end. I'm stubborn as a Missouri mule, she thinks. I'll accept things up to a point, and then I won't budge.

The way her kids turned out. What will happen to her garden. What they will do with her things. She doesn't care about her things. Junk. She'd rather be outdoors. She never cared about housekeeping.

Playing in her uncle's creek when she was little . . . meeting Spence down in that creek . . . years later when his tractor got stuck in their own creek, hauling him out with the truck. The way he plows her garden lickety-split, clumsily uprooting the precious new slips. She and Spence have spent a lifetime growing things together.

On the wall, the crucifix goes out like a light and there's a strange calm in the corridor, like the hush in church before the preacher begins.

19

In the growing morning light, Spence can hear the airplane coming, a little chug like a hummingbird's surprising motorcycle rumble. He fastened up the calves last night. He hasn't seen Abraham this morning, but Oscar is on the porch with Spence. The tiny single-engine plane flying along the creek line appears so light Spence is sure a good tail wind could make it do a somerset. He watches as Bill flies up and down the largest field, trailing brownish clouds behind him. The wind is from the south, blowing away from the house, so Spence cannot smell the spray. His head is stuffed up from the air-conditioning in the hospital. The plane lifts above the first tree line, barely missing it, then dips down into the second field. At the back, just before reaching the corn, the plane turns and plows back into its own trails of fumes. If Lila dies from that operation and her funeral is Sunday, he could go up in that plane Monday, and if it crashed he would spare Nancy from having to make a separate trip home for his funeral. He had a bad night.

The telephone is ringing. Spence runs inside and grabs the phone, expecting bad news. He has never gotten over the early association between bad news and the telephone.

"Well, how's Lila doing?" a shrill-voiced woman asks. She must be someone Lila knows from her trips with the senior citizens. "They said she was having her neck operated on," the woman continues.

"Yeah. Today—about one o'clock," Spence says, longing for whole minutes of blissful forgetting.

"Lila was looking bad," she says.

You old bat, he thinks, wishing the doctors would saw on *her* neck.

He tells the woman, "Lila's sassing the doctors. Can't nothing hold her down. She's raring to get home and do up her pickles."

"Well, I just wanted to know how she was," the woman says, hanging up abruptly.

It is past seven o'clock. Spence takes a capsule the doctor prescribed for Lila when she had bronchitis back in the winter. The bottle says, "Take one capsule after supper for breathing." The steam from his shaving water helps clear his nose. In the refrigerator, tan beads of glistening moisture dot the sinking meringue of the coconut pie. Nancy and Cat didn't take much of the food. Spence lays four strips of bacon on the bacon rack in the microwave and punches the time buttons. He watches the bacon curl, like time-lapse photography of flowers blooming and dying that he has seen on TV. He stops the oven just before the bell rings. He hates the sound—ping!—like a pebble from a slingshot hitting a hubcap. In the distance, the airplane's engine is receding. Through the window, Spence sees Abraham on the porch licking orange dust from his fur.

After breakfast, he pauses in the doorway of the spare room to look at some of Lila's things—a row of old dolls on a quilt. She bought old dolls at yard sales and cleaned them up and sewed clothes for them. She found a porcelain doll head in the junkhouse behind the barn and made a body for it. Lila can take a scrap of anything and work it into something pretty. The day before, while the girls were freezing the corn, he thought he heard her call him, but it was Cat, and he realized that if Lila died he would hear the girls talking and he would catch an echo of her voice in theirs and think it was her.

At the hospital, she says, "I had a hard night. I didn't sleep a week." She meant wink. She's silly from the drugs. "I'm drunker'n a two-tailed tom," she says, trying to raise her head. After they wheel her away to surgery, Spence strides down the corridor toward the elevator, passing a young woman who says to an older woman, "He wants to get Stevie one of them three-wheelers, but Renée don't want him to have it." A man in a hospital gown trudges down the hall alone, wheeling his I.V. and carrying his piss bag in his hands, carefully, like a baby. The prisoner is out walking too, pressing a folded blanket against his stomach, as if he has had surgery again. He is pale and weak, his eyes buried under those brows that jut out like awnings. He looks half dead.

Downstairs, Spence buys a Coke from the machine and sits at a table by a window in a corner of the cafeteria. Coke always settles his stomach, and the Coke acid helps clean his dentures. The window opens onto a little gray enclosed area—a triangle of grass framed by the angles of the two wings of the building. An updraft suddenly catches some trash and begins spinning it up in the air. A plastic bag and a foil potato-chip bag are dancing and circling, battling each other. As they rise in the updraft, they seem like cartoon characters. They seem alive, a young courting couple chasing and pursuing each other, then falling exhausted to the grass before rising up with renewed energy for the chase again. The dance keeps going on for so long Spence sits there, mesmerized.

He loses track of time, and Nancy and Cat find him there.

"Come on, let's eat," says Cat. "When I'm nervous, I have to eat."

Nancy grabs his elbow. "Come on, Dad, they have a lot of food you like. They have corn bread and green beans."

Nancy and Cat travel through the line, knowing exactly what they are doing. Spence hates cafeterias. There are too many choices. As they approach the cashier, he regards with chagrin what he has taken from the salad bar: corn bread, salad with bacon bits, cottage cheese, pineapple, peppers, shredded cheese, cherry tomatoes, dill pickles, crackers.

They sit at a table near the back of the cafeteria, away from the crowd.

"Do you want some of these tommytoes?" he asks Nancy, shoving the cherry tomatoes at her.

"No. I like those fresh tomatoes from Mom's garden. We brought her some the other day, with an onion."

"She saved some of it in a drawer for supper, and you could smell that onion all over the hospital," says Cat with a laugh. "Hey, there's Mom's preacher, Dad."

Spence spots the preacher from Lila's church speaking with a man on the far side of the cafeteria.

"Tell me something, Dad," Nancy says. "I remember the Pentecostals around here never would wear jewelry and makeup. But the PTL Club is Pentecostal, and they decorate themselves like Christmas trees. Why is that?"

"TV commercials," he says.

"I guess so."

"That reminds me. I heard a great joke, Dad," says Cat. "If you scrape off all of Tammy Bakker's makeup, do you know what's underneath?"

"What?"

"Jimmy Hoffa."

Spence can hardly eat. Cat is eating out of nervousness, not missing a bite. Nancy is picking at salad.

"Where do you hear jokes like that, Cat?" asks Nancy. "I never hear jokes."

Cat shrugs. The preacher is headed their way. He stops at their table and lays his hand on Spence's shoulder, saying, "I've got some sick here to look after, but I want you to call me this evening and tell me how she's doing."

"All right," says Spence, cringing. He hates to use the telephone.

The preacher's hand is still on Spence's shoulder, and now the man starts working the muscle. It's supposed to be a friendly and caring gesture, Spence figures, but it makes him nervous. He has never known a man who caressed anybody's shoulder that way. Cat and Nancy are staring at the way the preacher is rubbing on Spence's shoulder.

"I'll be praying real hard for Mrs. Culpepper," the preacher says. He is a young fellow who reminds Spence of the Cards' utility infielder. Spence can't remember the player's name.

20

With his children, Spence sits in the second-floor waiting room, a small corner area with a Coke machine and a telephone and a TV.

The Cards are playing the Astros, and Lee seems absorbed in the game. Nancy is reading a book. Nancy would probably read a book during a nuclear attack. Cat would reach for food, and Lee would go to sleep. Lee always slept when something was bothering him. He would sleep so long it was like a deep illness.

"Dad, what size bra does Mom wear?" asks Cat, who is filling out a form.

"I don't know. Big ones." Five-pound flour sacks.

Nancy says, "When that phone rings, I'm going to jump out of my skin."

Cat folds the form and picks up a women's magazine. A red-white-and-blue Fourth of July cake is on the front. She says to Nancy, "Look at this article, 'How to Warn Your Children About Strangers Without Scaring Them.' I'm at the point where I'm going to have to trust Krystal to know what goes on. I think she's smart. I think she knows what goes on."

In a TV commercial for *Time* magazine, the Pope appears momentarily, holding a strange animal Spence can't identify. "I didn't know the Pope was allowed to have pets," he says.

"He probably needs *some*thing," says Lee, dragging on his cigarette.

A couple about Spence's age enter the waiting area and sit down on a vinyl couch. They stare at the TV. The woman's eyes, with sagging pouches under them, are red from crying. She holds her pocketbook like a lap cat and rubs the material of her skirt nervously. The man, in short sleeves, seems cold. Spence can see the goose pimples on the man's arms.

"Is Joe Magrane pitching today?" the man asks.

"Yeah. He's starting," says Lee, not taking his eyes from the screen.

The man says, "Saint Louis sure goes for those lefties."

"The Cards wouldn't know a right-handed pitcher if he knocked 'em in the head," says Lee.

Jack Clark is up, and he hits a double for the Cards. Spence tries to lose himself in the slow, careful movements of the game. Baseball is the same situations over and over, but no two turn out alike. Like crops and the weather. Life.

When the telephone rings, Cat grabs it. Nancy shuts her book on her thumb and lowers her reading glasses. Spence sees Cat's intake of breath, then her affirmative nod toward them.

"She's O.K.," Cat says, hanging up. "But he thought at first she might have had a slight stroke. When he woke her up, her speech was a little slurred for a minute."

"Her words are always slurred when she's sleepy," Spence says. "That ain't nothing."

"Well, he decided she was all right. He wanted to wake her up as soon as he could, just to see if she had any nerve damage."

"She's O.K. then," Nancy says, breaking into a smile. "God, I'm relieved!" She holds her book at arm's length. "Look how I'm shaking."

Spence realizes he is shaking too—all the way to his knees.

"Thank God," says Lee. He jams his cap down on his head and turns toward the elevator. "I have to get back to work," he says. "I'll see y'all tonight."

Lila will be in intensive care that night, and they will have to wait until nine o'clock to see her. They will be allowed to see her for fifteen minutes—no more than two persons at a time. Spence decides to go home for a few hours.

In the car, the radio plays "Hearts on Fire" and he sings along with it. Then Phil Collins comes on. Spence can't stand Phil Collins, with his high-pitched yapping, like a pup fastened up in a shed. He turns the radio down. When he drove to the hospital that morning, his head had been full of intolerable imaginings—a funeral in two days. Now his relief empties out his mind, and he drives all the way home as if in a dream.

At home, a loaf of homemade bread wrapped in tinfoil sits on the deck, with a note, "From Hattie Goebel." It is still warm. He stuffs the loaf in a kitchen cabinet, then goes out and cranks up the push mower. He mows the patch around the orchard that he missed a few days before. The mower needs oiling. It keeps sputtering. He's proud of the appearance of his place—well cared for and not trashy. The new siding on the house looks good. After mowing, he reads the newspaper and tries to take a nap, but he can't get to sleep. He gets up and puts on his boots and heads for the back field with a tow sack and a bucket and a shovel.

"Come on, Oscar," he says. "We've got work to do."

For half an hour, he works at transplanting the marijuana plants from the corn row over to the back edge of Bill's land across the creek. He doesn't want to get in trouble with the Frost boys. Maybe Bill thought he was being neighborly, telling Spence about the plants when he might need help with his hospital bills, but it makes Spence angry. He doesn't want a handout. He has never borrowed, and he has always made good on his farm. But the plants in his corn have been bothering him—not the risk, so much. He doubts if the law would find these few plants; they go after major offenders, and he could always claim the seeds strayed from Bill's crop. And it's not that he is being especially virtuous. There's just something about growing them that seems out of character for him. Instead of being an outlaw, he would actually be in fashion, and he never wanted to follow the crowd. It would be like borrowing to buy a combine, or spraying his fields, or getting a credit card, or mortgaging his house—getting in deeper and deeper, like everyone else. He felt helpless when Nancy lectured him about the plastic bottles, but at the moment he feels he can do something. He can imagine the whole farm planted in this stuff someday; it could take over, like jimsonweed and burdock. But not yet.

He waters the plants with buckets of water from the creek. He props a drooping plant against a cornstalk. Oscar, wet and muddy from splashing in the creek, flops down at Spence's feet, spraying water on him.

"Oscar, you sure love to work, don't you, boy?" Spence says, pulling a cocklebur from the dog's shaggy chin.

Spence walks back to the barn in a state of suspension—the worst over but an air of uncertainty remaining, like waiting out a drought.

After feeding the calves, he eats a bowl of cereal and a piece of baloney and drinks a glass of milk. The news is on. He washes his teeth and runs the dishwasher. He waters the hanging plants on the deck. He feeds Abraham a can of turkey and giblets. Spence dreads calling the preacher.

When he returns to the hospital, Lee is waiting for him in the lounge.

"They moved her to the fourth floor, to the intensive care ward in the heart unit," Lee says.

"What's wrong with her heart?" His own heart somersets.

"Nothing. They just didn't have enough beds in the main unit."

"Oh. You liked to scared me there for a minute."

They crowd into the elevator. There is a hush and a giggle when three more people squeeze in. "The limit's sixteen!" cries a nervous woman in lime-green pants. "Reckon it'll quit on us?" someone asks. Spence squirms. "We've got too many overweight folks in here!" another woman says cheerfully.

In the corridor, Spence asks Lee, "Could you do me a favor and call the preacher?"

"What for?"

"He wanted to know how she was."

"Why can't you call him?"

"He makes me nervous."

The walls of the fourth floor are painted shades of pink, light tones of blood, like blood you spit out when brushing your teeth. As they walk down the hall, Spence says, "Preachers have this act they go into—one for the sick, one for the grief-stricken, one for weddings. They just switch from one to another like they was dialing a TV channel. And then the bull they start in on is like those get-well cards."

"That's their job," says Lee.

Nancy was right. Spence should have taught Lee to farm. If he spent some time out in the fields, he might have a chance to think about things and he wouldn't make so many excuses. Lee's always taking up for the wrong people.

Nancy and Cat are already in the lounge. "She's doing fine," Nancy says. "A nurse just told us she's awake."

Cat's hair is swept up on one side and fastened with an old-fashioned turtle-shell comb. "Did you eat supper?" Cat asks Spence.

"Some cereal and a piece of baloney."

"We went to that new Italian restaurant by the mall," Cat says, making a face at Spence's supper. "It was real good."

"I don't like Italian food," said Spence, wrinkling his nose back at her. "Pizza. Ugh!"

"Heartburn City," says Lee to Spence with a grin.

"We didn't have pizza," says Cat. "We had calamari."

"What's that?"

"Squid," Cat says, eyeing Lee. "I'm surprised I had the nerve to eat it, but I decided to go for it."

The waiting room of the heart unit is large and pleasant, with comfortable chairs and a huge television—a thirty-six-inch, Spence guesses. There is probably more money in heart bypasses than other kinds of surgery, he realizes. People with money probably have more heart trouble because making money is so stressful. The people with stomach problems on the second floor seemed poorer than the people on the fourth floor. A nun slips past the door, almost a hallucination—a penguin. Spence has seen very few nuns, except on TV, but once he saw a nun driving a tractor along a main road, and he puzzled about that for years, inventing histories for her.

He sits there, the music from a rock-and-roll program on TV going through his veins. No one else is watching except him and Cat. If Lila had died during the operation, he thinks now, he would hear rock-and-roll at her funeral. It would be in his head. Lee laughs at him for listening to rock music, but Spence doesn't care. He doesn't really care what people think most of the time. Yet he knows he couldn't have that music at her funeral because of what people would think. If she gets through this illness he might take her dancing again—if his back doesn't act up.

Cat says, "I've got this record. This group is great."

Some long-haired group is swinging bright-colored guitars flamboyantly.

"Their hair looks like they've been rolling around in cow mess," says Spence. Nancy has plunged into her book again, oblivious. "Is your book good?" he asks.

She nods. "Uh-huh."

He should read more, but reading gives him bad headaches. Since he got cable, though, watching TV is an education. When the news shows people in a foreign country, you can tell what the weather is like by what they are wearing. His favorite show is *National Geo-graphic*. He gets to see places he'd never go to—the ocean floor, the North Pole, Siberia, Australia. He loves seeing unusual animals from all over the world. His grandchildren are smart because of all they are exposed to on TV. Sometimes he is flabbergasted by how much they know. They know about dinosaurs, the Japanese yen, satellite communications—the most unlikely subjects.

At nine o'clock a nurse says, "Two of you can go in for ten minutes and then the other two can go in."

"Come on, Lee," Cat says. "Let's you and me go first."

They follow the nurse, and Spence says to Nancy, "She'll be half asleep, on them tubes. She won't even know they're there."

A moment later he says, "You're right. I should have learnt Lee to farm."

When Nancy and Spence take Cat and Lee's places at nine-fifteen, Lila is awake but too weak to raise her head. She smiles faintly.

"Get out of that bed and rattle them pots and pans!" Spence bellows at her. "We've got to go milk."

"Oh, shoot! I ain't about to get up and go milk," she says. "I've milked enough cows in my time."

She groans and he keeps teasing her, while Nancy places a washrag on Lila's forehead and gives her some water to sip. Her hair is tousled, and she has on no makeup. Tubes are taped to her wrist, and down her neck is the fresh wound, a long slash clamped together with metal staples. The loose flesh under her chin is pulled tight.

Suddenly Cat rushes into the room. "You're missing Mick and Tina!" she says, turning on the small TV that extends from the wall on a long metal neck. She pulls the set toward Lila's bed. "Mick Jagger and Tina Turner!"

"Oh, you don't want to miss Mick and Tina!" Spence says to Lila, clasping her arm.

On the flickering screen, Mick Jagger and Tina Turner are dancing a sexy dance, each singing to the other in a taunting but strangely loving way.

"Look at 'em!" Spence cries, excited by their movements.

"I can't see." As she turns, Lila's tubes dangle before her face. Spence pushes the tubes aside and tilts the TV closer.

"Look at 'em go!" he says gleefully, watching Tina's heavy black body—her big boobs and long legs and wide hips. She's wearing a black leather skirt and fishnet tights. She stomps around in high heels, with her pelvis thrust out. She's like a pickup truck, Spence thinks. Jagger, in contrast, is a lanky beanpole. His big rubbery lips remind Spence of a cow's screw hole.

"Who are they?" says Lila groggily.

"Mick Jagger and Tina Turner," says Nancy.

Spence has a sudden memory—dancing with Cat to Ike and Tina Turner and the Ikettes on the radio. Cat must have been no more than nine.

"How can she be so sexy?" Cat says. "She's no taller than I am and look how wide her hips are."

Tina Turner turns Spence on, the way Lila does—Lila's large, warm, sexy body. Tina is wearing a crazy Halloween fright wig. Her boobs shaking on the screen make him want to cry.

"Hand me that water," Lila says. "I can suck a little ice."

Spence pushes bits of crushed ice between her lips and she crunches it. Then her I.V. unit starts beeping. The fluid isn't getting through the tubes. Nancy fiddles with the tubes, but the machine keeps beeping.

"Where's the nurse?" Spence says impatiently.

Cat goes to look for her. If Lila were a heart patient and the beep signaled danger, she could be dead by now. Intensive care doesn't mean what Spence thought it meant. The nurse ambles in, punches some buttons and jerks the tubes.

"Just two of you are supposed to be in here," she says.

"I'm leaving," Cat says, but her eyes are still stuck to the TV screen.

The amazing thing, Spence realizes now, is that Lila's color has returned. Her face is rosy and full, lighting up every blemish of her complexion, each freckle and age mark and wrinkle. Her face is restored, the way raisins plump up in water.

"Your color looks good," Spence says, holding her hand. She moans a little, a seductive moan, out of place here in the hospital. He is too happy to speak.

He takes the washrag from Nancy and lays it on Lila's forehead. She gazes at the TV. "Who are they?" she says.

And then an incredible thing happens. Mick Jagger grabs Tina Turner's skimpy black leather skirt and rips it off of her and throws it across the stage. There she is in her fishnet tights and black panties, still dancing as if nothing has fazed her. Spence's mouth drops open. "Did you see that?" he says.

"Uh-huh," Lila says. "A colored woman showing her butt." She tries to laugh and her hand goes to her throat, to the ridge of stapled flesh down her neck.

Lila's color looks so good, her face warm and full like a ripe peach. The blood is flowing to her face again. He keeps gazing at her, and she says, "I'll be glad when I get home and don't have everybody staring at me all the time."

Her words sound right. She's not paralyzed. The stuff didn't flow to her brain and damage it.

The nurse reappears, her arm bent so that her watch faces them. "It's been fifteen minutes," she says.

Spence squeezes Lila's hand, and he touches her face. "Your color looks good," he says. The nurse switches off the TV. Mick and Tina have finished their wild dance, and Spence turns to go. "See you tomorrow," he says happily to his wife.

21

The airplane rumbles and shakes, the propeller whisking the dirt from the airstrip along the edge of Bill's pasture. Spence holds his ears as Bill urges him to climb in. Bill has an oil-stained satchel with him—probably tools to fix the airplane in case it conks out in midair.

"Buckle up, Spence."

"A lot of good that'll do!" yells Spence, fumbling with the seat belt. He's sitting in front, just behind the nose, and Bill is in back, with the dashboard and controls. This is like horse-and-buggy days, with Spence as the horse.

The takeoff reminds Spence of the stock car races at the fairgrounds. Somewhere, Spence heard that certain racing cars were so fast they had to have a parachute in the back to help them brake, and Spence figured it also kept them from taking off into the air.

The airstrip is bumpy with stubble. The plane buck-jumps. "Shake, rattle and roll," Spence sings to himself, feeling a new meaning in that song.

"Here we go!" Bill cries as he points the nose up.

Spence is out of his head to go up with Bill. But it's a joyride. Lila is out of danger, and she will be home on Friday, two days from now. The inspiration came to Spence at 3 A.M. two nights ago. He was dreaming about flying. Enemy planes were spraying the whole ocean with a deadly poison to kill the ships. He was in a Navy fighter, having to decide in a split second whether to live or die. In the dream, he was brave, as fearless and determined as those pilots in the war. He woke up, shaking with the horror of it, but he thought if you knew you were going to die, you should soar. It's true, he realized. We know we're going to die—sooner or later. He felt he had to go up in Bill's plane then, to prove he could face the possibility of death as bravely as Lila had. Of course, when Lila hears about this little adventure, she'll kill him.

Up in the air, it's a little smoother. The trees shrink, the fences become lines, the highway a ribbon. A school bus creeps along the highway like an inchworm. Then the airplane dips down and flies lower.

"There's your place, Spence." Bill is shouting, but Spence can barely make out his words above the engine's noise.

They are just above the tree line at the back, where Bill's property joins Spence's farm. To the left is the Frost place. They are flying so low Spence can almost spot the marijuana plants he transplanted into Bill's corn. They cross the line and gain altitude. Spence's farm lies before them. The house squats at the far end. It's pale green with brown shingles. The colors blend into the ground and the grass. The corncrib is barely visible through the woods; the barn sags; the old, un-used henhouse seems out of place, parked in the center of the or-chard.

All his life, Spence has had a conception of the size and shape and contours of his farm, but whenever he studies the topographical map, it seems somewhat off, not exactly what he knows to be true. Now, above the place, seeing it whole, he realizes it resembles the map after all. The twists and turns of the creek surprise him, though he knows every feature by heart—the little plum tree on a triangular island, the stand of scaly-bark hickory near the crossing, the cluster of birches, the honeysuckle vines that stay green all winter—all the particulars. But up above, they lose definition and become small parts of some-thing much bigger. His children used to paint pictures by the num-bers, and now the farm looks to him like a large design for paint-by-the-numbers. The lone oak tree in the middle field was al-ways so majestic, but now it seems small, a weed. The soybeans are a rich green rug. He is reminded of those giant designs the ancient Indi-ans made in South America. He saw them on a special last year and couldn't get them out of his mind. Those Indians could never have seen their designs whole—big frogs and turtles and cats—yet the out-lines were laid out perfectly.

The plane rides rough, but Spence doesn't care. He loves it, the way he used to love riding a cranky mule. Below, the calves are frisk-ing through the pasture, running at the sound of the plane. From up above, they are like puppies playing. Spence smiles. He feels great. Calves playing have always been one of his favorite sights. A surprise for Lila forms in his mind. It's time to stock the pond again. He'll slip some large catfish, two- or three-pounders, in with the little finger-lengths. He wants to see the look on her face when she catches such a big one. She won't expect that. He loves to see her when she's hap-pily surprised. She always laughs so big.

Bill turns the plane and swoops back down over the farm. Spence gazes at his land, his seventy-three acres—cut through by the creek and a stand of trees—and suddenly he sees something new about the layout. The woods are like hair, the two creeks like the parting of a woman's legs, the house and barn her nipples. Spence laughs to himself. He has been sending out a cosmic message to alien explorers and didn't even know it. He wonders if Bill has noticed this configuration—probably not, or he would have pointed it out. Spence wonders if he's losing his mind. Maybe seeing the land that way only means that his mind is on Lila coming home.

At the edge of the upper bean field, Spence notices something else—a tinge of brown. The row of trees at the edge of the field is turning brown. Spence realizes the trees must have been burned by the pesticide. Bill must have flown too low over those trees, or failed to turn off the nozzles when he flew over them, or miscalculated the wind and the distance. The leaves are burnt, the trees endangered. Spence feels sickened, and for a moment he can taste those fumes. He notices the tall oak barked up by lightning in an electrical storm last year. It is dead.

Bill banks the plane and Spence's stomach flips. Then Bill straightens out of the turn and heads toward the largest bean field.

"Hey, Spence!" yells Bill.

Spence turns and sees Bill fumbling at the buckles on the satchel he brought. He's not even steering the plane.

"Hey, watch what you're doing!" Spence cries. They're flying over the creek.

But there are no other planes in the air, not even any birds. The plane is up high enough that they won't crash if they hit a bump of air. It feels like driving down an immense, vacant highway—fast and wild because there is nothing to hit. Then from the satchel Bill takes out something familiar—a coffee can. It's that can of seeds. With a grin, Bill snaps the top off the can and pinches some seeds between his finger and thumb. The seeds fly out the window into Spence's soybeans. The first thought that goes through Spence's mind is that he can't strangle Bill here on the spot because they have to get the plane down.

"You crazy idiot!" Spence yells. "You're the one that planted those things in my back field, not the Frost boys!"

"Can't hear you, Spence!" Bill flings out some more seeds into the field, and the plane zooms on, aiming at some target of its own.

"Stop it. I'll turn you in!"

Cackling with laughter, Bill shouts something Spence can't make out.

Spence yells back, "Well, they won't grow! I'll pull 'em up. You said they need a lot of water." The forecast that morning called for rain. They are due for a good soaking rain, at last. Bill is laughing so much he's paying no attention to flying. They are diving down, heading for the tree line near the barn.

"I'll get you back for this," Spence says. "Set this thing down."

Bill doesn't hear him over the noise of the airplane, but he cuts back on the throttle and the engine seems to stop. He makes a broad swoop just above the trees, then begins turning, heading back, aiming for his airstrip. Below, a herd of Guernseys at the Campbell farm scatters like pieces of a breaking dish.

22

"I'm real proud of you for quitting those cigarettes," says Cat as she combs Lila's curls.

"I'm not coughing anymore. I can't get over that." Lila plucks at her blouse, holding the material out on the right side.

"If you do that, people will notice it more," says Cat, slapping at Lila's hand. "Stop it! Don't do that."

"I can't help it. I feel so self-conscious."

"You look pretty, Mom," says Nancy, who is gathering up Lila's things.

Lila is in pants and a blouse for the first time in two weeks. She feels warmer with something on her legs. Cat is wearing a wrinkled white cotton dress with a dropped waistline and patch pockets. The dress has threads hanging from the hem and Lila wants to snatch at them.

"That dress needs ironing," she says.

"It's supposed to look wrinkled."

Lila laughs. "All those years I spent ironing. I could have just let y'all go out in wrinkled clothes."

"When you get healed up you can start wearing this." Cat holds up the sample prosthesis that woman left.

"The sandbag," Lila says with a grin. It's still in its plastic envelope, with the pamphlets and letters.

"Here, Nancy, let's don't forget this," says Cat, tossing the package to Nancy. Cat lifts Lila's overnight bag and says, "I'll go get the car and bring it around to the front. When the nurse gets here to check you out, I guess we'll be ready to go."

Nancy stuffs the package into a paper sack with the water jug, the lotion, the extra Kleenex, all the items that came with the room. She sets the bowl of houseplants from Mattie and Eunice and the basket of artificial violets from Glenda on top of the other things in the sack.

"Do you want to keep these get-well cards, Mom?" she asks.

"Yes. I didn't get to read all the verses."

"People send these cards because they can't think of what to say on their own."

"Well, it's the thought that counts."

But it occurs to Lila how true it is that people either won't or can't come out with their feelings. She appreciates all the cards and the visits from the preacher and the kinfolks and her friends. But there's something wrong, like a wall she's slamming against, like those ocean waves Spence sometimes dreams about. She recalls Rosie clamming up and hiding in herself, for years, where nobody could get to her. Lila married into a family that never knew what to say. Spence is all bottled up and Lee and Nancy are just like him. All those books Nancy reads, and she never has much to say about what she really feels.

Lila says, "You girls sure have been good to me."

"You've been through a lot, Mom," says Nancy, curving her arm around Lila, giving her a tender hug. Lila holds on to Nancy, clutching her close.

"I can't say what I want to say," Lila says. "Maybe I should mail those letters that woman left."

"You don't have to do that, Mom. We understand."

"I never would have thought you all would care this much about me as you've shown," Lila says. "I was always used to doing for y'all, and I never expected you to do for me this way."

"But you deserve it."

It's not words Lila wants. Holding her child is enough, and Nancy is clinging to her, the way Lila once held her baby and read her those meaningless words, those letters from the ocean.

"I guess Spence figured he could get out of coming to the hospital this time," Lila says after Nancy lets go.

"He's busy with a surprise for you," Nancy says, rubbing away a tear. "We offered to come and get you." She glances at her watch. "I'll go find the nurse. This is ridiculous."

It is strange how happy one can be at the worst times. When Spence was on leave from the Navy, before he was sent overseas, Lila felt happy just to be able to see him once more, knowing she might never see him again. Now she feels exhilarated. When the cleaning woman comes in with a cart of equipment and starts talking about her son whose wife suddenly left him, Lila listens eagerly, as if it were the most fascinating story she'd ever heard. The cleaning woman, who is fat, with hair that sprouts out in tufts, says, "His wife left the kitchen in such a mess he had to get me over there to help clean it up! She'd spilled the meat-grease can all over the stove and it was all down in the burners."

The woman begins swabbing the commode with a rag, using her bare hand. Spence would gag if he saw that.

The woman says, "He was in shock. He thought she cared about him, and then she just up and left."

"It can be the other way around too," Lila says happily. "You think your family takes you for granted and then you find out they care a whole lot more than you thought they did."

"I bet that criminal down the hall don't have no family that's standing behind him," the cleaning woman says.

"Wonder what's wrong with him."

"I heard 'em a-talking and they said he swallowed razor blades, and they went in and didn't get 'em all and had to go back in again."

"Law! And I thought I had troubles!"

"What did they do to you here?" the woman asks, as she swishes her rag in a bucket.

"Oh, I've been through the wringer!" Lila cries. "I've had my tit cut off and my neck gouged out and steeples put in, and I've been stuck with needles all over like a pincushion and put down in cold storage long enough to get pneumonia. And they stole my cigarettes—I ain't had one in two weeks. Did I leave anything out? Oh, and I need new glasses!" Lila pauses to laugh. "I'll be glad when I get out of this place!"

"We sure are going to miss your laugh," a nurse says.

She backs the wheelchair into the room, and Lila sits down. The nurse buckles Lila in, and she feels as if she is in that airplane taking off for Hawaii. As she goes wheeling down the hallway, for some reason she remembers playing ball with the neighbor boys on Sunday afternoons at Uncle Mose's. They liked to pick fights with her, teasing her so much she would beat them up. Her breasts had gone through a short growing season, like something shooting out fast after a long, wet spring. "Been eating sassafras buds, Lila?" they would say, and she would fly into them. She could beat those boys to pieces. She loved that.

23

"I can't go to bed," Lila protests to Spence that afternoon at home. "I don't care how weak I am. I'm sick of laying."

"You've got to build your strength up," Spence says. He didn't go to the hospital that morning because the man was coming to deliver the fish he had ordered. He stocked the pond with fifty fingerlength catfish and twenty-five crappie and an extra twenty-five two-pound catfish, barely finishing before Cat and Nancy got home with Lila. The girls have left but will be back soon. Lila was mad at him for not coming to the hospital to get her. "Was a ball game on?" she accused him. He feels clumsy and nervous with her at home, as if she must be expecting more than just ordinary life now, after her ordeal.

Lila has just discovered the state of the refrigerator and she is ready to clean his plow. "You didn't even touch any of those vegetables I cooked! And I reckon that ham's ruined."

"No, it's not! We eat on it and Lee took some ham and tater salad and half of a cake. And Nancy and Cat eat some when they were here. There was too much grub—we couldn't make away with all of it."

"Who made this coconut pie?"

"I don't remember."

"I love coconut pie better than anything, but that one looks like a tire gone flat."

She opens the back door and steps onto the deck.

"Where are you going?"

"Out here in the sun. I'm glad I'm back here where I can get warm. I've been cold as a well-digger's butt for two weeks."

"We could go to Florida," he says, following her. "Back to the Everglades."

"No, I ain't never going down there again! That's where I got sick."

"The sun was warm there. It dried out my sinuses and I didn't have any trouble breathing."

"It made me dizzy," she says.

Abraham jumps onto the deck from the milkhouse roof, landing at Lila's feet. He immediately rolls over onto his back, curling his paws and looking at her upside down.

"Well, there's my youngun!" cries Lila, sitting down in the slatted deck chair. "Come here, baby!"

The cat jumps into her lap, purring, and she hugs him. He wriggles away and turns circles in her lap, then jumps down again and rolls over.

"That means he's happy to see me," says Lila proudly. "Did you miss me, Abraham? Law, you've fallen off. You ain't nothing but skin and bones."

"He's been busy," Spence says. "Catching grasshoppers and mice. I see him out in the beans early in the dew, and he comes in looking like a drownded rat."

"He loves them mouses, don't you, Abraham," Lila baby-talks.

The night before, Oscar woke Spence up, barking ferociously at something. From the thrilling sounds of the barks, Spence knew Oscar was excited over an animal, not a human intruder. He wondered if it could be the wildcat. As he lay awake, he thought with pleasure about the fish he was going to put in the pond. He remembered that the first time he ever laid eyes on Lila was at her uncle's pond. She was fishing. Her bare legs were long, like a crane's. Now he's nervous about his surprise and longs to tell her about it, but he has to save it.

Suddenly Lila is down the steps and striding along the driveway. He has to hurry to catch up with her.

"Where do you think you're going? You're not able to be going out for a hike."

"I'm going to check on the garden," she says, picking up speed. "I just want to see it."

He walks along with her, her legs working fast—her dancing legs. Abraham trots along with them, his tail a bottle brush sticking straight up. Oscar joins them then, scooting out from his dust hole under the car. When Lila arrived from the hospital, they had to hold him to keep him from jumping on her.

"Them vines are firing up," she says.

Despite the recent rain, the garden is drying up in the midsummer heat. Some of the Kentucky Wonder vines have dried up, and the corn is starting to turn brown, but the field peas are thriving among the corn. Lila plunges into the garden, between the okra and the peppers, and leans over to check a pepper.

"That one's ready to pick," she says, snapping it off. She straightens up and twists off a sharp-pointed okra from a stalk. Suddenly Spence realizes she is yanking up weeds and fishing out dirty, stunted cucumbers from beneath dying vines. She snaps off another fuzzy okra, grabs tomatoes.

"Check that corn, Spence. I bet it's hard. It's overgrown, but the field peas look nice."

"What do you think you're doing!" cries Spence. "You ain't got no business out here working in the garden."

"The girls didn't do a thing about those beans like I told 'em to."

"You don't have no gloves on! The doctor said you couldn't handle dirt without gloves. You might get a sore infected and then your arm'll fall off without those lymph nodes."

Lila's hands are full of vegetables, and she cradles them in her left arm. Beads of sweat have popped out on her forehead. She's smiling. "Look at that punkin, would you!" she cries, pointing. "That's going to be the biggest one we ever had! Well, I'll say!" She lets out a big laugh. "That's going to be one for Cinderella!"

Spence stands there, while the sweat on her forehead changes from drops to a moist, smooth layer. Her face is rosy, all the furrows and marks thrusting upward with her smile the way the okra on the stalk reach upward to the sun. Her face is as pretty as freshly plowed ground, and the scar on her neck is like a gully washed out but filling in now. He thinks about the way the soybeans are going to grow those little islands of marijuana, like lacy palm trees waving above the beans, hummocks like those in the Everglades, mounds like breasts. And then he imagines the look on Lila's face when she catches one of those oversized catfish he has slipped into the pond.

"These cucumbers is ready for pickling," Lila says.

"You sure were gone an awful long time," Spence says, his lips puckering up. "I thought to my soul you never *was* going to come home." He takes some of the vegetables from her. "I've got a cucumber that needs pickling," he says.

The way she laughs is the moment he has been waiting for. She rares her head back and laughs steadily, her throat working and her eyes flashing. Her cough catches her finally and slows her down, but her face is dancing like pond water in the rain, all unsettled and stirring with aroused possibility.

1994

Proper Gypsies

In London, I kept wondering about everything. I wondered what it meant to be civilized. Over there, I was so self-conscious about being an American—a wayward overseas cousin, crude and immature. I wondered if tea built character, and if "Waterloo" used to be slang for "water closet" and then got shortened to "loo." Did Princess Di shop on sunny Goodge Street? And why did it take high-heeled sneakers so long to become a fashion—decades after "Good Golly Miss Molly"? I wondered why there was so much music in London. The bands listed in *Time Out* made it seem there was a new wave, an explosion of revolutionary energy blasting from the forbidding dance clubs of Soho. The names were clever and demanding: the New Fast Automatic Daffodils, the Okey Dokey Stompers, Tea for the Wicked, Bedbugs, Gear Junkies, Frank the Cat, Velcro Fly, Paddy Goes to Holyhead. But the dismal, disheveled teens who passed me on Oxford Street made me think there could be no real music, only squall-pop, coming out of the desperation of the bottom classes. Yet I wondered what rough beast now was slouching toward its birth. I had an open mind.

However, I wasn't prepared for what happened in London. I was cut loose—on holiday, as they said in Britain. I had little money and no job to go home to, so this was more of a fling than a vacation. I had abruptly left the guy I was involved with, and now he was on a

retreat (on retreat?) at a Trappist monastery. He had immersed himself in Thomas Merton books. Andy was very serious-minded and
had high cholesterol. Actually, I believe he found Merton glamorous,
but I always remembered the electric fan in India, or wherever, that
electrocuted him—an object lesson for transcendental meditators, I
thought. I was separated from Jack, my husband. New Age Andy had
been my midlife course correction, but now he was off to count beads
and hoe beans, or whatever the monks do there at Gethsemani. When
he was a child, my son saw the dark-robed monks out hoeing in a
field, and he called the place a monk farm. I didn't know what I'd do
about Andy. He was virtuous, but he made me restless. I knew I was
always trying to fit in and rebel simultaneously. My husband called
that the Marie Antoinette paradox.

I was all alone in London, so in a way I was on a retreat, too. I had
a borrowed flat in Bloomsbury for a month. My old college friend
Louise worked in London as a government translator, and she was
away, translating for a consulate in Italy. Back in the sixties, the summer after our junior year, Louise and I had gone to Europe together—
"Europe on $5 a Day." During that miserable trip, Louise's mother
died back in Jacksonville, and she was already buried by the time the
news reached us in Rome. We didn't know what to do but grimly
continue our travels. We ended up in England, and we took a train to
the Lake District, where we met some cute guys from Barrow-on-
Furness who had never seen an American before.

Louise's flat was on a brick-paved mews just off Bloomsbury Avenue. It stood at the street level, and all the flats had window boxes
of late-fall blooms. There was no backyard garden—just as well,
since I didn't want to mother plants. I wasn't sure what I wanted to
do. I was supposed to be thinking. Or maybe not thinking. I wondered if I should go back to Jack. I didn't want to rush back automatically, like a boomerang—or a New Fast Automatic Daffodil.

Two days after my arrival from JFK, I still had my days and nights
mixed up. On Sunday, I slept till well past two. After breakfast I went
walking, a long way. I walked up Tottenham Court Road, past all the
tacky electronics stores, to Regent's Park. I walked through the park

to the zoo. When I got there, the zoo was closing. I decided not to proceed farther into the dim interior of the park but walked back the way I had come, on the wide avenue. The last of the sun threw the bare trees into silhouette.

As I walked back toward the flat, I kept thinking about Louise. I hadn't seen her in five years, and we were never really close. She was always following some new career or set of people. She thrived on people and ideas, as if she hoped that any minute someone might come along with a totally new plan that would radically change her life. Her closet was a dull rainbow of business suits, with accessories like scarves and belts and necklaces looped on the hangers and a row of shoes below. Big earrings were stashed in the jacket pockets. There was nothing else in the flat that seemed personal, no knickknacks or collections. She was without hobbies. No stacks of magazines, only some recent issues of *Vogue* and a lone *Time Out*. There was nothing to be recycled or postponed. The cupboards had only a few packages of Bovril and tea, and the refrigerator had been thoroughly cleaned out for my arrival. A maid was due each Thursday. I knew no one back home who hired someone to clean. In my neighborhood, in a small city on the edge of the Appalachian Mountains, if you hired somebody to clean or cook or mow, people would figure you had a lot of money and hit you for a loan, or they would gossip.

Louise's place was like a lawyer's reception room. The art on the walls was functional—a few posters from the National Gallery and a nondescript seascape. But in the hallway between the living room and the bedroom was a row of eight-by-ten glossy color photographs of plucked dead turkeys. The photos were framed with thin red metal edges. In the first one the turkey was sitting upright and headless, its legs dangling, in a child's red rocking chair. In the second, the turkey was sitting in the child's compartment of a supermarket cart. I could make out the word "Loblaw's" on the cart, so I knew the photographs were American. In the third, the turkey was lying on a rug by a fireplace, like a pet. In the last, it was buckled into a car seat.

I longed to show Jack these pictures. He was a photographer, and I knew he would hate them. The pictures were hideous, but funny, too, because the turkeys seemed so humanized. I had a son in college, but Louise had no children and had never married. Was this her creepy vision of children?

It was almost dark when I reached the flat. A sprinkle of rain had showered the nodding mums in the window box. Clumsily, I unlocked the outer door with an oversized skeleton key and switched on the light in the vestibule. Beyond was a door with a different, more modern key. I opened the second door; then a chill ran all over me. Something was wrong. I could see my duffel bag on the floor. I was sure I had left it in a hall closet. The room was dark except for the vestibule light. Frightened, I darted back out, pulling both doors shut. I jammed the skeleton key into the lock and turned it. At the corner, I looked back, trying to remember if I had left the bedroom curtains parted slightly. Was someone peeking out?

I walked swiftly to the nearest phone box, a few blocks away, and called the number Louise had left me, a friend of hers in case I needed help. It was an 081 number—too far away to be much use, I thought. A machine answered. At the beep I paused, then hung up.

I might have been mistaken, I thought. I could be brave and investigate. I walked back—three long blocks of closed bookshops and sandwich bars. It would be embarrassing to call the police and then remember I had left the bag on the floor. I had experienced deceptions of memory before and had a theory about them. I tried hard to think. Louise had assured me, "England is not like the States, Nancy. It's safe here. We don't have all those guns."

I had some trouble getting the outer door unlocked. I was turning the key the wrong way. I had to try it several times. When I got inside, I fit the other key to the second door, but it pushed open before I could turn the key. It should have locked automatically when I closed it before, but now it was open. I could see my bag there, but I thought it might have traveled six inches forward. Now I realized that the outer door may have been unlocked, too. My courage failed me again. Turning, I fumbled once more with the awkward skeleton key. Then I rushed past the bookstores and the sandwich bars to the call box, where I learned the police was 999, not 911.

"I think my flat has been broken into," I said as calmly as I could.

A friendly female voice took down the information. "Please tell me the address."

I gave it to her. "I'm American. I'm visiting. It's a friend's flat."

"Right." The voice paused. The way the English said "Right" was as if they were saying, "Of course. I knew that." You can't surprise them.

"I thought London was supposed to be safe," I said. "I never expected this." In my nervousness, I was babbling. Instantly, I realized I had probably insulted the London police for not doing their job.

"Don't worry, madam. I'll send someone straight-away." She repeated the address and told me to stand on the corner of Bloomsbury Avenue.

I waited on the corner, my hands in the pockets of my rain parka. People were moving about casually. The scene seemed normal enough, and I was aware that I didn't believe anything truly calamitous could happen to me. This felt like an out-of-body experience, except that I needed to pee. Soon four policemen rode up in a ridiculous little car. I had heard they didn't go by the name "bobbies" anymore. (Not P.C.? I had no idea.) Two of them stayed with the car, and two approached me, asking me questions. They took my keys.

"Stay here, please, madam, while we check out the situation." The bobby appeared to be about twenty. He was cute, with a dimple. His red hair made me think of Jack when we first met.

They whipped out their billy sticks and braced themselves at the door. It was a charming scene, I thought, as they entered the flat. I didn't want to think about what the cops in America would do. In a few minutes, the older of the two bobbies appeared and motioned me inside.

"Right," he said. "This is a burglary."

Inside, the place was like a jumble sale. All the drawers had been jerked from their havens and spilled out. The kitchen cupboards were closed, but the bedroom was a tornado scene. My clothes were strewn about, and Louise's pre-accessorized suits lay heaped on the floor, the earrings and necklaces scattered. I was so stunned that I must have seemed strangely calm. The police might have thought I had staged the whole affair. Louise's place had been so spare that now with things flung around, it seemed almost homey.

"Was there a telly?" said the bobby with the red hair.

It dawned on me that the telly trolley was vacant.

"Why, yes," I said, pointing to the trolley. "And there was a radio in the kitchen."

"No more," he said. "Was there a CD player or such?"

I shook my head no. Louise never listened to music. How could she like languages and not music?

"The TV, the radio, and about a hundred dollars cash—American dollars," I told the policeman after I had searched awhile. The cash had been in a zippered compartment of my airline carry-on bag. I had no idea what hidden valuables of Louise's might have been taken. My traveler's checks were still in the Guatemalan ditty bag I had hidden in a sweater. The burglars must have been in a rush. I had probably interrupted them. The phone-fax was still on the desk. The turkey pictures were hanging askew.

The bobbies wrote up a report. They gave me advice. "Get a lock-smith right away and have the lock changed," Bobby the Elder urged.

Bobby the Younger beckoned me into the vestibule. "You see how they got in? The outside door should have been double-locked. See the brass plate of the letter box? They could poke an instrument through the slot and release the door handle inside. Then it was a simple matter to force the lock on the second door. It could be done with a credit card."

"It could have been Gypsies," Bobby the Elder said. "There's Gyp-sies about quite near here."

"Be sure to double-lock the outer door," the Younger reminded me when they left a bit later. He seemed worried about me. I tried to smile. I coveted his helmet.

Consulting the telephone book, I chose a locksmith named Smith because the name seemed fitting. His ad said, "Pick Smith for your locks." While I was waiting, I tried to clean up the place. I hid Louise's kitchen knives behind the pots and pans. I looked for clues. Under a book on the floor, I found a framed photograph of Louise's parents. They stared up at me as if I had caught them being naughty.

Smith came promptly, arriving with a tool kit and a huge sand-wich—a filled bap, like a hamburger bun stuffed with potted meat. He set it on the dining table.

"You'll be needing a few bolts," he announced, after examining the doors.

"Could I ask you to block up the letter slot somehow?" I asked. I explained how the door could be opened through the slot.

Smith flipped the brass plate a couple of times. He frowned. "How would you get the post?"

"I'm not expecting any letters." Andy might write, but that didn't matter. Jack didn't even know where I was.

"I could screw it down," Smith said begrudgingly. He was a heavyset man who looked as though he worked out at a gym. He wore clean, creased green twill. Between bites of his bap, he shot an electric screwdriver into the lock plate of the living-room door and removed some screws. The sound was insect-shrill.

"Likely this was committed by some Pakis," he said, pausing in his attack. "The Pakis are worse than the Indians."

"I wouldn't know," I murmured. I was trying to remember where Louise's parents belonged. I had tried them out in the bedroom, but they looked too disapproving.

"We have some very aggressive blacks," Smith went on. "Some of them look you right in the eye."

"I wouldn't jump to conclusions," I said. I plumped a sofa cushion.

"But you know how it is with the blacks in your country." A screw dropped to the floor.

I didn't know what to say. I wasn't used to hearing people talk like this, but as an American I didn't seem to have a right to object. "Have you ever been to America?" I asked.

"No. But I long to take the kids to Disney World." He scooped up the screw. "Maybe one day," he added wistfully.

After that, I toured London by fury. I walked everywhere, replaying what had happened, hardly seeing the sights. I walked right past Big Ben and didn't notice until I heard it strike behind me. "Eng-a-land swings, like a pendulum do, bobbies on bicycles two by two"—that song kept going through my head. I walked the streets, dread growing inside me. I saw signs on walls of unoccupied stores: FLY STICKERS WILL BE KNACKERED! It sounded so violent, like "liquidated" or "exterminated."

I found that I was talking to myself on the street. A teapot was a grenade. A briefcase could be a car bomb. There *were* guns. I remembered the time Jack and I went with our little boy to see the crown jewels. It was 1975, at the Tower of London. We were waiting in a long line—Louise would say queue—to see the royal baubles, and an alarm went off. A group of baby-faced young men in military uniforms materialized, their M-16s trained on the tourists. Any one of us might be an IRA terrorist.

The cacophony on the major streets was earsplitting. On the Pall Mall, the traffic was hurtling pell-mell. The boxy cabs maneuvered like bumper cars, their back wheels holding tight while the front wheels spun in an arc. A blue cab duded up with ads screeched to a halt right in front of me and let me trot the crosswalk. Still angry, I marched to Westminster Abbey, aiming for the Poets' Corner. I had a bone to pick with the poets. Where were these guys when you needed them? I had to elbow through a crowd of tourists earnestly working on brass-rubbings. A sign warned that pickpockets operated in the area. I never followed directions and now I refused to ask where the Poets' Corner was. I was sure I'd find them, lurking in their guarded grotto. I walked through a maze of corridors, stepping on the gravestone lids of the dead. A great idea, I thought, walking over the dead. I stomped on their stones, hoping to disturb them. Then I saw an arrow pointing toward the Poets' Corner. But a velvet rope and a man in a big red costume blocked my way.

"Why can't I see the poets?" I demanded.

"Because it's past four o'clock," he said.

I didn't know the poets shut up shop at teatime. Slugabeds and layabouts. Pick a poet's pocket—pocketful of rye? Would prisoners have more self-esteem if their bars had a velvet veneer? I wended my way past a woman in a battery-powered chair that resembled a motor scooter. I skirted the suggested-donation box and plowed around a crash of schoolchildren.

I left the poets to their tea.

At the Virgin Megastore on Oxford Street I searched for music. Everything was there, rows and racks of CDs and singles of folk and gospel and classical and ragga and reggae and rock and pop and world. The new Rolling Stones blared out over the P.A. No moss on Mick! Then a group I couldn't identify caught me up in an old-style rock-and-roll rhythm. I had to find out what it was. It was a clue to the new music, all the music I had been reading about but couldn't hear in the soundless turkey décor of Louise's flat.

"What group is playing?" I asked a nose-ringed clerk.

"Bob Geldof and the Boomtown Rats, from their greatest-hits CD," he said, smiling so that his nose ring wiggled. "Circa 'seventy-eight, that song."

Where had I been all these years? Why didn't I know this? Did this mean I was old? The song ended. The Virgin Megastore was so huge and so stimulating I felt my blood sugar dropping. There was too much to take in. Whole walls of Elvis.

At the British Museum, I stared at ancient manuscripts. I saw something called a chronological scourge. It was a handwritten man-uscript in the form of a "flagellation," an instrument used in ritual self-discipline for religious purposes. The chronicle was a history of the world, written on strips of paper streaming from the end of a stick. There was a large cluster of the shreds, exactly like a pompon. I wondered if Andy was flagellating himself at the monastery. A paper scourge wouldn't hurt. It would only tickle and annoy, like gnats. Birch-bark twigs would give pleasure. Rattan would smart and dig. Barbed wire would maim.

For two days, I kept telephoning Louise, getting no answer at the villa in Italy where she was supposed to be. Then I got an answering ma-chine, Louise in Italian. I guessed at the message, heard the beep, and blurted out the story. "Don't worry," I said. "There wasn't any dam-age. Just the telly and the radio and nothing broken. I had to change the locks." I asked her to let me know about the insurance. I didn't tell her about the gagged letter slot and how I found her mail littering the mews because I kept missing the postman. I knew she would say "telly" and not "TV." Louise had gotten so English she would probably have tea during an air raid.

I sat in a cheap Italian trattoria and drank a bottle of sparkle-water. The waitress brought some vegetable antipasto. Then she brought bread. I ate slowly, trying to get my bearings. I knew what Andy would do: Purify, simplify, and retreat. He'd listen to his Enya records, those hollow whispers. I felt a deep hole inside. The family at a table nearby was having a jovial evening, although I could not make out most of their conversation. A young man, perhaps in his thirties, had apparently met his parents for dinner. The father ordered Scrumpy Jack and the son ordered a bottle of red wine. The mother pulled out a package from a bag. It was gift-wrapped in sturdy, plain paper. The young man opened it—underwear!—and discreetly repackaged it. He seemed grateful.

Another young man arrived, carrying a briefcase. The two young men kissed on the lips. Then the new arrival kissed the mother and shook hands with the father. He sat down at the end of the table—diagonally across from the birthday boy—and removed a package from his briefcase. It traveled across the table. Some kind of book, I thought. No, it was a leather case filled with what looked like apothe-cary jars. The birthday boy seemed elated. He lit a cigarette just as a young woman swept in, wearing a long purple knit tank dress with a white undershirt and white high-heeled basketball shoes. Her hair was short, as if Sinead O'Connor hadn't shaved in a week or two. She handed the boy of the hour a present. I decided she was his sister. But maybe they weren't even a family, I thought. Maybe I was just jump-ing to conclusions, the way the locksmith did.

My main course arrived. Something with aubergines and cour-gettes. I couldn't remember what courgettes were and couldn't iden-tify them in the dish. I didn't know why the Italian menu used French words. I wondered if Louise had learned Italian because Italy was where she learned of her mother's death. Maybe she had wanted to translate her memories of those foreign sounds we heard that unforgettable day at the American Express office, near the Spanish Steps, when she got the news from America.

Finally, I spoke to Louise on the telephone. "Don't worry about this little episode, Nancy," she assured me. She had no hidden valuables that might be missing. We discussed the insurance details. I'd get my hundred dollars, she'd get her telly.

"The police said it might be Gypsies that live nearby," I offered.

"Oh, but those are proper Gypsies," she said. "They don't live in the council estates."

Council estates meant something like public housing. "Proper Gypsies?" I said, but she was already into a story about how a cultural attaché's estranged wife showed up in Rome. The Gypsies must live in regular flats like Louise's, I thought. In America, no one would ever use a phrase like "proper Gypsies." Yes, they would, I realized. It was like saying "a good nigger."

"Louise," I said firmly. "I'm very disturbed. Listen." I wanted to ask her about the Indians and Pakistanis, but I couldn't phrase it. Instead, I said, "Remember when we went to Europe on five dollars a day?"

"More like six," she said with a quick little ha-ha.

"You know how I didn't know what to say to you when your mother died? I was useless, not a comfort at all."

"Why are you upset about that now?"

"I just wanted to tell you I'm really sorry."

"Look, Nancy," Louise said, in mingled kindness and exasperation. "I know you're unnerved about being burgled. But you got the locks changed, so you'll be O.K. This is not like you. I believe you're just not adjusted to your separation from Jack."

"It's not that," I said quickly. "It's the world. And the meaning of justice. Major stuff."

"Oh, *please*."

"*Ciao*, Louise."

At a little shop, I bought detergent and a packet of "flapjacks," just to find out what the Brits meant by the term. I went to a laundrette.

How did Louise do her wash? The laundrette had a few plastic chairs baking in a sunny window. Two Indian women cleverly bandaged in filmy cotton were washing piles of similar cotton wrappings. They were laughing. One said, "She was doing this thing that thing." She had beautiful hands, which she used like a musical accompaniment to her speech. It dawned on me that Louise's maid did her wash, probably taking it home with her to her own neighborhood laundrette. I wondered if the proper Gypsies had maids. Technically, wouldn't a proper Gypsy be one that fit all the images? Gold tooth, earrings, the works? I sat on one of the hot plastic chairs. In my pocket I had a fax from Andy—a fax from a monastery! I didn't think I would answer his simple-Simon missive. I couldn't imagine a monk faxing. I waited in the laundrette, eating the "flapjacks." They were a kind of Scottish oat cake mortared with treacle. The Scottish called crumpets "pancakes." They had tea very late, giving the impression they couldn't afford dinner. But the English had afternoon tea just early enough to make it seem they didn't have to work during the day. The English said "starters" for appetizers, preferring a crude word to a French word. Their language was proper yet at times strangely without euphemism. They ate things they called toad-in-the-hole, bubble-and-squeak, spotted dick, dead baby. They ate jacket potatoes and drank hand-pulled beers. I couldn't decide whether this was terribly strange or very familiar.

I threw my jeans and T-shirts and socks into a spin dryer called The Extractor. It was a huge barrel encrusted with ancient grime and thick cables of electricity. It looked like a relic of a brutal technology. Dark satanic mills.

At Trafalgar Square, trying to get from Nelson's Column to Charing Cross, I got caught up in a demo of some kind. With my plastic bag of laundry, I squeezed among a bunch of punks with electric-blue and orange Mohawks. Spiritless teenagers in ragged, sloppy outfits propelled me through a flock of pigeons. I kept one hand on my belly-bag; the pickpockets from Westminster Abbey were probably here. Maybe poets, too. I couldn't tell what the protest was, something about an employment bill. I saw turbans and saris, and I heard hot, rapid Cockney and the lilt of Caribbean speech and the startled accents of tourists. I could hardly move. My plastic bag of laundry followed me like a hump. Although it was scary, there was something thrilling about being carried along by the crowd. I felt all of us swirling together to a hard, new rhythm. My hair was blowing. I could feel a tickle of English rain. A man next to me said "Four, four, four," and the woman with him beat time in the air with her fists. Her earrings jangled and glinted. The scene blurred and then grew intensely clear by gradations. It was like the Magic Eye, in which a senseless picture turns into a 3-D scene when you diverge your eyes in an unfocused stare. As you relax into a deeper vision, the Magic Eye takes you inside the picture and you can move around in it and then a hidden image floats forward. Inside the phantasmagoria of the crowd, everything became clear: the stripes and plaids and royal blue and pink, the dreadlocks and Union Jacks. I saw T-shirts with large, red tie-dyed hearts, silver jewelry, gauzy skirts, a large hat with a feather, a yellow T-shirt that said STAFF. I saw a coat with many colors of packaged condoms glued all over it. The surprise image that jumped into the foreground was myself, transcendent. All my life I had had the sense that any special, intense experience—a sunset, the gorgeousness of flowers, a bird soaring—was incomplete and insufficient, because I was always so aware it would end that I would look at my watch and wait. This was like that, in reverse. I knew the crush of the crowd had to cease. It was like an illusion of safety, this myth of one's own invincibility.

Finally, I reached a crosswalk where a policeman had halted traffic and was rushing people across the street. I landed in front of the National Gallery. I joined a smaller throng inside and found myself staring at some sixteenth-century Italian crowd scenes and round Madonnas. The thumping piano of "Lady Madonna" surged through my head.

I thought about the first time I visited England. It was in the summer of 1966, and I was alone in London for a few days because Louise had gone on ahead to deal with her mother's effects. It had been five weeks since her mother died. I was left alone, emptied of Louise and her grief. I was going home soon. The Beatles were going to America, too, to begin what turned out to be their last tour there. Their records were being burned in the States because John Lennon had commented offhandedly that the Beatles were more popular than Jesus. I figured he was right. The morning newspaper gave their flight number and departure time. It was a summons to their fans to wish them well on a dangerous, heroic journey. The Beatles' vibrant rebellion had taken a somber turn. I decided to go to the airport and try to get a glimpse of them because I was young and alone and I loved them fiercely, more than I'd ever loved Jesus. I took the tube to the Heathrow station, then had to catch a shuttle bus. While I was waiting, a motorcade turned a corner right in front of me. It was a couple of police vehicles, with one of those black cabs sandwiched between them. I realized it was the Beatles being escorted to their flight. I could see vague shapes in the back of the cab. I waved frantically. Through the dim glass I couldn't tell which was which. But I believed they saw me, and I knew they were thinking about America, cringing with dread at the grilling they faced. They were looking at me, I was sure, and I was looking at my own reflection in the dark glass.

The rest is history.

2002

The Heirs

1

*I*n February 2002, in the attic of her grandmother's house, Nancy found a packet of letters and a small stick of dynamite in a shoe box.

Nancy was born here at the Culpepper homeplace in 1943, and she had grown up on the farm, but she had not lived there for many years. Now all the older generations of her family were gone, and the family farm had come to her, to be split with her younger brother and sister. The land was now rented out to soybean farmers, and the house, unoccupied for a year, had deteriorated. Whenever she returned to the farm, she always felt intimate with it, filled with an overpowering love for the familiar contours of the fields and the thick fencerows and the meandering creeks. The farm had shaped the family for generations, as if each individual had been carved by the wash of the creek and the breeze of the heavy oaks. It was the place she had always called her real home, and it had endured. Yet it had changed over time, just as she had herself, and now the farm would pass from her life. She wanted to approach the impending sale to a development consortium with some detachment. She could not live here. Her parents were dead. And the greatest old oak trees had fallen, split by lightning. The barn had burned. The other house, the small wood-frame where she had grown up, had been razed. The smokehouse, the corncrib, and the henhouse disappeared years ago.

In a motel room on the bypass around the small town, Nancy filled the ice bucket with water and set the stick of dynamite in it. The stick, about eight inches long, was rust red, crumbling slightly on the rim. Perhaps it was only a Roman candle, she thought. She remembered fireworks at Christmas when she was a child—never on the Fourth of July, when the family always stayed home because of holiday death tolls.

Nancy placed the shoe box on the bed, with her laptop and book satchel. She felt comfortable in the anonymity of motels, where she could be alone, uninvolved with her surroundings. She unlaced her hiking boots and slid them off. Settling herself on the bed, with the pillows behind her, she began to examine the contents of the box. She forced herself to contain her eagerness; she wanted to savor the details. She was hoping for family secrets, for clues that would illuminate her own life. Along with the letters was a newspaper clipping, an ad for Detroit Special overalls: "They wear like a pig's nose." In the bottom of the box were a pink self-covered button, several large hairpins, and a small booklet about a corn drill. She flipped through the booklet, recalling how as a teenager she rode on such a drill behind her father's tractor, helping him plant corn one spring. She could almost feel the metal seat—hard, punctured with holes arranged in a daisy design. Holes to aerate one's bottom. She remembered sitting there for hours, operating the seed hoppers. A day of labor seemed like a year, and her sunburn got infected.

The letters were tied with a selvedge, which was frayed and yellowing. Tucked beneath the string was a note handwritten on lined tablet paper: "Take care of these as we are saving every scratch of the pen."

Nancy cut the selvedge and the letters fanned out. They were addressed to Mrs. Nova Renfroe and Miss Artemisia Smith, Nancy's great-aunts. She had heard her grandmother speak of her two sisters many times—in a tone of both melancholy and mystery. Nancy's father, who was fond of his aunts, had once told her that Aunt Mezhie had epilepsy, but Nancy's grandmother would never confirm that.

Nancy hadn't realized until now that Mezhie's name was actually Artemisia. She had hoped to find personal letters in the box, but most of them were from the Syndicate of Edwards Heirs, with various return addresses. The first envelope yielded two receipts for donations of a dollar each, with a note of acknowledgment. As she read through more of the letters—mostly pleas for donations—she grew both reflective and excited. She recalled that her grandmother used to say, "We were supposed to heir a fortune, but we got cheated out of it."

She found another loose item in the box, a family history published in a booklet on thin paper. She began reading.

> *My name is Alonzo Green. I will chronicle what is known of the family history to the best of my ability. It all commenced in 1642 when an Englishman called Thomas Hael, or Hall, purchased a large tract of wilderness in Nieuw Netherland. This is the land in question, which came down to our great-great-great grandfather Robert Edwards. We have the deed from the Dutch Colonial Government: "a certaine parcell of land in ye Island of Manhattan, stretching on the North River, betwixt Old John's Land on the south and Jan Rotterdam's Road north and about 1 thousand rodds wide from the river." Thomas Hael explored his boundaries with a heavy heart, wondering at the wisdom of the acquisition. A year earlier, he had married loquacious, dumpling-shaped Anna Mitford of Bristol, England, and the pair sailed to the New World to seek connubial joy and religious adventure. Poor Anna! She contracted a virulent sea sickness and did not survive the journey. Not much is known about the status or pecuniary expectations that Hael may have brought with him to Nieuw Netherland or about how he provided for himself after his arrival. But by wintertime, the grieving widower paid a thousand Carolus Guilders for this unpromising stretch of dark forest and sand dunes below Old John's Land and married a robust young Knickerbocker. Her name is not remembered. She gave him five daughters, who showed little appreciation for the lonely, fearsome landscape*

surrounding them. The nubile maidens hovered indoors in the fledgling village of Nieuw Amsterdam until one of our more jejune kinsmen, Thomas Edwards, an asthmatic seafarer, arrived, with a shine in his eye. He was captain of a broad-bottomed, wide-beamed three-master called the Society. *After a brief but vigorous courtship filled with Morris dancing and demonstrations of nautical knots, he was forthwith betrothed to the oldest Hael daughter. Thomas Hael, or Hall, lacking a son, bequeathed to his oceangoing son-in-law his "wearing clothes" and a paper entitling Edwards and his heirs to Hael's patch of ground—surveyed as seventy-seven acres, three rods and thirty-two perches. This is rightfully ours.*

Thomas Edwards, out on the high seas raiding Spanish galleons for Queen Anne, was too busy to settle down, and he left this land to his grandson Robert Edwards. But Robert, who was also a seafarer, had no use for the New York property, which was burdened by rising taxes and gargantuan boulders, so he leased it for ninety-nine years to the notorious Cruger brothers for a thousand pounds and one peppercorn per year. In the agreement, his descendants were to take possession of the estate when the lease expired, in 1877. But Robert Edwards, without issue, was killed in a freak shipwreck off the coast of New Zealand, and the ninety-nine-year lease tied up the property until it was almost forgotten. Robert's heirs were some brothers—William, Joshua, Jacob, John, Leonard, and Thomas—and a sister, Martha (called "Mackie"), but by the time the lease expired they were all dead and their offspring flung along the Great Wagon Road and out to the Territories. It is true that the ninety-nine-year lease itself was so severely damaged in the 1860 basement leak at the Bouwerie Hall of Records that not a legible cipher remains, but an affidavit from one Mr. Murphy, a lugubrious liveryman, attests to his memory of the wording of the lease. Although the actual facts may be hard to pluck from the folds and twists of time, descendants

*far and wide have over the years painstakingly assembled
the evidence of our inheritance. Anyone descended from the
brothers of Robert or the obscure sister, "Mackie," is in line
to be an heir. Some years ago in New York, Edwards descendants were especially aroused by the famous troubadour
Valentine Edwards, who mumbled an obscure-sounding
shipwreck ballad, ending with the refrain "Ninety-nine years
and the land is ours, / Ninety-nine years is all . . ." The song,
"The Wreck of the Mangel-Wurtzel," became a national sensation after Valentine Edwards performed it before
Theodore Roosevelt at the Music Box on Twenty-third
Street in 1908. The Edwards family lore—the stories handed
down about the privateer and the Dutch deed and the
lease—was stirred afresh by kinsman Valentine Edwards'
shipwreck ballad into a surfacing, as if memory itself were a
form of wreckage strewn along the floor of a distant sea.*

*The Edwards claim is a tribute to memory, to continuity,
to the supremacy of kinship!*

*And so, from the end of the last century, and through the
Roosevelt years, and on up to the present Harding years, the
Edwards claim has gained ground and amassed authority.
Edwards families have held conventions, reunions, and
church picnics celebrating the illustrious history of our clan.
There were some doubting Thomases until 1919, when a
document discovered in an old hair trunk in a colonial-era
attic in Orange County, North Carolina, verified the bucca-
neer's ninety-nine-year lease to the Cruger brothers, who
had sublet to the Trinity Church. Therein lies our proof.*

*As an earnest petitioner and family historian, on behalf
of the Edwards family of America I submit claim of owner-
ship of the land described. The estimate of wealth has en-
larged beyond our capacity to account. Old John's Land
bordered Greenwich Village. Jan Rotterdam's Road is now
arrayed with mighty structures climbing skyward. The vast
Edwards holdings, a lopsided rectangle on the bottom of the
island, includes the Woolworth Building, the Federal Build-*

ing, the New York Stock Exchange, and the whole of Broad-
way. Respectfully submitted,
        —*Alonzo S. Green, Kokomo, Indiana, Sept. 10, 1921*

Nancy leafed through a printed document from the Board of the Syndicate of Edwards Heirs, describing the Supreme Court's rejection of the Edwards petition. The property delineated in the document seemed to be most of lower Manhattan, from Christopher Street, Greenwich Village, on down to the tip of the island. Nancy was eager to tell Jack about this. How amazed he would be to learn of the expectations of her modest family! When they first met, Jack had pictured her rural Southern upbringing as a scene from the distant past—like the Depression world of her great-aunts. She laughed aloud. She could have told him her family owned the World Trade Center.

Nancy knew with certainty that in 1932 she would have sent her money in, too. If she had been a farm wife in the Depression—or perhaps her spinster sister, in a diaphanous dress on a summer Sunday, awaiting a gentleman caller (a crude youth with no prospects except setting out some tobacco in a corner of his father's land)—she would have built up the dream of the inheritance to such a frenzy she would have had to be locked in her room. She knew she would have answered ads in the back of magazines, entered contests, conspired with cousins on ways to escape a country woman's lot. Her yearnings frothing over, Nancy would have waited impatiently for the mail to bring some deliverance. With the promise of the Edwards fortune, she would have hitchhiked to New York to claim the city. But she recognized her tendency to exaggerate, to blow up some detail the way Jack used to enlarge a segment of a photograph in his darkroom before he went digital.

An envelope spilled out two receipts for membership in the syndicate—twenty-five dollars each. Nancy was astounded. She knew that farm people didn't have cash during the Depression. She wasn't sure, but twenty-five dollars might have been like two hundred and fifty dollars now. How could they have made such sacrifices? She pictured her great-aunts, worn into submission by the steady routine of farm work, their thin cotton dresses clinging to their heavy, biscuit-fed bodies. She thought of the tyranny of men—their expectations of meat and pie on the table and clean, starched shirts.

She could imagine the remade dresses, the wool coats of a generation's wear cut into strips and woven into rugs, the fresh beans simmered with hog jaws for an entire day. She remembered such images from her grandmother. How tantalizing the letters about the inheritance would have been! The aunts' imagination would have stirred the kings, queens, and jacks on the playing cards to life. The aunts would have dreamed of the bustle of the city, with the opera and fine millinery shops. But Nancy thought perhaps they did not even know what to dream of. Did they have sexual fantasies? She tried to imagine their sex lives—dutiful, simple gropings in the dark.

There was one more letter—an envelope from the U.S. Postal Service addressed to Bealus Renfroe. Nancy thought he was Nova's husband, but she wasn't certain. And to her surprise, Nancy discovered three photographs in an envelope in the bottom of the box. She held one up to the light—a large group of men and women and children fashionably dressed, the women in dresses with hems rising toward the knees. The twenties? She had sought details of her family history for years, but they were not a family of storytellers, and the Culpeppers had few old photographs. She held the second picture close to the dim lamp. A man in overalls was standing on a stump. What was pleasing about this picture was how good-looking the man was. He stood erect, his thumbs in his pockets, and faced the camera with confidence. He had a farmer's hands, but his face was smooth, with strong features and dark, straight hair spilling from under a striped cap. He stood like a prized specimen on display, an excellent, prized ram at the fair.

The third picture was two attractive women in sailor middy blouses and hats with upturned brims. Their faces were plump ovals. They stood arm in arm in front of a rough-hewn picket fence, and the shadow of the photographer fell on the grass beside them. It was winter—the grass stunted, the trees leafless. There was a barn in the background, with a tree shaped like a Y nearby. The women stared into the face of the camera with the intensity of predators. The woman on the left had her mouth open in a smile—even, pretty teeth. The other one smiled without opening her mouth. Nancy located the two women and the handsome man in the group photo; he was flanked by the middy-bloused women, and his arms embraced their shoulders.

Jack could enlarge these pictures for her, and she would study them for clues, like the guy in *Blow-Up,* a movie that had seemed so sophisticated and profound when she was young. She was aware that in her work as a historian, her habit was to re-create the past by dwelling on a pink button loose in a box, an old washed-out photograph of an unidentified man posing on a stump. Her mind leaped around, as if it were a magic wand and she could make these images come to life.

2

In the spring of 1929, two women, sisters, were toiling in a tobacco patch in western Kentucky. They were suckering dark-leaf tobacco—pinching off the sticky buds, smearing the gum on their aprons. Bealus Renfroe had sent them out to work after breakfast in the still, blazing air. Nova, his gangly, high-spirited wife, kept a careful eye on her sister Artemisia, who had a habit of banging her head on a fence post when she began to grow agitated. Nova had learned to say soothing things to calm her sister, even though Nova herself was full of fire much of the time. But her sister's horizons were restricted. Artemisia didn't go to the store or visit anyone except family.

At midmorning, the mailman, Early Otto Kilgore, arrived, his Model T stirring a cloud of dust for half a mile. Early was his true name, not a nickname, and he was often true to his name—early with the mail, which was most often only some tradesman's plea. His horn blared, and the sisters heard him holler, like a farmer summoning field hands. They ran down the tobacco rows and jumped over a stile, their hems dragging, to see what surprise Early Otto had brought. He handed Nova a thick envelope from a cousin, Joe, who had moved to Calloway County. She ripped it open, while Early Otto remained, his engine bleating, to learn what news he had brought. Joe's letter was brief, but his voice leapt off the tablet page like that of a revival preacher ranting of glory. Nova read the letter aloud. " 'Look at this, girls. Read the enclosed pamphlet careful. Pay attention to what Mr. Alonzo Green says, for he has researched it. He says our fortune is coming. If we can prove we are Edwards. That's easy, for you know that our great-grandmother was a Edwards. That makes us legible to get in line to heir a fortune. I figure a million dollars!' " Along with the printed pamphlet, Joe had sent two application blanks for membership in the Syndicate of Edwards Heirs.

"Don't neither one of y'all tell this to Bealus," Nova said, after glancing through the pamphlet, fancy-printed in tiny type. "We'll study on this and surprise him. He would never let us join up. It says here it costs a dollar for more information."

Early Otto seemed to know something. He nodded, with a silly smile, and said, "You can count on me, gals. I won't breathe ne'er a word."

"Mezhie, don't *you* tell Bealus!" Nova said.

"I won't tell *no*body," said Artemisia, who thought of herself as Artemisia, even though she would deign to answer to Mezhie.

As they made their way back to the tobacco patch, Artemisia said, "We ought to been rich ladies." She smoothed her gummy apron. The tobacco made a stain like a thousand squashed roach bugs.

"Life used to be better in the old days, I've heard tell," Nova said. "They always told how Mammy married beneath her, even though everybody liked Pappy."

"She used to have fine things—a peacock and a silver brush."

Their mother, long dead, had china dishes and a Hoosier pantry and a shelf filled with books—stolen by a bachelor cousin who had an abnormal interest in Latin and physiognomy.

They studied the document later, the next chance they had of being alone in the crowded household. That night, Nova crept up to Artemisia's room, a sweltering nook in the attic. Nova was always afraid her sister would have one of her spells and fall down the stairs, but Artemisia stubbornly retreated to her little garret, where she hoarded her few possessions (especially prizing her tooth cup and hair combs). Artemisia had read the fine print in the pamphlet.

"Look, Nova, they've quoted Ezekiel," she said. She read aloud, " 'Thus saith the Lord God: Remove the diadem, and take off the crown: This shall not be the same, exalt him that is low and abase him that is high.

" 'I will overturn, overturn, overturn it, and it shall be no more, until he come whose right it is, and I will give it him. Ezekiel 21: 26–27.' "

"It's only right," said Nova. Then she whispered hoarsely, "Just think, how we'll surprise everybody."

" 'Dear Miss Artemisia and Mrs. Nova,' " Artemisia said, as if she were reciting a monologue or acting in a play. " 'It is our pleasure to inform you that you have heired a million dollars; enclosed is our check.' Do you reckon it'll be more than that?"

A period of watching and waiting began. Within a month, the sisters completed two application blanks and mailed them in with a dollar apiece, saving postage by placing everything in one envelope. They had to filch the dollars from the egg money, but they compensated by denying themselves a second egg at breakfast. No one noticed their sacrifice. The household was large—with Nova's three children, a couple of Renfroes and their wives and several other children, as well as a hired hand who slept on a pallet on the back porch. The human swarm made some secrets easier, but Artemisia's attentiveness to the arrival of the mail was inescapable. Bealus teasingly accused her of waiting for love letters. "She's slipping around, hoping for some bowlegged, lovesick goof to carry her off," he declared with a wink. He kept up his teasing, and the sisters let his suspicion stand as a convenient cover. Early Otto was in on their secret, revealing that he was an Edwards heir himself. His great-grandmother was a cousin to their great-grandmother.

A letter arrived. A Mrs. March wrote to Nova and Artemisia personally, on stationery from a hotel in Nashville, explaining that the organization subsisted on donations, a dollar or two a month. And for their claims to be represented in the courts, they each had to send a twenty-five-dollar membership fee. "I can also work up your family tree, which you will need in order to be represented," Mrs. March wrote. "But we don't need to worry about that yet." She wrote informally, in a zestful, cheery tone, on a typewriter. The sisters' disappointment was palpable, and for days they drifted on a cloud of gloom. They yearned to join, but fifty dollars was out of reach. The tobacco crop might not bring that much, and the cash would go for the necessary store goods. But a seed had been planted in their minds. For weeks afterwards, while ironing or canning peaches or hoeing, or even while ensconced in the two-seater meditation shack behind the house—whenever they could snatch private moments—Nova and Artemisia entertained themselves by imagining Mrs. March in a hotel, writing letters on her typewriter and researching people's family trees. They created a picture of a widow in silk, who moved in society but was down-to-earth and chatty, having once been penniless. Artemisia said, "Mrs. March loves March flowers, and a hired hand totes flowers up to her room every day. And she plays the piano in the grand hotel lobby."

Artemisia's enthrallment with the fortune had been a corrective, Nova observed. Lately, her sister had not had any of the fits that had started several years before, after she got a lick on the head from a wagon tongue that knocked loose and flipped backwards. Her fits were like those of dogs in August, when the heat crazed them and caused them to dance in circles and froth at the mouth. The Renfroes, who had been good enough to take Artemisia in because she and Nova were inseparable, wouldn't acknowledge that there was anything wrong with her. It was just temperament, they said. "She sure has got a wild temper." "She knocks herself out sometimes just a-busting her head on a wall." "What makes you that way, Mezhie?" Bealus and his brothers scolded her after her spells. But Nova wouldn't join in. She believed that her sister had a demon she had to get out of her, that she had to slam her head on something in order to release the offending spirit. Artemisia never seemed to remember the falling and flailing and frothing. When anyone mentioned mad dogs, she changed the subject.

"Beware of false rumors about this case," Mrs. March warned. "People are trying to horn in or discredit the true claimants. Don't speak of this to outsiders!"

Mrs. March wrote that it would take a long time to get the case to the Supreme Court. She begged for patience—and another dollar or two donation to keep the effort going. The sisters were desperate with longing, their frustration tangled like yarn, spinning out in knots. The potato crop came in short, with nothing extra to sell. In the fall, the children needed shoes. A calf died.

All through the farm community of Locust, word had circulated about the Edwards heirs. Several of the pamphlets had turned up, stirring excitement like a gathering storm. A good number of the community could claim some Edwards kin, but few could afford the fee to support a claim. Nova heard Bealus scoff at talk of the inheritance, and she feigned indifference. Early Otto brought word that he had found proof of his Edwards connection all the way back to New Amsterdam. His grandmother Novella Wyatt remembered her grandmother talking about some land in New York. He had not saved up his fee yet, and his anxiety had affected his driving. He ran into a ditch twice.

Bealus Renfroe was a proud man, a rationalist who thought his pretty wife flighty, but he often indulged her whims—even when her outbursts of passion appeared daresome, unheard-of among the men of his acquaintance. He did not share details of his privilege with the congregation of men behind the barn or at the stockyard, where they routinely reviewed the intricacies of the female anatomy along with wheat prices and the mating habits of bulls. They spoke of women's bodies in an abstract way. They told jokes. ("They call Bessie a washerwoman." "Why's that?" "Her face is long as an ironing board; she's got a chest that's flat as a washboard, and a bottom like a wash kettle.") Bealus, suspecting his wife of some secret, worried that Nova had a loosened flap in her brain and might be in danger of developing the same malady her sister had. He feared Nova's collapse, even though Nova had never lost consciousness, had never banged her head on a fence post, had never slobbered, even on the pillow. She awoke bright and alert, like a wound-up cock-a-doodle-do, bounding out of bed and romping through her morning work with a fervor that seemed to parallel her energies in bed the night before. They had produced their three children effortlessly ("with our eyes closed," he said), but despite Nova's passion, her fertility seemed to have halted in the prime of her productive years. He sensed that this knowledge liberated her. She could dance a jig and bake a cake and set a hen almost in the same breath. But he worried that her infertility might also have the opposite effect; it might work a fever upon her brain.

Still, her lust flooded him, just to think of it. When he was plowing a field with an old mule he called Sidey-o, his mind was dancing with visions of Nova's soft flesh.

Out of the blue, she had begun to perform special, unmentionable acts upon him—things he'd never been able to get her to do before. She rendered him helpless. Afterwards, she would ask him for a quarter, or occasionally a dollar. She said she was saving the money for a surprise for him and the family. Christmas was coming, she said, although she couldn't promise the surprise in time. She made the secret seem irresistible, as orgiastic as the pleasures she offered now. Normally strict and thrifty, now Bealus grew easy and profligate. He could give her a few quarters after a trip to town. He could spare a dollar after he hauled turnips to the market, wheat to the mill. Bealus was known around the courthouse square in Hopewell, where he went to trade. Everyone knew he indulged his wife, but he let that be known in such a way that he would be seen as proud and fair and benevolent—like a good master, not a hen-pecked weakling. Of course, he would not reveal the secrets of Nova's special new gifts, because he did not want anyone else to get any ideas. He plowed the fields in a daze, forked hay to the cows while in a dream. Not since his early youth had such passion invaded his whole being; her new skills caused paroxysms to shout through his being, and in the fields he throbbed until night fell and he could bring a quilt over her head again, holding her until she came up for air.

In a year and a half, the sisters saved the fifty dollars for the two membership fees. It was enough money to provide a year's worth of store-bought goods for the household. They did without dry-goods such as muslin and sacking. Bealus was not able to buy new overalls or shoes for himself, but he did not complain. He did not know that they were dipping into the church tithe. The sisters sent in their applications just after Christmas, drawing upon some of their Christmas allowance by refraining from buying oranges and nuts for the holidays. To the howls of disappointment, Nova smiled sweetly. "These are hard times," she said.

Mrs. March sent a handwritten letter, acknowledging the memberships and enclosing receipts.

One early-spring day Nova told Artemisia what she had done to get those dollars from Bealus. Artemisia was an old maid, over thirty, and no man would have her. Nova told her story with great pleasure and animation. When Nova elaborated, in some detail, on what it was like—the proper procedure, the way she built up to the pleasure—she anticipated that Artemisia would simply not believe her. She expected merely to amuse her sister. She had innocently wanted to share her delight and to reveal the source of the savings, but she had not imagined Artemisia's reaction. Soon after Nova had exhausted her lively description, Artemisia commenced to staring at a knot-hole in the pine wainscoting, as if she were a cat watching for a mouse, and then she began that familiar guttural moan, like an animal trapped in a deep well. She slid against the pine wall into a heap, with her tongue catching her bonnet strings. As she wallowed and began to throb, the bonnet strings curled around her tongue.

"Mezhie!" Nova squatted next to her. She pulled the bonnet strings from her sister's mouth and removed the bonnet from her head. By then Artemisia was thrashing, quietly during the prelude, then building to a crescendo.

"Mezhie!" Nova began to moan herself, her voice rising until she was bawling like a cow, moaning with the deep anguish she often felt for her sister.

Artemisia's thrashing reached symphonic proportions, and after an eternity she began the slow subsiding, the diminuendo, the hush of her music. With a sorrow that squeezed her soul, Nova remembered how Artemisia had ached to learn the piano. But there had been no one to teach her after Mrs. Bledsoe took palsy.

For months, no word came of the inheritance, except four short notes asking for more donations. Mrs. March suggested one or two dollars per month, each, for expenses for the lawyers to press their case to the Supreme Court. They needed five hundred dollars for their trip to Washington. Any month now, the results of the case might be known. The sisters sent in what donations they could afford, and they waited, with growing apprehension, for news. Although Early Otto could not send in his own membership dues, he had already made plans to buy some acreage and livestock as soon as the inheritance arrived. Early Otto believed firmly in the Edwards claim, and he itched to gab about it more freely, but he kept his word and didn't reveal to Bealus that the sisters had applied. Artemisia, drained by the sheer effort the dream of riches required, decided that all she wanted out of the estate was a piano, and she spoke incessantly of it to Nova and the mailman.

Bealus said to her, "I heard you talking about a pi-anner. Is that what your sweetheart's bringing you? I imagine we'll see him hauling it up the road any minute now."

"I never said any such thing," Artemisia said, every notion of music plunging into hiding.

"You'd come nearer a-building one out of kindling sticks yourself," Bealus said.

Later, when they were sorting dress pieces to start a quilt top, Nova sought to reassure her sister about Bealus's ways. "Nobody would ever hope there could be a piano if we didn't have this reason to believe," she said.

"I'm just weary with a-waiting," Artemisia said. "Purely weary."

On a bleak December day, when the weather had begun to turn and the leaves had fallen and hog-killing day was imminent, a letter arrived from Mrs. March, apologizing for the long silence. She was writing from a hotel in Birmingham, Alabama. "I have distressing news," Mrs. March wrote. One of the principal lawyers employed on behalf of the claimants, she explained, was in prison, having been indicted for fraud—charges not related to the claim. "This development means that we cannot proceed at present. However, our organization is not dissolved, and we hope the claim can go forth soon, when we can replace Mr. Worth. Meantime I know you have been very eager to complete your genealogy, which would need to be done before any claim could be verified. The regular fee of any genealogist is twenty-five dollars, but I'm prepared to do the work for you for ten dollars each—since your trees will be the same. I have a special interest in your line, because the information you have given is similar to other records of Edwards claimants who can trace their interest back to our Robert Edwards, shipwrecked sailor. Please let me know if you want me to get up your family tree for you, so that when the case resumes you will be represented and can take possession of your share of the estate more quickly." Mrs. March enclosed two family-tree forms to be filled out with what names they knew.

The sisters were despondent, and no amount of coming Christmas cheer would raise their spirits. Nova was afraid that Bealus was expecting something extraordinary to come of all the money he had given her. She knew he had little cash to spare. And yet she and Artemisia needed more, so that Mrs. March could verify their connection to the original property owner in New York. The sisters' disappointment was like the emptiness left by a stillbirth.

They heard from Mrs. March a month later, the day the hogs were killed. She had been called to Memphis, on urgent business. She wrote, in handwriting, "We are proceeding with claims. Mr. Jack Hopkins has joined the team, and all preparations are being made for the journey to Washington. Please let me know if you decide to have me go ahead with your family tree. There is much work to be done on your family record, but I feel sure we can take care of you, in case of further success. But please keep your business on this matter strictly to yourself, as you know *some* people do not want us to have success. Refuse to show anything or talk to strangers and outsiders."

Nova squeezed Artemisia's hand silently as they read over this letter for the fourth time. It was late at night, and Artemisia's garret was chilly. Their hands were raw from handling sausage and chitterlings and other hog parts all day. Two butchered hogs hung in pieces out in the smokehouse, while a hickory fire smoldered beneath them.

Artemisia said, "We can't stop now."

In the autumn of 1932, Nova fell ill and was confined to her bed. For some time, she had felt lassitude and loss of verve, which she blamed on disappointment about the inheritance, for nothing of substance had been learned. A knot that had been in her breast for a year had grown larger, and another appeared under her arm. At first she thought the knot would go away, but when the second one formed, she was filled with dread. A poultice did not shrink the knots. Nor did prayer, although Artemisia scoured the Bible for pertinent passages. Nova hadn't called attention to the knots, but Bealus found one. The discovery made her worry that he might suspect she had hidden some secret pleasure from him. She had withdrawn her intimacies. She thought perhaps he would take the knot as a sign of some betrayal, but he did not accuse her. So she decided the knots were her punishment for hiding the secret of the inheritance, for wheedling his dollars and quarters out of him in such an un-Christian way. Bealus didn't suggest having the doctor until the knots began to sap her strength, like pregnancies requiring extra nourishment. Artemisia said they were mad-stones, the same as sometimes found in deer stomachs and used for divination.

"Mad-stones are harder than this," Nova said. "And I can't divine a thing from them but suffering."

When the pain began, she couldn't help gather the corn at harvest. Her older daughter, Betsy, quit school to help cook for the men. She did the patching and some of the housework.

Artemisia, suffused with melancholy, sat by Nova's bed. "If we heir that fortune, we can carry you to a famous clinic, and they can fix you."

Artemisia continued to meet Early Otto every day, waiting for news of the inheritance, but little came. They had sent in their twenty dollars, most of it earned by peddling dried-peach fried pies to ladies in town. Mrs. March had finished the family trees, establishing their straight line to the shipwrecked sea captain, and the court dates had been delayed.

When she felt she might be dying, Nova said to Artemisia, "I want you to ask Bealus for anything you need. Bealus will take care of you. And Betsy will help." Nova had difficulty swallowing, and her speech was broken into uneven phrases.

"I'll be all right," Artemisia said. "When we heir the money, we'll be all right. I can set up housekeeping. I'll buy myself a mansion and new pots."

"Keep after the fortune," Nova said. "Don't let Bealus . . ."

She fell asleep, and Artemisia tucked Nova's hand under the quilt, out of the draft.

When she knew for certain she was dying, Nova said to Bealus, "I want you to do one thing for me. Just one thing I ask and that is all."

"Anything." Bealus was half-crazed, primed for reckless promises.

"You'll be needing a wife. I want you to marry Mezhie."

Bealus jumped, as if he had been kicked in the face by a mule.

"I don't want her to go to the asylum," Nova said, her voice a harsh whisper. "I don't want her to end up by herself and no family."

"I can take care of Mezhie," Bealus said. "She can live right here— but *marry* her? I couldn't think it."

Nova said, "You need her to take care of the children. If she's in the house, sooner or later there will be temptation. It won't be right. So you have to marry her. The mad-stone's working now, and I can foretell the future. I can tell you I'm going to die, and I have to make plans: what to do about you and what to do about Mezhie. So I figured it out, and that's it. That's what you have to do. You're a man, and if she's under your roof and you have no wife, you'll want her."

"But—"

"She'll love you, even though she doesn't know it now, and she'll remind you of me. You won't know the difference after a while."

In the end, Nova resigned herself to the Lord's care, and when the pain made her scream, she imagined she was having one of her sister's fits, sharing with her that excruciating agony she had witnessed so many times and which now, for far too long, she kept expecting to turn into oblivion.

Out of Christian duty, Bealus Renfroe meant to honor his wife's dying request—in his own way—if he could figure out a suitable plan. But his fear of Artemisia throttled him. His grief was at odds with his sense of honor. A man wanted to bring out a certain amount of frenzy in a woman, it was true. But not unconsciousness and a slathering tongue caught in the strings of her nightcap. Artemisia's fits frightened him with their supernatural depth. Her spasms reminded him of a religious exercise in the old days when penitents fell over from the church benches and jerked themselves senseless, until they lay stiff as boards.

But then Bealus slowly opened his mind. On a spring afternoon, Artemisia rounded a corner of the house, unaware that he saw her. Her mouth was moving, as if she were pantomiming a conversation; she threw her hands up in surprise, although she hadn't seen him. She was deep into her pantomime. He saw that she was pretending to talk to her sister. He recognized the way the two sisters chattered together. She was taking both sides of the conversation, going back and forth. He recognized Nova, her expressions, her modest "Aw, pshaw!"—as well as the flirtatious dips and tosses of her head, her hand brushing the wings of her hair. Artemisia was playing both parts, as though she had two personalities, as though she had Nova in her.

He didn't reveal that he saw her at her game. He had believed Artemisia to be a stray mooncalf, possessed by enigmatic visions. Now he saw that Nova inhabited her, and memories of Nova rose unbearably in his mind.

When he went to Artemisia in her garret, he meant to do so tenderly, without impertinence or dishonorable intention. He wanted to know if Artemisia had any liniment.

"I didn't know where Nova kept the liniment," he said. "She always had liniment. She rubbed my sore back with liniment." His tongue caressed the word, drawing it out long.

"I'll show you the liniment," she said, catching her nightdress around her feet, holding it up as she descended the stairs. With the lantern, he went ahead of her, half turned to catch her if she stumbled.

Bealus observed her gathering the hem of her nightdress, squatting to fetch the liniment from a cupboard it shared with the bluing and the starch. She held the hem bunched around her feet. As she searched for a rag, her hair fell across her eyes like a shadow, and she seemed to peek from behind it, wary of him, but perhaps beckoning. He was aware that his trousers were held up by only one gallus.

"I'll tear you a rag," she said, poking into another cupboard for an old shirt, which she ripped in half. She tore out a sizable swatch and handed it to him, and he touched it, without taking it from her.

"She'd have done it for you," she said. "She would have reached where you can't reach. Where's it sore?"

He guided her hand behind his dangling gallus toward the small of his back.

Pulling up his shirt, she rubbed circles on his back with the liniment-soaked rag, and its strong smell, like turpentine and cloves, washed over him, a fragrance that filled him with Nova's presence. Her sister's touch was delicate and steady, not like a person who might suddenly slump to the floor and begin to thrash and drool. He saw how steady she was, how nimble her knuckles.

She eased his soreness, and they left the kitchen.

"Thank ye," he said to Artemisia as she ascended the steps to her garret. In the dark shadow at the top of the stairs he could imagine he saw the ghost of Nova.

In six months, they announced their betrothal. He believed her fits had slacked off, although he was in the fields most of the day and couldn't witness her behavior. She seemed to hold an aura of beatitude when she was around him. No one in the household reported any spells. His brother's wife, Ethel, ran the house, and Artemisia answered to her, until Bealus told Ethel that from now on Artemisia was the lady of the house and everyone would answer to her. Bealus knew the gossip throughout the community of Locust transcended mere talk of Artemisia's spells. It was that she lived in his house. Nova had known what would happen, and she had told him what to do. Nova was right. The preacher married them in the parlor, in front of the portraits of his parents on the wall. Bealus stood with Artemisia where he had stood with Nova fifteen years before, and where Nova had been laid out so recently, holding a lock of his whiskers tied with a baby ribbon. During the marriage service, Bealus felt a wave of emotion stir through him—like the giggles, but not mirth. Grief. He told himself sternly that it was not appropriate to feel grief on his wedding day. "I do," he said, his voice husky.

Artemisia was filled with surprises. Where she once scurried meekly, she began to behave more forthrightly—deliberate and unhurried. She presented him with the choicest samples of fried hen and squirrel, and she prepared hot, bubbling cobblers from the Indian peaches that grew along the creek. And, to his amazement, without any coaxing from him, Artemisia repeated what Nova had done to arouse ripples of pleasure, with the same little flourishes, her tongue alive and slithery on him. He imagined a comfortable swirl of mating snakes—not an unpleasant thought, for he admired snakes. He did not mention snakes to her, though, for he knew she would be frightened. He had grown to appreciate her timidity, so different from Nova, yet he knew she harbored Nova's capacity for uninhibited delight. She continued to act out her conversations with her sister, and he half-believed she was in communication with her, for her gestures included so many of Nova's passionate and spontaneous mannerisms.

"I have something to tell you," Artemisia told him one day.

Of course, she meant she was pregnant. He hoped not, for he feared a child inheriting her affliction.

"We might heir a fortune," Artemisia told him.

"What?"

"I'm an Edwards. Nova and me. We sent in to be heired."

"That Edwards thing that Early Otto and them's so worked up about?"

She nodded eagerly. "We kept it a secret from you that we sent in."

"Do tell," he said, amazed by this information—so inconsequential, yet such a secret. "Why in the world did you keep it a secret?"

"We wanted it to be a surprise." She didn't reveal that she and Nova had donated so many ill-gotten dollars.

Artemisia tried to be a good wife; she was agreeable, unlike her sassy sister. She did what Bealus wanted, and she offered him all the pleasures her sister had instructed her in. She wanted to ask an occasional quarter or dollar from him the way Nova had, but shyness forestalled her. She regretted telling him the secret. Once she had told him about the inheritance, he crushed her hopes. He made little of it and shamed her, refusing to reward her.

Before long, a letter arrived, wanting a dollar, and she did not have it. She fluttered her eyelash against his tender tumescence—a butterfly aquiver. His throbs gave her hope, but later when she worked up the courage to say she could use a dollar for some new ribbons, he said, "You know there's no dollars to be had. Don't you know times is hard? Where's your head living at, pretty little girl?"

She stewed about the matter. Her mistake had been in offering herself freely from the start. She should have introduced the request for quarters first, before indulging him. She was so used to keeping the secret, that now it was known she felt shame, her nerves agitated. The secret was turned inside out like a snakeskin, as if it had been something inside her, nourishing her, keeping her soul together. She cried inside, wailing, but ever so silently. Bealus did not believe in the inheritance. He did not believe it would ever materialize. "It's a dream for fools," he said. She knew it had dawned on him what Nova had done with the money she solicited from him, money he could have used to trade for a cow or a mule, or to buy shoes for his children.

Artemisia felt her small life enclosed by the split-rail fences of Bealus's sixty acres. She craved a few things in life, but she had never demanded anything. Now her desires bloomed. She longed not only for a piano but also for some books, and for some silk material to make a dress. She wanted silk that would feel as fine on her skin as her subtle tonguings had been on Bealus's flesh. Her imagination churned with these little wants, so much removed from the grease can, the slop jar, the iron skillet, the lye soap, the snot-nosed, supercilious children of Nova's, the patronizing church members who all regarded Artemisia as a freak of nature. Her mind wound around and around, craving a velvet weskit and a feather boa, books to read, paper for writing, a man from a newspaper to talk to her about the world, to bring her news of the world, the world that spun around and around and around.

Bealus found her among Nova's dresses in the garret. He had been in the fields from sunup to sundown, and Betsy had brought his dinner at midday. She said Artemisia was lying down, resting. In truth, Betsy had not looked for her but had whipped up the dinner herself and dragged the buckets on a child's wagon to the fields. That night he found his wife, twisted out of shape, her tongue bitten, the satin dress with which she pillowed her head still damp. He buried his head in her unfurled hair, as if to extract the essence of her gentle caresses in one last draught. He cried until he was hoarse and her hair a soaked mop. In repose, her face was sweet and childlike, drained of desire and insufficiency. He could see more than ever the features of Nova, the shape of Nova's mouth.

A few weeks after Artemisia's funeral, Early Otto brought a letter from the U.S. Postal Service, addressed to Bealus. Bealus sat on a stump beside the road to read it. The letter inquired if he or any members of his household had received any letters regarding inheritance claims. The Postal Service was investigating fraud. There was a form to fill out and a return envelope. After a morning of forking potatoes, Bealus was weary, his heart heavy as a bushel of seed corn. He slid the letter into his pocket. He did not want to answer this query. After all, the two women he had buried might have been right. The inheritance might come. He felt he had no right to put a stop to their hope. He had to honor their dream. Bealus waved to Early Otto, who was sitting in his Model T by the mailbox, his engine hiccuping, waiting, as if Bealus might have something to tell him.

3

Nancy rearranged the pillows behind her, wishing she had her microwaveable heat pack to ease the stiffness in her back. As a child, she had slept with a hot brick on cold nights, a brick warmed on the coal stove and then wrapped in newspapers. She clearly recalled the sensation of its warmth, the smell of hot paper. Then the weight of her heritage came rushing through her mind, as if the brick, a straight aim from those two desperate women, had been thrown at her. A shadow of raw grief descended, wrapping scarecrow arms around her, and she wept for the loss of her parents. Like Bealus, her father was cunning and strong and detached, carrying a world in his head.

Like Nova, her mother burned with frustration and desire. Nancy cried because she had gone away and had not shared her life with them, except in her imagination.

She heard the ice machine roaring in the hallway, and a man and woman laughing, and in the parking lot a horn blast.

The last letter, the one from the U.S. Postal Service, contained a notice of fraud investigation, with several inquiries about the Edwards estate. Included was a return-reply envelope. Evidently Bealus Renfroe had never answered the inquiry—out of embarrassment? Humiliation? Artemisia and Nova had stored the letters in the shoe box—with a stick of dynamite?—for a future generation to pursue the claim. Nancy supposed her grandmother, Nova and Artemisia's sister, had preserved the letters. Her grandmother saved everything—string, pins, scraps—for the sake of saving, it often appeared, not for any true purpose. It occurred to Nancy that her grandmother was capable of saving a stick of dynamite.

Nancy saw herself in this group of people, lives that had passed from the earth as hers would too. She felt comforted by the thought of continuity, even if a stick of dynamite could be called an heirloom.

In her mind's eye Nancy gazed at a spot of ground behind her grandmother's house. Inside the old wash house, her mother was feeding print dresses through the wringer of the washing machine. Outside the wash house, Nancy's grandmother was stirring boiling overalls with a broomstick, while a fire smoldered beneath the iron kettle. Nearby, Nancy, a child, was flinging underwear and washrags onto the thorny, overgrown quince bush to dry. Beyond was the expanse of fields, with a pointillist splotch of Holsteins grazing. And far in the distance, beyond the second tree line, in the corner of the landscape, her father rode his tractor, like a bug crawling on the painting, like Icarus falling unnoticed from the sky.

Over the following weeks, this image would stay in Nancy's mind, long after the Culpepper family farm was sold for an industrial park and Nancy and her sister and brother had retreated with the profits.

2005

The Prelude

$\mathcal{N}$ancy was waiting in Windermere for Jack's train. With its grassy splendor, the Lake District was an ideal place for a marital reconciliation, she thought. She hadn't seen him in almost a year. He was flying from Boston to Manchester, then catching the train.

In the ladies' room at Booth's, next to the station, she fussed over her hair and her eye makeup in a way she never had when she and Jack started out together, in the sixties, when her hair was long and straight. Now she used hair mousse and eyeliner. She no longer knew how to interpret the face she saw in the mirror.

If it were 1967 again and she knew what she knew now, how would she behave? She liked to imagine herself as a young woman, going north to begin graduate school, but this time she would be carrying confidence and poise as effortlessly as wheeling ultralight luggage. If she had had a sense of proportion back then, would she have married Jack?

She bought a fat double-pack of Hobnobs. She remembered how much Jack had liked those oat biscuits when they were in the Lake District together, long ago—rambling amongst sheep and bracken through the Furness Fells. Now she was on a Romantic kick, she had told him on e-mail. She was tracing the footsteps of Coleridge and Wordsworth, trying to capture in her imagination the years 1800–1804, when the two poets were involved in a romantic upheaval in their personal lives. It was not true that Dorothy Wordsworth and her brother William had an incestuous love, Nancy thought; Dorothy was surely in love with Coleridge. Samuel Taylor Coleridge—a married man, peripatetic, unhealthy, an excitable genius. But Coleridge was obsessed with another woman. Dorothy, doomed never to know the love of a husband or a child, gathered mosses and made giblet pies and took notes for her brother's poems. That was the story that kept coming to life in Nancy's imagination, and once it had sparked in her mind, she couldn't stop it. When Nancy and Jack were young, pairings and commitments were casual and uncertain, and Nancy even wondered later if she had really been in love with Jack. But the passionate love triangles—and trapezoids—in the Lake District two centuries before seemed desperate.

Early in their marriage, when Nancy and Jack traveled to England, their passion was unadulterated. After arriving in London, jet-lagged, they collapsed in the afternoon, then awoke at 3 A.M. Not knowing what else to do, they made love, after dropping a shilling into a wall heater, as if it were some kind of condom dispenser. They always thought that their son, Robert, was conceived in England, perhaps on that occasion.

Or maybe it had been a few days later, here in northern England. Jack had an assignment to photograph cottages. Nancy, who had written a paper on the Romantic imagination for a history course, had brought along an anthology of Romantic poetry. But the poems seemed old-fashioned, with their hyperbole and exclamation points, and she read few of them. Jack was shooting landscapes, and throughout the trip he goofed around trying to sound as if he were from Liverpool, like the Beatles. Nancy had a cold, and she was hungry, but when they arrived in the town of Kendal late on a Sunday, there was no place to eat. They bought Hobnobs and overripe pears from a chemist, who directed her to a preparation on a dusty lower shelf—a fig syrup that was good for colds, an analgesic.

"It's a very old remedy," the chemist said. "We've used it for generations."

At a bed-and-breakfast on a hillside of houses with long front gardens, Mrs. Lindsay served an elaborate tea, with little sandwiches and biscuits, enough to call dinner. She sat by the fire chatting about her flowers, her youth, her son the stevedore in Cardiff. Nancy sat entranced, her slightly feverish warmth dissolving into a comfortable ease. Mrs. Lindsay was seventy-five—very old, Nancy thought, thinking of her frail, taciturn grandmother in Kentucky.

Upstairs with Jack, Nancy swigged fig syrup and blew her nose. The syrup made her sleepy, and she slept well in the deep feather bed with piles of fluffy coverlets. At breakfast downstairs, Nancy studied the lace curtains, the flowered wallpaper, the ornate china cupboard, while Jack wrote in his notebook.

"Did you see Dove Cottage, where Wordsworth lived?" Mrs. Lindsay asked as she poured hot milk into Jack's coffee.

"We're going today," Nancy said.

"When I was a wee one in Grasmere I heard the old ones talk about Mr. Wordsworth."

"You knew someone who knew Wordsworth!" Nancy was astonished. The Romantic period was ancient history.

Mrs. Lindsay set the coffeepot on the sideboard. "They remembered him walking over the hills, always walking, with that stick of his," she said.

Nancy's interest in the Romantic poets went dormant after that and didn't reawaken until the past year, after she and Jack sold their house in Boston and agreed to live apart for a time—until desire reunited them, they said. Alone in the Lake District, Nancy revived the image of Wordsworth and his stick. She carried it with her, supporting her thoughts of the friendship of Coleridge and Wordsworth, as she imagined the pair hiking in the surrounding landscapes. Her mind dwelled on those characters, seizing each clue to their reality. If Wordsworth was a steady walker, Coleridge was an intrepid pioneer trekker, the type of person who today would have written a Lonely Planet guide. In his fight against an opium addiction, he would trot out boldly into the wild, with his broomstick and his green solar spectacles, daring to walk the drug out of his system. On at least one occasion Coleridge hid out in an inn at Kendal, maybe on Mrs. Lindsay's street. He went to the chemist for his opium, a mixture called Kendal Black Drop. Nancy smiled to herself, remembering now the fig syrup, pushed to the back of the dusty shelf.

Nimble Jack bounded down from the train. When he saw her, he dropped his blue duffel. Still clutching his camera bag, he jumped up and clicked his heels in the air.

"I can still do it!" he cried.

Nancy burst into laughter. She loved the attention he attracted. Her husband—a grown man, a middle-aged man, a kid. His face was a little harder and thinner. Their embrace was long and tight, with embarrassed squeals and awkward endearments.

"I don't know how I got along without you," he said, holding her against the wall of the track shelter.

"We're both crazy," she murmured.

"What have you been doing up here?"

"Getting Hobnobs for you," she said, producing the package.

He laughed. He probably hadn't thought of Hobnobs in thirty years, and maybe he didn't even recognize them, she thought.

In the taxi, Nancy gestured toward the glistening lake and the gentle green mountains, but Jack was chattering about his flight and his sister Jennifer's family in Boston. He had a nervous catch in his voice. Then he apologized for that.

"It's all right," Nancy said in a soothing tone. The tone was a bit new for her, she thought. She rather liked it. "We're going to be fine," she said.

"Thank God for e-mail," Jack said. "How did couples ever work out their differences in the past?"

"They went walking," Nancy said.

"Up here for the walking, are you?" the taxi driver, a woman in Bono sunglasses, asked. She said she was a native and had walked all over. "This is the best place in the world," she said. "I've just been to Spain and walked the Sierra Nevada. Really enjoyed that. But I wouldn't trade the Lakes."

As they neared Ambleside, Jack began to consider the scenery. But the view now was throngs of tourists. Nancy had insisted they did not need a car. Cars were discouraged because of the traffic, she told him.

She had been there for a week, walking miles every day, just as Dorothy Wordsworth did before she lost her mind.

The lobby of the hotel in Grasmere, where Nancy had been staying, was barely large enough for Nancy and Jack to stand together at the counter. Nancy could have afforded a posh hotel, but she had resisted, uneasy about spending her inheritance on luxuries her parents never had.

"Oh, is this your hubby?" the desk marm burbled, pronouncing it "hooby." She smiled pleasantly at Jack. "Enjoy your stay, luv."

As they climbed the soft-carpeted stairs, Jack said, "I brought my boots. You said we were going to climb a mountain a day. Do I need a walking stick?" He joked, "Maybe I need a cane."

"We're not old."

"If you say so," he said. "That reminds me. I've got some news."

"Oh, what?" She couldn't tell if he meant good news or bad. Jack had perfected an enigmatic expression.

"Robert and Robin took me to the airport. Robin sent you something. It's in my bag. But that's not the news."

"So is Robert going to marry that girl?"

Jack shook his head. "Who knows?" he said, with a slight flicker of a grin.

"She's nice. I like her."

Robert had been living with Robin for two years. Nancy thought Robin was an improvement over his ex-wife, the post-colonial feminist academic from Brattleboro.

In the modest room, Jack glanced around at the evidence of Nancy's life there—books, hiking boots, a periwinkle fleece neck gaiter—as if he was seeing a side of her he didn't know. Although he was still slim and athletic, she could see his face was older, but she was already getting used to it. His familiar face jumped back into place. Probably he saw the same aging in her, but he regarded her tenderly, as though he hadn't noticed the white down that in certain lights was beginning to show on her chin.

"I was afraid something would happen to you here, out walking alone," he said, hugging her once more.

"It's not dangerous here. Tourists, tourists everywhere."

"I still didn't like it."

"Tell your news?" she asked.

"We need to wait a little for a better moment."

"A Romantic moment?"

He grinned. "I get it."

"The poets have been keeping me company." She laughed.

"Aren't they a little old for you—dead, maybe?"

"Historians always get crushes on dead guys."

Nancy vowed not to bore him with her latest obsession. She was putting away her jacket, making a place for his luggage. She felt a bit flustered, as if she was going to entertain a near-stranger. They hadn't really kissed yet.

When Jack came out of the bathroom, she went in. Beside the sink she had made a wall display of Lake District scenes—Grasmere, Loughrigg, Derwentwater. Tourist postcards, not art. He probably disapproved, she thought. She hadn't always understood his photography. "What is it a picture *of?*" she always wanted to know, but he wouldn't tell. "History majors!" he would say. Yet she thought a photograph of knives laid in bomber formation lacked subtlety. Was it supposed to be a statement—about war, say—or was it the simple shock of surreal juxtaposition, as facile as a video on MTV? Even MTV was a generation ago, she thought now. She could hear the telly. Jack had turned on BBC 4.

She had once told him his pictures were cold, and that hurt him. He was actually warm and loving, much more so than she was. Still, the pictures *were* cold somehow, she felt. But was that a good reason for the breakup of a marriage?

He was standing by the window, watching the swift, narrow rush of the River Rothay below. His hair was thinner, sandier, but not really gray. Her own brown hair had an auburn sheen, and in bright light she could still find individual rust-red hairs, as if they had been borrowed from Jack.

Turning from the window, he embraced her and they tripped around in a clumsy little circle on the thin floral carpet. She thought his news would be about his photographs, and she wanted to show affection, offer praise. She had been rehearsing. Never good at small talk, she had always found it difficult to issue congratulations or happy, encouraging words. She was often preoccupied; she was laconic; she didn't elaborate or waste words. It did not occur to her to say, "Good job, honey." She had never called him "honey." But of course she had always loved him. He knew that.

Now Nancy, the grad student miraculously possessed of style and a sense of proportion, and ready with appropriate words, smiled. Jack had opened the curtain and was gazing across the fast-flowing water at the church tower. The Wordsworths lay in its shadow, in the graveyard.

"Robert and Robin—it's their news," Jack said, turning to her. "They're having a baby."

Nancy gasped. "Well, knock me down and call me Popeye!" It was something her mother might have said. The phrase shot foolishly through her newfound poise. She sank onto the bed. "Wow. I'm speechless."

"I was surprised. Bowled over. Thrown for a loop. You could have knocked me over with a feather. I'm agog. I'm stupefied. I'm—"

"You had time to rehearse that!" Nancy cried. Jack's trick of reeling out synonyms had always amused her. Now she started to cry.

"It's O.K.," he said, curling his arm around her shoulders. "Robin is a sweet girl. Robert's old enough to make us grandparents. Not that we're old! You just said that."

"Stop," Nancy said through her tears. "I'm not crying over that. I'm crying because of the synonyms."

"Want me to go on? I was dumbfounded. I was nonplussed. I was—"

"That's one thing I missed. I missed that so much."

"I begged Robert and Robin not to tell you yet, to let me bring the news, because it's *our* news too. I wanted to share it with you, to see the look on your face."

She smiled, but only slightly. She had a sense that she was somewhere off to the side, observing her happiness. She held back, for fear of ruining it.

———

The bed slanted downward, and the shiny duvet on the comforter made crinkly sounds. The bed was unfamiliar to their marriage. And the time of day was unusual, too. Robert, their child, was becoming a father. This was how it was done, she thought, as she and Jack reenacted the moment of creation. She couldn't get away from the surprise: a bit of her and a bit of Jack, combined once, now recombined with something else to initiate a new generation. The phrase "recombinant DNA" floated through her mind, although she wasn't sure what it meant.

Jack sat on the edge of the bed. "I'm sorry," he said. "I was slow. You used to call me 'Speedy.' "

Nancy patted him. "It's all right. We're out of practice." She smoothed the goose-down comforter in place. The thing was surprisingly warm. "Ejaculation," she said suddenly. "Jack off! I never thought of that before. People used to say ejaculation when they meant exclamation."

"They said erection too. Builders would call a house an erection." Jack pulled on his T-shirt. He said, " 'My mighty erection,' he ejaculated slowly."

"Don't worry about it," Nancy said. She couldn't think of what else to say.

Soon after she left Jack, a year ago, she visited Northampton, Massachusetts, where they had first met. She drove her old history professor around the countryside. Professor Doyle—she still wanted to address him that way—was still passionate about the Transcendentalists. "I hate time!" he wailed. Nancy was unnerved. She remembered how in class he pumped his fist in the air for emphasis, making history come alive, as if it were a timeless possession in his mind.

Nancy pulled over in front of a post office across the road from the house where she and Jack used to live. The green saltbox, now painted brown, was for sale. The field where she and Jack once ran with their dog had sprouted a monochrome faux–New England housing development. Nancy entertained a quick fantasy of purchasing the house and moving in with Jack, starting over.

"History is imagination," Professor Doyle said, with a tinge of bitterness.

Jack napped while Nancy read snatches of Wordsworth's *The Prelude,* his long paean to Coleridge, in the light from the window. Wordsworth was reviewing his life, gearing up to write his magnum opus, not knowing that most of his great works were already behind him. She absorbed the fleeting scenes of youth, when the two poets had connived to whiplash the imagination. Wordsworth wrote about the eloquence of rustic people, who didn't use proper English and who toiled with bent bodies, people like those from Nancy's past. The poets, in their quest for what they called the sublime, thought nothing of walking the length of England. With Dorothy, they went for midnight rambles in the dead of winter. Nancy could not stop wondering about Dorothy's boots.

Robin's gift was a box of chocolate mice from Boston, and Nancy nibbled several down to their inedible tails. Jack seemed unusually tired, and she let him sleep.

The light was fading when he stirred. Nancy knelt by the bed and nudged him awake. "Come on, Jet-Lag Jack," she said. "You'll get your days and nights mixed up. It's time to go downstairs for dinner."

Jack groaned and sat up. "What time is it?"

"Eight-ten. You don't want to miss sticky-toffee pudding." She grinned as he grimaced.

Jack roused himself from bed, fumbled through his duffel bag, and found a wadded shirt. He began to change into it. Then he reached for Nancy, who was slipping into her black running pants and clogs—her dinner outfit.

"Actually there's more news," he said, holding her arm. "I have prostate cancer."

"*What?*"

"The prostate," he said.

"Oh, Jack!"

"They have to do some more tests, but they want to do surgery."

Nancy realized she was now sitting on the floor, clutching the side of the bed. He sat on the side of the bed, and she raised herself to sit beside him. "Maybe it's not really cancer?"

"The doctor did a biopsy. I should have waited to tell you after I get all the results."

She recognized her numbness, the clicking into detachment mode. The news would not sink in for some time. She started to tell him that he was crazy to travel overseas instead of going for surgery right away. But she refrained.

She saw her emotions lying around her, in heaps, like children flung from a Maypole.

Holding her tightly, he told her the details. He had been worried for some time. Perhaps he had come back to her out of a need, she thought, but it was also possible that he knew there was no time for recriminations and separation. Now she was called upon to exert that confidence she had imagined in herself, to say the right things. But she didn't know exactly what. She was sitting in his lap, her head on his shoulder. Somehow they were now in the easy chair.

"I won't ever leave you again." The words didn't sound like hers. "I'm not just saying that," she said.

"I know. I'm not asking you to come back because of this."

"I wanted to come back anyway. You know I did."

"I was afraid to ask you, afraid it wouldn't be authentic."

"Let's not worry about the authentic. We've always pressured ourselves to be authentic. Let's just be ourselves."

He smiled. "Whatever that means." She rubbed his neck. "I missed you," he said.

"I'm glad."

He said, "I don't want you to come home if you don't really feel—"

"Home? We have no home." She ran her fingers through his hair. "You know, it doesn't necessarily mean doom. Some people just live with it."

"Unless I have the Frank Zappa kind."

Nancy reached for her fleece shirt, but she wasn't sure she was cold.

"Bopsy," Nancy said.

"What?"

"Mom pronounced it that way—when she had breast cancer. Biopsy. Bopsy."

"Bopsy, Mopsy and—Cottontail?"

She slid from his lap and stood. "You *know* I love you," she said. "It's *time* that I hate."

Jack's news hit her again. It was illogical, unreal.

She wondered if Mick Jagger ever worried about his prostate.

While Jack was in the bathroom, she roamed through a small paperback he had brought about the prostate. The walnut-sized gland—always described as a walnut, like something a squirrel would hide. The inconvenience of it, such a silly thing to harbor in one's body. A tumor in itself.

Her whole life with Jack was reconfigured in a couple of moments, its arc becoming a circle, like the circle implied in a rainbow or a sunrise.

The downstairs dining room, looking out on the river, was almost deserted. Their table for two was in a corner across from the sideboard of fruit and pudding. The table setting included three china patterns, Nancy noticed.

"The cuisine is strangely inventive here," she told Jack. "Nouvelle Borderlands."

She chose an Italian eggplant dish with cubes of smoked tofu and a pasta called orecchiette—fat blobs like collapsed hats. Jack ordered the plaice. The pasta came with roasted potatoes and carrots on the side, while the plaice had mashed potatoes, carrots and courgettes.

As they ate, Nancy talked rapidly, spilling out everything she had saved to tell Jack. They were ignoring his prostate, but her thoughts had adjusted like blocks of text rejustifying on a computer screen.

"Do you like the plaice?" she asked.

"It's fine—I guess what you always called a charming, cozy hotel."

"I meant the fish."

He grinned. "If I'd said the fish was good, you would have said you meant the hotel."

They laughed. "Maybe you know me better than I thought you did," she said.

———

In the gray morning they walked, in rain gear, under the soft, dim sky. Jack had slept through the night and declared his jet lag deleted. Dumped. Vanquished. Atomized. But his eyes still looked tired.

"The beans want sticking," Nancy said to Jack in the garden behind Dove Cottage.

"What?"

"Dorothy wrote in her journal, 'The Scarlet Beans want sticking.' It's the same way my grandmother talked. And my mother too. They grew scarlet runner beans, and they had to find sticks for the vines to hold on to. Dorothy wrote about William gathering sticks to stick the peas."

"You're still thinking about your past," he said, not unkindly.

Nancy was thinking of the time Coleridge stopped in at Dove Cottage, while Dorothy and William were away. Coleridge went into the garden, picked some peas, and cooked them. He dressed them, he wrote in his notebook. Nancy's mother used that word. She dressed eggs, dressed a hen. Nancy was pleased to find this cultural connection to her parents and grandparents, but she wouldn't mention that to Jack now. Nancy followed him down the cobbled lane past Dove Cottage, where he occupied himself with taking photos of some small-animal skulls displayed on the side of a stone house.

She said, "Did it ever occur to you that Wordsworth would have an accent, that he would have sounded like the Beatles?"

"Give me a line."

" 'My heart leaps up when I behold a rainbow in the sky'?"

Jack tried it but didn't quite get it right. They laughed. She wondered if he was remembering their other trip to the Lake District, but she didn't ask.

A World War II–era Spitfire appeared suddenly, low in the sky over Grasmere. Jack fumbled with his zoom lens and took several shots. "Damn," he said. "I wanted to get it against that hill over there. I just got sky."

"There were fighter jets every day last week," Nancy said.

Early in their marriage, in their rural phase, Nancy grew vegetables. It seemed a moral obligation to grow something if there was good ground. But one night she found herself up at midnight preparing English peas for the freezer. And it occurred to her that she had left home in Kentucky to get away from the hard labor that had enslaved her parents. She was meant to use her mind. But her mind wandered, and she never had a successful career, because she shied away from groups, with their voluble passions. A career was more important to Jack, and she knew he sometimes felt a failure because he hadn't exhibited at the Museum of Modern Art.

Eventually they sold their place in the country. Jack craved the stimulation of artistic friends, and Nancy had grown restless. They moved to Boston, which Nancy loved for its history, and fell in with a set of articulate, intellectual dabblers. But she found something myopic in their ways, how they stirred and sifted the doings of the day as if they were separating wheat from chaff, passing judgments on everyone who came to their notice. Their gatherings, although bohemian, were little contests, a show of strained witticisms. They never made crude remarks or talked about sex or money, and they assumed that everyone in the nation knew who Susan Sontag was.

"I should have made a big pot of chicken-and-dumplings, complete with the yellow feet sticking up," Nancy told Jack once after a miserable dinner party when she had cooked fried chicken. "They would jump right in if it was Chinese. But if it's Southern, it's unacceptable."

Jack just sighed. "There you go again, Nancy. They ate."

"Don't laugh at me," she said.

Kentucky wouldn't release her. She wouldn't let it. She fought Jack on this, and he always accused her of being held back by her culture. She and Jack had often been apart for considerable stretches of time—her many trips to Kentucky; a former job that kept her on the road; and then a serious separation a decade ago. She went to England then, too, but that trip held no good memories. It was only a midlife crisis, she and Jack assured each other, when they reunited. Then a few years back, her parents died, in a ghastly six-month period—cerebral hemorrhage and massive stroke. Nancy broke from Boston then and began living part-time in Kentucky while she reconsidered herself and waited for her grief to subside. She supposed that

9/11 freed her from her own personal grief, but she never said so, for fear of sounding melodramatic. After her parents' farm was sold, that hard rural way of life that had endured for centuries passed away. Nothing held her there, except what Jack called the guilty-daughter syndrome, her conviction that she had betrayed her parents in a hundred ways and that she had never really explained herself to them.

Now Nancy stood in Dorothy's garden and gazed at the yew tree beside the house, a tree that had been there two centuries ago.

Her parents were gone. Their farm was gone. She was herself. It was the twenty-first century.

Heavy rain hit at lunchtime, but by afternoon it eased and the sky brightened slightly. They walked to Easedale, past Goody Bridge. The rain-swollen stream was rushing and high under the bridge. They walked along a boardwalk with the water lapping at the edges, then crossed a sheep pasture to the rocky trail that ascended the mountain. Tall granite fences, the ancient work of farmers and shepherds, made hard lines up the mountain. The rock steps of the path were carefully laid, now worn smooth by generations of walkers. The ascent up to Sour Milk Gill was not difficult.

"Are you sure you're all right?" Nancy asked Jack.

"I'm O.K. Fine. Couldn't be better."

"Maybe we should have trekking poles," Nancy said, indicating a young couple with backpacks who were descending at a fast clamber, their metal-tipped poles clicking rapidly against the stones.

"I knew I should have brought a cane," Jack joked.

"We're not old," Nancy said.

They walked steadily for about a mile, Nancy following Jack's lead. They paused just before a steep ascent and drank some water. Nancy stood on a large, smooth rectangular stone that served as a small bridge over a streamlet. As she gazed across at the waterfall, she thought she glimpsed her own image, outsized, with a halo, in the mist above the water. She felt she was in one of Coleridge's "luminous clouds." The sudden sensation faded as she said all this aloud to Jack. "The poets called it a 'glory,' " she explained. "It's accidental, not something that can be forced. It just swoops in, like a bright-feathered bird landing inside your head."

"I've read about that," Jack said. "It's caused by a tiny seizure in the brain."

"Well, then, I'm having a tiny seizure."

The path veered close to the tumble of the waterfall, which was known long ago as Churn Milk Force. Nancy, watching the crash and spray of water, suddenly felt a rare burst of anger as she pictured the days lined up ahead, days that could descend into a dark tedium. Churning through her mind was an intolerable parade of flash-card images—a hospital corridor, a shrunken body, falling hair, a coffin. She would not be able to endure it.

"Stand still. I want to take your picture." Jack lifted his camera and pointed it at her. "I like the way your hair seems to be in motion."

He fiddled with his lenses, paused to let a hiker past, and began snapping.

"What are you thinking?" he said, shielding his camera in its case.

She hesitated, unzipping her jacket partway. She heard a sheep bleat. "I was remembering when we were in the Lake District before," she said. "In Kendal. Remember Mrs. Lindsay and how when she was small, the old people would tell about seeing Wordsworth walking around with his walking stick? Just think—we knew somebody who knew somebody who knew Wordsworth! I've never forgotten that."

"Only three degrees of separation."

"Isn't that amazing?"

"That's important to you?"

She heard the judgment in his voice. The "so what." But she sped along.

"Don't you remember Mrs. Lindsay? I'll never forget her."

"Vaguely."

"I counted forty-eight dishes and pieces of silverware on her breakfast table."

"What a thing to remember," Jack said. "You amaze me."

"Our minds are different."

He nodded, then zipped his camera into its pack. He moved away from the path and sat down on a large rock, his hand gesturing for her to sit beside him.

"I've done a lot of thinking in the past year," he said.

"Me too."

"We weren't paying attention to each other—for a long time."

"I know."

"Because our minds *are* so different," he said. "I get it now."

"We knew that."

"I know, but we were so busy going in different directions, we just didn't make time. You were always doing your puzzles—I mean your scholarly studies."

"Same thing."

"And I was translating everything into some formal meaning." He sighed. "What the hell am I trying to say?"

"You don't have to explain."

"I just mean that the tracks stopped crossing. And we forgot to say hello."

"It's pretty typical," Nancy said, then laughed. "I hate that. I hate to be typical."

"Let me tell you something that happened," Jack said, reaching for her hand. "I was in New Hampshire. Robert and I went to Franconia Notch. And I was overcome with a memory of when we went there years ago. Franconia Notch wasn't at all the way I remembered it."

"You and I were together there with Grover."

"Grover." Jack seemed about to blink out a tear. Grover had been his most beloved dog. "I remembered how we played hide-and-seek in the Flume. Grover and I hid from you. We had such a great time hiding from you. All those big boulders down there."

"The Flume was so narrow and dark," Nancy said. "And I remember a man gave me a hint—where you were hiding. I must have seemed lost. But I found you."

"God, that was such a great memory." Jack put his head in his hands. "And then I realized that all this time I've been hiding from you."

Nancy put her arm around him. "But it is a good memory. And Grover was at our wedding!"

"Life was grand then," he said.

"It was very heaven." Quickly she added, "Wordsworth."

At the top of the waterfall, the scene opened to the tarn, the small mountain lake leaking down the side of the mountain. The lake's surface was shiny and smooth, the reflections of the surrounding mountains sharp. Except for the half dozen hikers in view, there was no sign of the modern world. The mountains—erratic brown-and-gray walls—rimmed the setting.

"This is incredible," Jack said. His camera case dangled from its strap, as if at a loss for pictures, as Nancy was at a loss for words.

"Dorothy and William walked up here at night," she said presently. "They walked everywhere at night. Even in the winter. In the snow and rain."

"I hope they had Gore-Tex," said Jack.

As Nancy pulled Hobnobs from her pack, explosive sounds burst from above—a pair of jet fighters blasting through the sky above the tarn.

Jack scrambled for his camera. But the jets were gone.

The trickle of the river was loud through the open window.

"Let's call Robert," Nancy said.

"Good idea," Jack said, glancing at his watch. "He should be home now."

Robert and Robin were at the house in the White Mountains where Jack's family spent summers. Robert did research at Dartmouth in molecular biology, and he had already published a paper of some significance on cell signaling.

After Jack dialed a long series of numbers from his telephone card, Nancy took the phone. Robert answered on the second ring. Hearing her son's voice filled her with an anxious pleasure. She sensed that whenever she talked to him she turned into a slightly different Nancy, seeing herself as he saw her. Now she turned into a giddy grand-mother, silly, talking to her son.

"Robin wants to keep her job," Robert was saying. "She can work at home."

"I hope you're happy," Nancy said. "I hope this is what you wanted." She wondered if they were still in love after two years of co-habitation.

"Dad told me some news too," he said.

"Oh?" Nancy sensed Robert's hesitation.

"He said you were getting back together."

"Did he know that?"

"You'd better ask him."

The coming together again seemed easy, she thought. Perhaps Jack's good news and bad news had canceled each other out, leaving them in limbo. While Jack spoke with Robert, Nancy examined her face in the bathroom mirror. More and more, she resembled her mother. This used to frighten her, but she had come to find the recog-nition pleasant. She would say a quiet hello. Now, as she gazed into her reflection, she could remember the stages of her growth in photo-graphs—the tentative baby-faced first-grader; the saucy high-schooler; the college adventurer, with her brows darkened and thickened, her lipstick lustrous, her hair briefly beehived; her unadorned sixties per-sonality (the "natural look," it was called); the thinner, more angular face as her son grew up and she weathered. She could see all her faces morphed together, each peeking out of the other, the guises through which she had acted out the scenes of her history. And, too, she saw her mother's turned-up nose and scared eyes; and her father's square jaw; and her grandmother's sagging jowls. She imagined other un-known faces of ancestors, and she saw her son, his mouth and warm coloring. And somewhere in her face was her grandchild.

She heard Jack winding up his talk with Robert. Again, she re-membered that first trip to the Lake District with Jack, at Mrs. Lind-say's in Kendal. When Coleridge returned to England in 1806 from a long escape to Malta, he didn't want to see his wife. He had gone to Malta to forget a woman he loved—not his wife, and not Dorothy. He returned to England after two years, intending to ask for an official separation from his wife, but he couldn't bring himself to go home to the Lake District. He remained in London for months. And then when he did go, he delayed the reunion even further by stopping at an inn in nearby Kendal. After he invited Wordsworth to supper, people heard he was back. His family and friends rushed forth to see him, because he had been gone for two years, and they loved him. But he was afraid, afraid to go home.

Nancy could see him reaching far back on the dusty shelf for his opium mix. *Kendal Black Drop.* The words beat on her ears.

That evening after dinner, Nancy and Jack walked down Stock Lane to look at the stars. They wandered out into the soccer field. Tiny Grasmere was sleeping, but a faint stream of music and laughter seemed to emanate from the mountains, or maybe the moon. The moon was hornéd, as it was in *The Rime of the Ancient Mariner.* The hornéd moon, an image Dorothy had contributed.

Coleridge often walked the fourteen miles from Keswick to Grasmere to visit Dorothy and William. In her journal, Dorothy wrote that she and Coleridge took this very walk, along Stock Lane. They walked from the cottage to the church in the moonlight. She wrote of lingering in the garden later with Coleridge, after the others had gone to bed. To Nancy, the spare notations resonated with desire.

Nancy and Jack stood in the soccer field, gazing up into the night sky. Nancy's mind was busily adjusting the details from Dorothy's journal to this spot. She felt the sorrow of separation and unrequited love and romantic obsession—all of life's romance blowing like a cyclone through those lives two centuries ago, when they were innocent of time.

"I don't think I could live this far from a city," Jack said. "But I like this climate. I don't have any sinus trouble here."

"Good."

"What about your guys?"

"What?"

"The poets. Any sinus trouble?"

"Coleridge had to breathe through his mouth." She laughed. "But his worst trouble was his digestion." She paused, trying to remember one of his descriptions. She said, "He wrote in a letter that he had been bathing in the sea and it made him sick. He said, 'My triumphant Tripes cataracted most Niagara-ishly.' " She spoke slowly, to get the syllables right.

He laughed. "Your pals are starting to be real to me."

She squeezed his hand. "They're here, like ghosts." She could feel them, young people struggling with the future.

The air was damp but not biting. They crossed the road to Dove Cottage. The windows were dark. Nancy imagined Coleridge stopping there in the rain, wanting solace and comfort from his friends; arriving late, past midnight, he was wet and anxious after his long tramp over Mount Helvellyn in the rain. Probably he needed to spew out all his ideas and affections—the treasure trove of a young genius, thrust forth like a hostess gift. His was a mind that never stopped whirling and somersaulting. Nancy imagined the stone floor in the front room, wet with the rain Coleridge brought in, and the urgent glee of his voice slamming the walls and the low ceiling. A man whose voice was music.

In the dark, by the garden gate, Nancy and Jack huddled together, his arm tight on her shoulders. He had come across the ocean for her.

"I missed you," she said. "I want you back."

"I want you back," he said. "But where? Where will we live?"

"I don't know. Where *can* we live?"

Nancy Culpepper

BOBBIE ANN MASON

A Reader's Guide

A Conversation with Bobbie Ann Mason

Reader's Circle: Nancy Culpepper, the title character of your story collection, moves around quite a bit—from Kentucky to the Northeast, then to London—trying to find her place in the world. In your own life, have you found that favored place where you feel most like yourself?

Bobbie Ann Mason: Like Nancy, I'm drawn to England, especially the Lake District. I feel most myself when I am alone—which is the best way to embark on the creative-writing adventure.

RC: Do you see shades of yourself in Nancy Culpepper?

BAM: Nancy is more like me than any other character I've ever created, but I see her at a certain distance from me, situated in a marriage that I can explore perhaps more freely than she can because I'm not married to Jack. It is her sensibility that I feel closest to.

RC: How is the art of crafting a short story different from writing a novel? Do you prefer one writing experience to the other?

BAM: A short story demands a focus, an intensity, and an economy that novels can't usually sustain, although I generally go about writing a novel in much the same way—with attention to detail and endless rewrites. I usually prefer writing stories because a novel is such a long struggle, but the ultimate gratifications of completing a novel are deeper.

RC: What about nonfiction? Does your voice change as a writer, depending on whether you are writing fiction or nonfiction?

BAM: Writing nonfiction is much more difficult for me, demanding as it does a logical mind and a fidelity to fact. I usually approach it as I do fiction: as an organic, intricately involved design rather than as a straightforward journalistic path. It's quite challenging to juggle textures, motifs, and all the subtle devices one utilizes in fiction when writing nonfiction.

RC: How do you set out to write a short story? Where does your creative process begin, and how does a story evolve?

BAM: A story often starts with something very small—an image or a phrase, or a tone I hear in my head. It evolves by happenstance and exploration and willingness to go into new territory. If bricklaying were the analogy, there would be no pile of bricks and no blueprint. I wouldn't even be building a wall, but rather hoping for something surprising to fall into place. Ultimately, I'd have to do a lot of rearranging and troweling to make my project work, but ideally, it would turn out to be a crystal palace and not a brick wall.

RC: Like Nancy, are you a fan of Mick Jagger? What or who are your creative influences?

BAM: The Rolling Stones have certainly been on the soundtrack of my life, but Mick Jagger isn't especially significant to me. It was the Beatles whose inventiveness grabbed me. My early musical resources include rhythm and blues, big bands, and jazz. The other "creative influences" are probably Louisa May Alcott first and then the literary voices I encountered in college—Salinger, Hemingway, Fitzgerald. In graduate school I seized on Nabokov and Joyce.

RC: What are you reading now? What are your favorite books?

BAM: I'm reading the poems of Samuel Taylor Coleridge and others of the Romantic era, and I'm reading Albert Camus' *The Stranger* in French, trying to figure out why the English translation I have read so many times is embellished so much. My favorite books include *Lolita, The Great Gatsby, A Farewell to Arms, A Portrait of the Artist as a Young Man,* and *Middlemarch.*

RC: Your story *Lying Doggo* features a wonderful canine companion: Jack's delightfully named dog, Grover Cleveland. Do you have dogs of your own? Are you an animal lover?

BAM: Yes, I love animals. I had a collie named Beowulf when Grover appeared in the Nancy stories. Little did I realize that Beowulf would one day face Grover's fate. I grew up on a dairy farm with plenty of animals, but I'm more of a cat person than a dog one.

RC: Recently, you've written in *The New York Times* about the environment, and the problems of mountaintop-removal coal mining in your home state of Kentucky. Can you tell us a bit about this?

BAM: Writers in Kentucky are trying to bring national awareness to the devastation that America's demand for coal is inflicting on our great national treasures, the ancient forests and mountains of Appalachia. The other main issue for me is animal welfare. The way we treat land and the way we treat animals are similar; the willingness to commit abuse knows many forms.

RC: Is there a way for people to become involved in these causes?

BAM: We must reduce our dependence on coal by saving electricity. Look for green energy alternatives. Use energy-saver fluorescent light bulbs. Get Energy Star appliances. Grow your own food. Get educated on the subject: Go to ilovemountains.org. Read *Lost Mountain* by Erik Reece, which dramatically documents what is happening to the land and its people. This is a national tragedy. Speak up! Go green!

Similarly, in terms of how we exploit animals, we can reconsider everything about how we live—what we eat, what we wear, what products we buy. Cruelty to animals is a sign of our worst impulses, and there's no excuse for it. Start with local rescue groups and animal sanctuaries. Spay and neuter. Trap, neuter, and release feral cats. Join some animal-welfare groups and find out how we can change our own habits. At the bottom of both issues is compassion and respect for our planet and its creatures.

RC: Turning back to *Nancy Culpepper*, what do you see as the big lessons of Nancy's life? What are you hoping that readers will take away from these stories, and from your work in general?

BAM: I don't think of a work of fiction as having lessons but rather aesthetic pleasures—in the language, the details, the characters, and the joy of reading. We get rewards from intimately observing other lives in action when we enter a world different from our own. Reading should be an adventure that enlarges our perspective and deepens our sympathies. I hope the reader will appreciate Nancy's adventures while she puzzles out her own identity.

Questions and Topics for Discussion

1. Linked stories have a long tradition in American fiction—Sherwood Anderson's *Winesburg, Ohio* and Ernest Hemingway's *In Our Time*, for instance. How do these stories about Nancy Culpepper work together? What threads unite them into a sustained narrative?

2. Photographs play an important role in the stories, from Jack's artistic compositions to the family photos that Nancy seeks. How is the relationship between Nancy and Jack suggested by the different ways they regard photographs?

3. There are several weddings and at least two long marriages in *Nancy Culpepper*. How is the marriage of Nancy's parents different from Nancy's marriage to Jack? How is it similar? How is a "good marriage" defined in the different generations and places, and what would your own definition be?

4. The cultural divide that Nancy feels is expressed in numerous ways. Where exactly does she live in her mind and heart? Is this "schizophrenic" sensibility familiar in modern life? Does her devotion to her parents and her home place hold her back, as Jack believes?

5. What happens to Nancy in "Proper Gypsies"? After the burglary and the conversation with the locksmith, Nancy tours "London by fury." How do we account for her state of mind in Westminster Abbey? In the music store? In the restaurant? In Trafalgar Square?

6. In the final story, "The Prelude," Nancy's history professor comments, "history is imagination." How does this comment apply to Nancy as a historian?

7. In "The Heirs," is the story of the farm women something Nancy imagines? How convincing is it? What do you see of Nancy herself in the story of Nova and Artemisia?

8. Images of garden vegetables, especially peas, appear in several of the stories. How do these images reflect Nancy's attitude toward her rural heritage? In "Spence + Lila," why does her mother want to remember to "tell Nancy about the peas" (page 138)? When Nancy is in the Lake District in the final story, how do the scarlet runner beans complete this thread?

9. Spence's view of his farm (page 131) informs his view of the world. Compare this to how Nancy understands the world, using the passage at the end of "The Heirs" (page 202), and the landscape Nancy remembers from her childhood.

10. Nancy goes to England several times over the years. Why do you think Nancy, in "The Prelude," was "on a Romantic kick . . . tracing the footsteps of Coleridge and Wordsworth" (page 205)? Where does the news that Jack brings her fit into her preoccupation? Does her obsession help her to deal with change?

11. Why is the last story called "The Prelude"?

BOBBIE ANN MASON is the author of *An Atomic Romance, In Country, Clear Springs,* and *Shiloh and Other Stories.* She is the winner of the PEN/Hemingway Award, two Southern Book Awards, and numerous other prizes, including the O. Henry and the Pushcart. She was a finalist for the National Book Critics Circle Award, the American Book Award, the PEN/Faulkner Award, and the Pulitzer Prize. She is writer-in-residence at the University of Kentucky.

About the Type

This book was set in Sabon, a typeface designed by the well-known German typographer Jan Tschichold (1902–1974). Sabon's design is based upon the original letter forms of Claude Garamond and was created specifically to be used for three sources: foundry type for hand composition, Linotype, and Monotype. Tschichold named his typeface for the famous Frankfurt typefounder Jacques Sabon, who died in 1580.

Join the Reader's Circle
to enhance your book club or
personal reading experience.

Our FREE monthly e-newsletter gives you:

- Sneak-peek excerpts from our newest titles

- Exclusive interviews with your favorite authors

- Fun ideas to spice up your book club meetings: creative activities, outings, and discussion topics

- Opportunities to invite an author to your next book club meeting

- Anecdotes and pearls of wisdom from other book group members . . . and the opportunity to share your own!

- Special offers and promotions giving you access to advance copies of books, our Reader's Circle catalog, and much more

To sign up, visit our website at
www.thereaderscircle.com
or send a blank e-mail to
sub_rc@info.randomhouse.com

 When you see this seal on the outside, there's a great book club read inside.

Printed in the United States
by Baker & Taylor Publisher Services